CUTTING THE CORD

Amanda Bateman

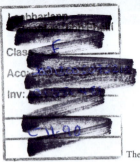

This is a work of fiction. Names, characters, businesses, places, events
and incidents are either the products of the author's imagination
or used in a fictitious manner. Any resemblance to actual persons,
living or dead, or actual events is purely coincidental.

Matador
9 Priory Business Park,
Wistow Road, Kibworth Beauchamp,
Leicestershire. LE8 0RX
Tel: 0116 279 2299
Email: books@troubador.co.uk
Web: www.troubador.co.uk/matador
Twitter: @matadorbooks

ISBN 978 1789016 093

British Library Cataloguing in Publication Data.
A catalogue record for this book is available from the British Library.

Printed and bound by CPI Group (UK) Ltd, Croydon, CR0 4YY
Typeset in 11pt Minion Pro by Troubador Publishing Ltd, Leicester, UK

Matador is an imprint of Troubador Publishing Ltd

CUTTING

THE

CORD

For my wonderful Dad.
Miss you so much.
Forever in my heart.
Always on my mind.

ELSIE

Friday, 13th December 1963

Elsie May Arnold opened her front door and ventured out into the snow. With her pregnancy almost at full term she knew she was taking a risk, but Elsie loved a risk and she certainly didn't like to be told what to do! So, carefully planting each footstep down, she made her way into town. The usual five-minute walk, however, took her fifteen. The snow and ice were more treacherous than she had first thought, and she'd almost ended up on her backside more than once. Finally, she was safe inside McGregor's, the local shop, which sold everything from eggs and bacon to hammers and nails. Elsie headed straight over to the record section. The Beatles' latest release was at Number One in the charts and she was desperate to own it. She was just leafing through the singles when a familiar voice called her name.

"Elsie Arnold, what on earth are you doing in here? You should be home in the warm, not out in this terrible weather in your condition," Mavis McGregor almost shouted at her as she strode across the shop towards her. Mavis not only owned the shop with her husband, Robert, but was the local midwife. Elsie had hoped she'd be out on her rounds, not helping in the shop today.

"I needed the fresh air and some time out," replied Elsie. "The kids have been driving me crazy and Harry's flat out at the garage so he's not much help. So, I decided a little walk into town would do me good."

"I understand what you're saying, Elsie, I really do, but this is no weather to be out in your condition. You could easily have fallen and who knows what consequences that would have had!"

"I know, Mrs McGregor, and I put on my good boots with all the grip despite knowing the snow would ruin them," replied Elsie. She really wanted to tell the nosy old bat to mind her own business but with the baby due any time she really did need to keep her onside.

"Well, I guess no harm has been done," began Mavis McGregor. "You finish your shopping then I'll walk you back, okay?"

"Thank you," Elsie replied. She really didn't fancy the idea of been escorted home like an errant child but if it shut her up and kept the peace she'd go along with it. Elsie spent several minutes more in the record aisle before heading off to the grocery section. If Mrs McGregor was going to be walking home with her she might as well make good use of her Elsie chuckled to herself. She then proceeded to load her basket with potatoes and tinned goods. Within a few minutes the basket was full and weighing Elsie down. She made her way to the counter, struggling with the laden basket, when a sharp pain shot from the middle of her lower back right round to the front, causing Elsie to drop the basket and fall to her knees clutching at her swollen stomach. Before she managed to catch her breath from the first sharp pain another followed, hot on its heels.

"Mrs McGregor," Elsie screamed out. "Mrs McGregor come quick, the baby is on its way." Elsie screamed out again, as yet another contraction racked through her. This was Elsie's fourth child and with each birth the labour had become quicker. Freddy, her eldest son, had arrived after ten hours of labour. Anne's labour had only been half of that and Charlie had arrived within two hours! Odds on, this baby would be born within the hour! Elsie let out a gut-wrenching scream as the urge to push engulfed her.

"For fuck's sake, will someone fucking help me?" screamed Elsie. Within seconds, Mrs McGregor, along with her husband, were either side of her, helping her to her feet. Elsie screamed out again as an even more violent contraction shot through her. The latest scream seemed to bring the other customers running to help lift and move this mad woman into the back storeroom before they were greeted with more expletives and ear-shattering screams.

No sooner had the helpers laid Elsie on the storeroom floor and made a quick exit than Elsie had an even more compelling urge to push and this time she didn't ignore it. With a hellish scream, Elsie pushed down for all she was worth. The pain was leaving her exhausted, but she had no choice but to summon up every ounce of strength she had and push again. With this last push, out came the baby, straight into the capable arms of Mavis McGregor. Elsie laid her head down on the floor and offered up a silent prayer, asking that the baby would be just like her other children. Meanwhile, Mavis went about her job, cleaning the little one's airways, delivering the afterbirth and cutting the cord. All the time, Mavis was struck by how milky-white this new little girl's skin was and what a vivid shade of red her mass of hair was. After all, Elsie was a true blonde and Harry had the blackest hair she'd ever seen. Two of their children had their dad's colouring, while the other had white blonde hair. But this baby had bright red hair. Maybe those rumours of Elsie playing away from home weren't rumours after all, thought Mavis. Maybe this little girl was going to be the undoing of Elsie Arnold, she thought. There was only one way to find out, so, wrapping the baby in a towel and making sure that her hair was clearly visible, Mavis, with her back to Elsie, urged her to sit up and prepare to hold her new daughter. Elsie propped herself up against a crate for support and made ready. Mavis turned with the child in her arms, its red hair shining out like a beacon. The look on Elsie's face confirmed what Mavis had suspected. It was a look of sheer horror. Elsie's prayers had not been answered. Elsie took the child from Mrs McGregor's arms and sent up another silent prayer. This time, she prayed that Harry wouldn't chuck her and her new daughter out in the cold.

While Elsie cleaned herself up a little, Mavis sent for

Harry and then made a pot of tea for them both. Elsie was now sitting in Robert's armchair in the shop's back office, breastfeeding the little one. They looked like the perfect picture of a mother and child, but Mavis knew differently. Elsie Arnold was anything but a loving mother. The only person Elsie May Arnold truly loved was herself. Mavis was interrupted from her thoughts by a knock at the back door. Now it was show time! Harry had arrived. Mavis placed her cup on the office desk and stole a quick glance at Elsie as she made her way across the room to open the door. There wasn't any need to tell Elsie who was knocking on the door, as the look on her face confirmed she'd already guessed. Elsie took a deep breath and braced herself, ready for whatever Harry was about to throw at her.

Harry strode across the room without uttering a single word to either Mavis or Elsie. The baby had stopped feeding, obviously sensing something was scaring her mother, and began to cry. Immediately, Harry scooped the crying child up into his arms and turned his back on both women to take a good look at the new baby. He instantly saw that his worst fears were being confirmed. He'd hoped against hope that it would turn out to be his baby Elsie had been carrying. But the red locks confirmed it was the mechanic he'd hired at his garage. He'd caught them at it in his storeroom back in the spring. Harry stared down at the crying baby. He began to gently rock her to and fro. Almost instantly the crying stopped, and she was asleep in his arms. Tears that had welled up in Harry's eyes now openly ran down his face. They fell like raindrops onto the little one's red hair. Harry took in her milky-white skin and, oh, how beautiful she was. He knew in that instant that, despite her not being his, she had already stolen his heart, just like his own children had, just like Elsie had. He turned back round to look at his wife and Mrs McGregor with tears still in his eyes but a smile on his face.

"She's the most beautiful baby I've ever seen," he began. "I remember my old grandad talking about a wayward great-aunt of his with hair the colour of fire and a temper to match. Look like she's made a return," he chuckled. "I'd like to name her Jane Elizabeth, if that's okay with you, Elsie? Jane after my favourite actress, Jane Mansfield, and Elizabeth after Good Old Queen Bess the First. She was a strong woman with flaming red hair. What d'ya say?"

Elsie was so pleased that she wasn't been thrown out into the cold that she'd have agreed to the baby being called BASTARD if that meant she still had a roof over her head.

"Jane Elizabeth it is," she replied. Cradling little Jane Elizabeth in his arms, Harry placed a tender kiss on her forehead.

"Welcome to the family, Janie," he said to her, then kissed her once more for luck; he had a feeling they were both going to need it.

Mavis McGregor didn't know whether the story about a red-headed great-aunt of Harry's was true or not but the look of love on his face for both mother and child was as clear as day. She just hoped, for Harry's sake and little Janie's, that Elsie realised what a lucky escape she'd had as everyone knew that Elsie Arnold played away from home on a regular basis!

HARRY

Saturday, 30th July 1966

Harry Arnold pulled the big garage door closed and slid the three bolts across to lock it. He didn't normally close his garage at two o'clock on a Saturday but it was the World Cup final today and England were taking on Germany. The local club had put on food and was playing the match live for all who cared to listen. Harry wasn't really a football fan, but he'd agreed to go along as it wasn't every day your country was playing in a World Cup final. He had been quite looking forward to it, but the past two days' revelations had put paid to that. Last night he'd had to lie to his family about why he was so late home from work and today he was not only going to have to lie to both his family and friends but try to stop the one person he loved most in the world from making the biggest mistake of her life. Harry held his head in his hands. When and why had his life all gone so wrong? Last night he'd come so very close to killing a man. A man he didn't know. Yet a man who was preparing to take his wife away from him!

Two days ago, a woman who he'd never seen before had pulled onto his garage forecourt. She'd addressed him by name and asked to speak to him in private. Harry had shown her into his grubby little office and there she had broken his heart. She'd informed him that her husband was planning to run away with his "SLAG" of a wife while everyone was busy cheering the England football team on. Seems she'd been having her "LYING BASTARD" of a husband followed for a few months now. Mrs Sheila Riley, as she called herself, was none too short of a bob or two and had taken it upon herself to employ a private detective on the advice of a well-meaning friend. Bob Spencer, it turned out, had been well worth his fee. Not only had he photographed her husband, Sidney, with this other woman but had even managed to get the table next to them in a small restaurant out in the countryside and eavesdrop on their plan. The cunning Bob Spencer had a microphone inside what looked like a hearing aid, so the loved-up couple had spoken freely, presuming him to be hard of hearing. Sheila Riley finished off the conversation by saying Bob Spencer had found out who the identity of this other woman was. She'd thought it her duty to inform this woman's unsuspecting husband of what the "DEVIOUS ADULTROUS" pair were up to. She'd also been kind enough to tell him where her "NO GOOD LYING BASTARD" of a husband would be that Friday evening. Then she'd promptly left, leaving Harry a broken man.

All day Friday, Harry had hummed and aarhed over what to do? Should he confront this Sidney Riley alone? Or should he just wait at the appointed rendezvous and confront them both? Sheila Riley had told him that her husband knew how to handle himself but that didn't frighten Harry. At six feet four he was no pushover. He lugged tyres around and hauled engines in and out of cars for a living. This meant he was in great physical shape. A lot of people referred to him as 'the Gentle Giant' but Harry was no saint. He'd had his fair share of run-ins over the years from people trying to get away with not paying for their fuel or his services. He'd even had to rough up a few of Elsie's admirers in the past. If he met up with this Sidney Riley things could easily get out of hand! But what was to say that by him turning up at their meeting place they wouldn't still bugger off together? Harry had finally decided it was best to square up to Mr 'FUCKING' Riley alone and make him see the error of his ways one way or the other. So, last night, Harry had gone to the local park where Mrs Riley had told him her husband would be. Apparently, Sidney Riley took a walk around the park's duck pond every Friday night at 6:30pm sharp. It was all part of his Friday night ritual. After arriving home from work, he'd eat his tea, take a bath, then take a quick walk around the duck pond before rounding the evening off with a game of dominoes in the nearby pub with his father. In the three months Bob Spencer had followed Mr Riley this routine hadn't changed so there was no reason why tonight would be any different. And last night had been no different. Except of course he'd been accosted by Harry!

Sidney Riley hadn't realised who Harry was until he'd been yanked off the well-trodden path around the duck pond, bundled into the woods and slammed hard up against an oak tree. He'd never seen a photo of Harry Arnold or met him before but by the look of sheer anger on this man's face it wasn't hard to guess who he was. Sidney had been rumbled, but by whom? Within five minutes he knew the answer! Sheila! Well, he had decided he wasn't going down without a fight. That was his first mistake! The second came after his nose had been broken when he'd told Harry that this wasn't going to stop him and Elsie from being together! He didn't make a third! With several broken bones and a warning to stay away from Elsie if he valued his life, Sidney Riley had conceded defeat. NO woman was worth losing your life over. Harry rubbed his sore knuckles. They were grazed and swollen on both hands, but his explanation had been easy and so had the lie he'd told. Too easy. He'd said he'd done it trying to get an engine back into a motor. Hence why his knuckles were a mess and he was late. Now as his two sons approached the garage forecourt he was about to lie again, and he hated himself for it, but he hated the thought of Elsie leaving him and the kids more.

"Dad, come on," shouted Charlie as he raced over to his dad. "We don't want to be late for kick-off, do we?"

"It's not for another fifty minutes, Shorty," Freddy remarked.

"I know," began Charlie, "but they're handing out sweets to the kids before kick-off, I don't want them to be all gone before we get there."

"In that case, you'll have to go on ahead of me, son. I've gotta pop home and change me shoes. Forgot to bring them with me and I don't want to be wearing these oily old boots in Arthur's Club, do I? He'd string me up if I got oil over his floor."

"I'd like to see him try," chirped in Freddy.

Harry smiled. "Go on, get off then before all those sweets have gone and save me a seat; I don't fancy standing all afternoon." With a promise of saving him a seat, Freddy and Charlie set off at a pace to the club and with a heavy heart Harry set off in the direction of home to confront his wife. As Harry turned the corner into their road he saw Anne walking towards him pushing little Janie in her pushchair.

"The club is in the other direction," shouted Anne as she strode towards her father.

"I know, sweetheart," Harry responded, "but I forgot to take me shoes to work with me this morning and I look daft in my Sunday best with these old oily boots on me feet." Harry pointed down at his work boots as he came side by side with his two daughters.

"I see what you mean, Dad, but I can't stop nattering to you, I've gotta drop our Janie off at Aunt Mary's and get to the club myself before kick-off." Anne took off at speed around the corner and out of sight. Harry was so glad that he'd made the decision to leave his shoes at home on purpose; it had made for a plausible excuse to be heading off home instead of the club. Turning to see that Anne hadn't backtracked either, Harry set off once more for home.

Quietly placing his key in the front door, Harry turned it in the lock and gently pushed open the door. The stairs were directly in front of him and he could hear drawers being banged up in his and Elsie's room. He quickly removed his boots, tiptoed up the stairs, crossed over the small landing and stood in the bedroom doorway. Elsie's back was to the door. She was obviously so intent on packing her belongings into two suitcases that she wasn't aware of a presence behind her. Harry watched her as she folded her clothes and placed them neatly into the suitcases. At that moment, he felt as though the very life of him was being sucked out and placed neatly alongside the clothes in the suitcase. But Harry knew he had to be strong and show not an ounce of weakness in front of this devious, lying woman. He had every intention of making her stay with him and their children. So, he drew in a deep, long breath. As he did so, Elsie became aware of someone behind her and quickly turned, expecting to find one of her children standing there. She had never for one minute expected it to be Harry.

Harry couldn't help but smile at the utter shock on his wife's face as she'd turned around. He'd guessed from the look of her that it had been one of the kids she'd been expecting to see. She hadn't planned on it being Harry. They both stood staring at each for several moments before Elsie found her tongue.

"I'm off on a small trip, Harry. I need a break. The kids are driving me crazy. You're never here. Always busy down that bloody garage of yours. Well, you can take care of them for a few days. I'm having me a nice break down the coast with Joanie." With that she turned her back on Harry and continued to pack.

"Awful lot of clothes that, ain't it, Elsie?"

"Well, you never know what the weather's going to like do you."

"I'm told this lovely warm weather is going to continue right through to September."

"Well, I don't trust those weather forecasts, always getting it wrong they are?"

"Bit like me then, eh, Elsie? Only I thought you was doing a runner with some bloke called Sidney Riley?"

Elsie froze for a moment than refolded a jumper. "I know Joanie has let herself go these past few months after her Ronnie took off but she certainly don't look like a bloke, Harry." Harry was surprised by how much he was enjoying this. He was also surprised by how quickly and easily the lies flew out of his wife's mouth.

"No, Elsie, I wasn't referring to Joanie at all. I'm talking about a Sidney Riley. Married to a woman named Sheila. Lives in Lilleshall and works as an accountant at the beet factory. Currently enjoying a few days recuperating at home after he had a run in with a very angry husband. Your very angry husband to be exact." Harry watched as his wife's shoulders slumped and the incessant folding of the jumper stopped. He waited for her to take it all in. For her to realise the game was up. Eventually she straightened herself up and turned to face him with pure anger on her face.

"You think you and your bully-boy tactics are going to stop me and my Sid from being together?" Elsie screamed at her husband. "Because it won't. Sidney will be at the bus stop across the road at three o'clock as planned and no one and I mean no one will stop us from leaving." Elsie's face had turned beetroot-red as she spat the words out. Harry started to laugh at her, at which point Elsie flew at him, raining her fists down on his chest. He let her get a few blows in then he slapped her hard across the face and pushed her away from him, so she fell onto the bed, landing on top of the open cases. Harry could see that had surprised her. Never before had he ever laid a finger on her. Oh! There had been many times over the years that he had wanted to land her one. To put her in her place. She'd shown him up numerous times and her lying adulterous ways had at times left him feeling like he could actually kill her. But, yet, he had always contained his anger, his hurt and his humiliation. Even when little Janie had been born, he'd lied to cover for her. He knew Janie wasn't his, yet he had accepted the child. Christ, he loved the very bones of her and why had he sucked up all this? Because he loved Elsie more than life itself. He worshipped the very ground she walked on. He'd shown her nothing but love and given her anything her heart desired but now enough was enough. Harry had stomached a lot of things from this woman, but he wasn't about to let this lying, dirty whore, because that was exactly what she was, abandon their children. They didn't deserve that, and he was damn well going to make sure it didn't happen. Harry looked at his wife. It was as if he was really seeing her for the first time and it hurt like hell. He stepped forwards, looming over her as she lay sprawled across the bed. Then, with all the venom and hatred he now felt for Elsie, he issued his warning.

"I'm going to say this once only, so you best listen carefully. You're going to unpack those cases and put every last thing back in its rightful place. Then you're going to tidy yourself up and we're going to go down the club and join our family and friends and pretend like none of this ever happened. And I want you to remember this, Elsie Arnold. You are my wife. You are mother to three of my children and one I've accepted as me own. And if I ever find out that you're slagging around with anyone ever again or try to fuck off again, so help me I'll kill you. I'll do time for you, Elsie, remember that, next time you feel like dropping your knickers for all and sundry. Now get to it, woman." With that Harry left the room and headed downstairs. He'd never felt so liberated in all his life.

Elsie waited until she heard Harry go down the stairs before she allowed herself to cry. She had never in all the fifteen years they'd been married been afraid of her husband before. But now she feared him with every ounce of her body. Elsie knew that Harry meant every word he said. She also knew he was more than capable of carrying his threat out. Slowly she raised herself up off the bed and began to unpack.

FREDDY

Christmas 1969

Frederick Henry Arnold stood patiently waiting in the bus shelter across the road from the Fox and Duck pub to see if his mother came out. He'd parked his Lambretta up behind the shelter, out of sight, and was trying desperately to stop the cold seeping into his bones. He lit another cigarette and cupped his hands around the end for a bit of warmth. He'd been told by a very reliable source that his mum was having an affair with a man working on the new shopping complex they were building on the outskirts of town. He'd told him this was their regular meeting place, so here he was waiting to see if it was true. He knew this Derek Collins was inside as his car was parked up in the far corner of the pubs car park. Paul Taylor had done his research well. Derek Collins was a twenty-eight-year-old electrician staying at The Hollyhocks B&B in Wellington. He drove a yellow Mini Clubman that Freddy could just about see from the bus shelter. So far Paul had been right, not that Freddy had any reason to mistrust him in the first place. He and Paul, along with his identical twin, Peter, had been friends their entire lives. But Freddy prayed that the woman that Derek Collins was snuggling up to wasn't his mum! If it was, all hell would break loose. As Freddy ground out his cigarette on the ground the pub door opened and out walked his mum as clear as day on the arm of this Derek Collins. Freddy watched in horror as they walked across the car park then, before helping his mum into the passenger side, Derek kissed her passionately. Freddy felt physically sick. His worst fears had been confirmed. He went round the back of the bus shelter and started up his scooter and headed off to the snooker hall in the hope of catching up with the twins to see what could be done about the situation.

Peter and Paul Taylor were in the middle of a frame when Freddy showed up. From the look on his face they sussed that he'd been down to the Fox and Duck.

"So, what you want to do next?" asked Paul.

"Ram that bastard's bollocks down his fucking throat," snarled Freddy.

"I ain't cutting anyone's bollocks off, mate, but I'm more than happy to give him the beating of his life. In fact, by the time I've finished with him, he'll be wishing I had rammed his balls down his fucking throat instead." Both Paul and Peter laughed at that, but Freddy just didn't feel like laughing. He just couldn't get his head round the idea that his mum was planning to do a runner again! Oh! He knew he wasn't supposed to know about the events that had taken place on World Cup final day, but he'd overheard his dad telling his sister Mary all about it in the office at the garage. What kind of a woman was his mother? She was a far cry from what he'd actually thought of her. Now he had to make sure that his mum didn't run off with this Derek Collins character or that his poor old dad didn't end up committing murder.

"Freddy, mate, you get off home. Make sure your mum knows you're on to her without giving the game away and we'll sort this Derek Collins out for you, okay?" offered Peter.

"Yeah, Freddy, we'll be his very own Father Christmas, delivering one hell of a present." Once again, Paul laughed at his own joke but this time all three of the friends laughed together.

"Is that you, son?" shouted out Freddy's dad as he let himself in the back door.

"Yeah, Dad, sorry I'm a bit late. Got caught up with the twins."

"I hope they weren't dragging you into their world of crime, son." Freddy walked into the front room as his dad spoke, and he settled himself on the opposite end of the sofa to his mum. She looked like butter wouldn't melt in her mouth, sitting there knitting without a care in the world.

"This ain't London, Dad, and Paul and Peter ain't Shropshire's answer to The Kray Twins."

"I'm not saying they are, son, but the police are round their gaff that often, they're thinking of running the police station from there."

Freddy thought, "What's with all the wisecracks tonight?" before he responded.

"That's because their old man is a pisshead, Dad, who likes to throw his weight around. The twins are only trying to protect their old mum, that's all."

"I know, son, but them boys ain't always protecting their mum and you and I both know that. So, what skulduggery were they up tonight?"

"A few frames of snooker then a quick trip out to the Fox and Duck." Freddy heard the pause in the clattering of his mum's knitting needles when the Fox and Duck was mentioned.

"Doing a bit of protecting out there, was they?" asked his dad.

"If you must know, yes! They've been asked to put the frighteners on some bloke, rough him up a bit. Make him see the error of his ways." Once again, the knitting needles stopped clattering, only this time his mum let them lie in her lap.

"What's he done, this bloke?" she asked.

"Seems he's knocking off someone else's missus and he's found out. So, he's asked the twins to sort it for him. They heard he was going to be at the Fox and Duck tonight but when we got there he'd already left."

"I wished you'd not gone with them, son; you don't want to get caught up in that sort of thing," remarked Harry. "Good thing for you really that he'd left."

"Yeah, I guess you're right, Dad, but don't worry, I'll make sure I'm nowhere to be seen when they catch up with him."

"Let's hope for their sakes they don't, son."

"I'm afraid they will, Dad. They know where he works and where he's living. I've got a feeling he won't be having a merry Christmas."

"Well, he'll only be getting what he no doubt deserves," Harry sighed. "Now, let's drop this line of talk and have us a Christmas drink; it is Christmas Eve after all. Elsie, go get some glasses; we'll have us a drop of port."

Elsie happily put her knitting away and headed off into the kitchen. She needed a moment alone to think. It was no coincidence her Freddy being up the Fox and Duck with those thug twins. It was her Derek they were after, no mistaking, and Freddy knew, that was for sure. She needed to warn Derek, but how could she? She'd only managed to get away for an hour tonight because every year she went for a quick Christmas drink with her best friend, Joanie. She knew she'd taken a big risk doing that. Joanie wasn't one to be fobbed of easily. She'd had to lie about using the time to collect a surprise gift for Harry. But tomorrow was Christmas Day; there was no way she could get away and it was simply out of the question to try using the house phone to warn Derek. The house would be full to the rafters with family members. In fact, she had no chance of getting word to Derek for the next two days. Elsie just hoped the twins were also spending Christmas at home!

Derek Collins spent Christmas Day and most of Boxing Day alone in his room listening to the radio and eating cold beans from a can. There had been a Christmas invite from the B&B's owners to join them for the festivities. However, it was only for breakfast and that had been served in total silence. He'd finally had enough of looking at the same four walls and his own company and decided to take a walk and see if he could find a pub open somewhere and perhaps someone, anyone, to talk to. By the end of the night Derek wished he'd stayed home alone. He'd paid out good money for some watered-down whisky in a flea-ridden pub and now he was lying face-down in some back alley having taken a beating from two thugs warning him to leave town and stay the hell away from Elsie Arnold. Well, he was most definitely down but he was by no means out. He was Derek Collins, aka John Walker, aka Walter Johnson. In fact, he had more aliases than he cared to remember. It had been a very long time since he used his real name, Kenneth Harlow. He'd done time for GBH and was wanted on several accounts of ABH down south. No jumped-up little thugs were going to scare him away. They'd just got lucky, that was all. Elsie Arnold was his bitch now and he was going to be leaving town with her! He spat out the blood that had formed in his mouth and with a harrowing howl hauled himself up off the ground and headed back to the B&B. There'd be no hospital visit for him tonight. Just a bottle of whisky and a long soak in a hot bath.

It was New Year's Eve. Earlier in the day, Elsie had packed a small holdall with some of her clothes and a few toiletries and had hidden it behind the shed down beside the back-garden gate. Harry and Freddy had already left for the club and Anne was upstairs bathing Janie. Freddy had informed her of Derek's beating on Boxing Day evening. She'd been furious, but she'd managed to sneak away the next day and phone Derek at his lodgings. He'd told her he was okay and that the sooner they left the better. So, the plan had been made. She wasn't going to be able to take as much has she'd hoped but that didn't matter. She'd be away. She'd be rid of all the demands these selfish bastards asked of her day in day out. Elsie put on her most loving voice as she shouted up the stairs to Anne.

"I'm off now, love, to meet your dad at the club. Don't wait up, I'm sure it'll be a late one. Oh, and Anne," she added as a cruel afterthought, "HAPPY NEW YEAR," and with that Elsie left by the back door, collecting her bag from its hiding place as she headed out of the back gate. As she turned the corner at the top of the road, she could make out the tail lights of Derek's car, idling in the lay-by. She hurried across the road and walked up to the passenger side of the car. As fast as she could, she opened the door, threw her holdall onto the back seat and climbed into the passenger seat. She looked across at Derek. His face was a mess, but she could see the swelling was already going down. She leaned across and tenderly placed a gentle kiss on his cheek.

"All set?" he asked.

"You bet," Elsie replied, then planted another kiss on Derek's cheek. With that Derek pulled out onto the road and into the night. Elsie never once looked back.

Freddy kept one eye on the clock and the other on the

door to the club. His mum should have been here a good hour ago, but there was no sign of her. He glanced across at his dad. He was chatting away to one of their neighbours, looking like he didn't have a care in the world. Poor bugger thought Freddy. It was no good: he'd have to go see what was keeping that slut of a mother of his. Freddy placed his glass down on a nearby table and headed off out of the club's main door to see if he could see her anywhere outside. He was just about to take a look around the back of the club when a hand was firmly placed on his shoulder. Freddy froze on the spot.

"It's only me, son," said his dad. "Come back inside and enjoy yourself; its New Year's Eve." Freddy turned to face his father.

"I thought I'd go see where mum has got to," he began. "I'm worried about her." Harry looked into his son's eyes and could plainly see all the love, hurt and anguish in them. He pulled Freddy close to him and hugged him as if he were once more that little boy who used to plead for one of his daddy's bear hugs. Freddy automatically hugged his father back. Finally, Harry released his hold and held his son at arm's length.

"She's not coming, Freddy. She's gone."

"What do you mean gone?"

"She took off about half an hour after we left, with that Derek Collins fella."

"But how…"

"How did I know? I ain't daft, son. I knew exactly who you were talking about on Christmas Eve. I even know that those thug twin friends of yours jumped him Boxing

Day night. Heard they gave him a good kicking an' all. But the poor bastard was too suckered in by that whore of a wife of mine to walk away. Well, now he's got her, the poor bastard. Now his troubles really do begin." Freddy could hardly believe his ears. His dad knew! His dad hadn't done anything to stop her? What in God's name was going on?

"If you knew, Dad…"

"Why didn't I stop her? Well, it's like this, son. It's not the first time. Christ, it's not even the second time your mum has played around. Ever since I got with her she's been playing me for the fool. We'd been dating for a few weeks when I found out she was engaged to some other sap. I walked away but she pursued me. Promised me it was all over. Like a fool, I not only took her back, but we were married within six months. By the time we'd reached our first anniversary she'd cheated on me twice. Twice, son." Harry was close to tears, so he drew a deep breath and then continued his sorry tale.

"I should have called it a day then but like the lovesick puppy I was I forgave her, though on the condition that we moved away. She reluctantly agreed. So, I took a job as a farm hand for Farmer Boyce. He was well into his sixties so there was no immediate temptation for Elsie. We lived in a small cottage on the farm for six years, blissfully happy. While we were there, you and your sister were born. Our cosy little cottage was quickly becoming a little too cosy."

"I remember collecting the eggs with Mum in the morning," Freddy broke in. Harry smiled at the memory.

"We moved not long after Anne was born, didn't we, Dad?"

"Aye, we did. We were rapidly outgrowing the cottage and your grandad had decided to retire. He and your grandmother bought their little bungalow, a mile down the road from the garage, and we all moved into my old family home and I took over the running of the garage."

"You sound sad about that, Dad. Didn't you want to run the garage?"

"Oh, I did, Freddy, more than anything, and of course Elsie was thrilled. She was moving back into a busy town. She'd be somebody, what with me now owning the family business and us living in the large four-bed detached house that came with it. But me, I had this awful feeling that our wedded bliss might not last. For a good many years thankfully, I was proved wrong. Elsie threw herself into turning the house into our family home and then Charlie came along so her hands were full. I'd finally let my guard down. Believed stupidly that all that carrying on was behind us but soon enough Elsie was back to her old ways."

"You mean there's been someone before this Derek Collins came along?" Freddy didn't want to let on that he knew about the World Cup affair. He was happy to just let his father get it all off his chest.

"Another two to my knowledge, son. The first was a mechanic I'd employed called Roddy McCuskey. Quick-tempered red-headed bugger he was but a bloody good mechanic. Caught him and your mum up to no good in my office, of all places. I gave him a good hiding and sent him packing. Few nights later, he turned up at the garage smelling of whisky. He came stumbling towards me. I thought it was the drink and reached out to prevent him falling. I got a knife in my guts for that." Freddy suddenly remembered the nasty scar his dad on the lower right side of his stomach. Harry had always told them it was an appendicitis scar.

"We thought it best to tell you kids I'd been taken into hospital with appendicitis than the truth. Sorry, son." Harry placed a tender hand on Freddy's shoulder.

"What happened to this Roddy guy?" asked Freddy.

"Got two years in the nick."

"What did mum have to say about all of this?"

"Told me she was pregnant while I was in hospital recovering from the stabbing. She admitted she had no idea who the father was. She was too far gone to have an abortion, so six months later our Janie was born." Harry paused to let what he'd just said sink in. It didn't take long for the penny to drop with Freddy. Freddy looked up into his father's eyes. For the first time in his life, Freddy could see all the heartache in them. He embraced his dad. Holding him close to him. Never before had Freddy felt so much love and respect for his dad. He'd always been a mummy's boy, favouring his mother over his father. But not now. All the love he'd had had been replaced by a burning hatred for her deep in the pit of his stomach. Freddy stepped back from his father before he asked the question he already knew the answer to.

"So, Janie is Roddy's daughter?" This instantly brought tears to Harry's eyes, but he didn't raise a hand to wipe them away. He just walked over to the two-feet-high walk that ran alongside the club's car park and sat himself down.

"He may be her biological father but I'm her dad and she's my daughter. Your mother turned me into a liar and now I'm going to ask the same of you, Freddy. I'm going to ask that you never tell a living soul about Janie not being mine. It would kill me if she ever found out and destroy her life too. I've made it my business to keep tabs on that scumbag. Didn't want him showing up causing trouble. Found out that within months of being released from prison he killed a woman. Beat her to a pulp. He's serving life in Parkhurst Prison. Our Janie doesn't need to know her father's a murderer." Freddy sat down beside his dad on the wall.

"I'm beginning to understand why you've decided to let her go now, Dad." Harry let out a spine-tingling chuckle. Freddy thought perhaps his dad was finally going mad.

"Having another man's baby didn't stop your mother, Freddy. Oh! For a while she was all sorry and attentive to all our needs. But that's not her way. She hates it when her needs don't come first. She's a selfish, lying, cheating whore and I should have sent her packing the minute I'd registered Janie's birth. But she was like some sort of drug I thought I couldn't live without, so I played the role she had me play. Only this time I wasn't so naïve to believe she'd changed her ways. As the saying goes, 'a leopard can't change its spots'. I got wind she was planning to bugger off with this bloke called Sidney Riley. The plan was for them to slip away while we all were cheering on England in the World Cup final. I collared him in the park and beat the living daylights out of the bastard. Had to stop myself from killing the cocky bastard, I did. He took some convincing to fuck off and leave well alone. World Cup day I snuck up on Elsie as she was packing to leave. Told her that lover boy wouldn't be showing up, so she'd best get unpacking and start thinking of her kids instead of herself for a change. And I'm not proud of it but I told her there and then that if I caught her playing away again I'd kill her. And believe me, son, at that moment in time I meant it. But here I am again! Folk round here called me the 'Gentle Giant'. I called myself the GIANT FOOL. But not anymore, Freddy. She's burnt her bridges with me this time. I wouldn't have her back even if my life depended on it. I'm done with the whore. It'll be 1970 in under an hour. A new year. A new decade. A new me. That worthless whore has taken up enough of my time, energy, life and money. From now on I'm going to invest all those things into you kids. I'm going to be all the parent you need. Now let's go back inside. Get ourselves a drink and make a toast to Derek Collins for finally taking that evil mare off my hands." With that, Harry stood up, swiped away the last remains of any tears and walked back into the club.

Freddy sat for several minutes alone on the wall with everything his father had told him playing round his head. How could he have adored this woman so much? This woman who was prepared to dump her husband and kids for a few cheap thrills. Well, good riddance to her. He just hoped she had the good sense to stay away from them all, especially sweet little Janie.

FREDDY

Summer 1970

The months following the departure of Elsie hadn't been easy at first for anyone. Rumours of Harry finally flipping out and killing his adulterous wife had been rife at first. Charlie and Janie had been taunted at school by spiteful children. Folk had tarred Anne with the same brush as her mother, openly calling her a little whore or slut. It had changed Anne and not for the better. Long gone was the sweet, caring young girl, to be replaced by a hard-faced bitch. As for Freddy, he'd been in more fights than he could count and had even been locked up on one occasion to cool off in the local police station's cells. But, finally, things were settling down into a nice easy pattern. The rumours had stopped and been replaced by kindness and sympathy for Harry. Charlie and Janie were no longer taunted at school and now had more friends than they really needed. Anne, she seemed to embrace the new-found hardness in her, and Freddy had finally excised his demons and was working full-time at the garage alongside his dad and loving every minute of it. But then Tommy Higgins came along!

Tommy Higgins was a couple of years older than Freddy, but his sister Joan had been a big friend of Anne's before their mum had run off. Joan couldn't stand the nastiness that Anne was always dishing out of late and had stopped calling round. Joan had recently been on the family summer holiday to Blackpool with her parents and while there she'd seen Elsie Arnold several times. Hence why Tommy had paid Freddy a visit. Joan had asked him to let Anne and her family know that, after a bit of holiday detective work, Joan had found out where Elsie was staying and working.

"She's working part-time at a big pub called The Manchester up on the front near the tower," Tommy began to tell Freddy. "She's living in a flat above a hairdressing salon called Betty's. It's on Windsor Avenue, a few streets away from the Pleasure Beach. She goes by the name of May Collins. Joan said a nice young barmaid there called Ruby Walters was very helpful. I'm only telling you all this because our Joan asked me to. Personally, I think you should just forget I ever said anything." Tommy shook Freddy's hand then left as quickly as he'd arrived, leaving Freddy in a dilemma. Should he tell his dad? Should he go see for himself? Or do as Tommy suggested and forget he'd ever heard a thing?

Freddy fretted over what Tommy had told him for days. He just couldn't shake off the way that she'd just packed up and started a whole new life for herself without any thought of the consequences it would have on all those left behind. The burning knot of hatred was back with a vengeance deep in his gut. Despite his better judgement, he just knew he had to travel to Blackpool. Track her down, like the dog she was, and tell her exactly what he thought of her. He doubted it would make the slightest difference to her but it sure as hell would make him feel a whole lot better.

Ten days later, on a sunny Thursday morning, Freddy was sitting on the seafront railings opposite The Manchester. He felt bad about lying to his dad about where he was going and why, but he really thought it was for the best. He'd said he was going to Manchester to meet up with a girl called May he'd met when he'd gone to Rhyl for the day a few weeks back with the Taylor twins. However, he'd told Paul and Peter what he really was up to and they'd only let him go on ahead alone with the understanding they'd be joining him on the Saturday.

At a little after ten o'clock a small brunette knocked on The Manchester door. Within minutes she was ushered inside. At 10:30am sharp the door to the pub was wedged open for business. Freddy remembered that Tommy had said she only worked part-time so Freddy assumed this wasn't one of his mum's shifts. He was just getting to his feet to go over and suss out the pub and this Ruby when his saw his mum come hurtling round the corner of the pub. She darted through the pub door shouting her excuses for being late that loud that Freddy could almost make out what she was saying from where he stood across the busy road. Freddy smiled to himself. Typical Mum. Last to clock in but first to clock out. Freddy set off to find some cheap lodgings. Elsie wasn't going anywhere until afternoon chucking-out time.

By two o'clock Freddy was back sitting on the railings eating an ice-cream. He'd found himself a lovely little B&B on Monrose Avenue, just a couple of streets away from the flat his mum was renting. Mrs Davidson had told him she ran a tight ship! Breakfast was at 8:30am sharp. Evening meals were at 6:30pm sharp! The front door was locked at 11pm sharp! No alcohol in your room. No unauthorised guests in your room. Accommodation had to be paid for in full on day of arrival. Freddy had paid for three nights for him and had also paid for a double room on the Saturday night for the twins. As Freddy waited for the pub to close its doors for the afternoon he came up with a plan. Today he would check out the rest of what Tommy had passed on. Tomorrow he would confront his mother, leaving Saturday free to have some fun with the twins.

Within minutes of the door closing Elsie came out. She stopped to light a cigarette then headed off down the front in the direction of the Pleasure Beach. Freddy watched her disappear out of view then he walked across the road to the pub. He'd just reached the other side when out of the pub came the young girl he'd seen going in that morning. Freddy thought this must be the Ruby, Joan had mentioned. He quickly caught up with her.

"Excuse me, Miss, I wondered if you'd be so kind as

to help me," Freddy began to explain. "Only I just saw you come out of The Manchester and wondered if you could help me, like. I'm only here for a few days and I promised my mum I'd try to track down her old mate May Collins for her. Mum heard she might be working here at the pub." Ruby Walters stared at the handsome young man before her. He had the blackest hair and bluest eyes she'd ever seen but for some strange reason there seemed to be something familiar about the way he looked. And this was the second time this summer she'd been approached about someone asking after May!

"Who'd told your mum that then?" Ruby asked. Freddy decided to embellish the truth a little.

"Young girl with plaits. Came on holiday with her parents few weeks back. Goes to school with me sister. Told her she thought it was May serving behind the bar and a barmaid called Ruby had confirmed it. She hadn't been too sure though as she'd only ever seen photographs of May with me mum." Freddy could hardly believe how easily the lies slipped from his mouth. He was definitely his mother's son, he thought. Ruby remembered the young girl. She'd stopped her by the toilets one lunchtime and asked who the older blonde lady was that she'd seen working there. She'd mentioned it being a friend or mum of someone then, but which way round she couldn't recall. She couldn't remember the girl's name either, but she did remember those long thick plaits she'd had. She also remembered that the girl seemed unsure of whether she'd got the right person as well. Seemed a little dipsy, she recalled. That was probably why she'd never mentioned it

33

to May. Not that she spoke much to her anyway. May was only interested in talking to men!

"Your sister's friend was right. May does work here but she only works the lunchtime shifts. Likes to keep her evenings free, does our May!" The minute it was out of her mouth, Ruby wondered what on earth had possessed her to be so spiteful about May to a complete stranger. Freddy noticed the look of horror on Ruby's face at the realisation of what she had just said and started to laugh.

"What's so funny?" asked Ruby.

"What you just said," replied Freddy. "My mum said I'd have to look for her in the day as she wouldn't be working in the evening if she knew May." Ruby smiled at Freddy.

"How long has it been since your mum last saw May?" enquired Ruby.

"Good few years, I guess," lied Freddy.

"She's not changed much then," smirked Ruby.

"Doesn't look like it, does it?" offered Freddy. For several minutes, they stood on the pavement outside The Manchester, neither of them in a hurry to leave but both waiting for the other to say something. Freddy decided he liked this girl Ruby a lot and asked if she'd like to take a stroll along the prom with him. She readily agreed and taking her hand Freddy guided her across the busy seafront road.

They'd spent the rest of the afternoon together. They walked along the sand. Played the machines in the penny arcades and chatted away like lost friends. They'd parted back outside The Manchester at just before six o'clock. Ruby had to be back at work for seven and Freddy needed to be seated for his evening meal back at the B&B by

6:30pm sharp. They'd arranged to meet again the following evening at 7:30pm down by the entrance to the Pleasure Beach as it was Ruby's night off. Ruby had agreed not to tell May that he was asking about her. He'd told Ruby he wanted to be a nice surprise for her. After his evening meal at Mrs Davidson's B&B, Freddy set off to find a good spot by Betty's Hairdressers where he could spy on the flat above without being seen. After walking around the area several times, Freddy settled on an amusement arcade that gave him a view of the side entrance to the upstairs flat and a good view of its windows at the front. He caught a glimpse of Elsie walking passed one of the windows almost immediately, so he knew she was still indoors for now.

Derek Collins was the first to leave the flat. He was dressed casually, and Freddy could easily make out that he carried a darts case in his hand. He watched as Derek quickened his pace and headed off in the direction of the tower. Ten minutes later Elsie was out on the street. She was dressed to the nines and was heading in the opposite direction towards the Pleasure Beach. Freddy let Elsie get a good way ahead before he started to follow her. Elsie was moving along at quite a pace, but Freddy still managed to keep her in sight. Finally, she turned into the Pleasure Beach fairground. Freddy knew he'd have to get closer now or else he'd lose her. He quickened his stride and now was only a few feet behind her but with the fairground packed with holidaymakers he was sure he'd still be able to go undetected. At the funhouse entrance Elsie came to a halt and started to look around. Freddy dropped his head, pretending to read a nearby kiosk's billboard. Slowly, after a few moments, he raised his head and looked for Elsie. His heart began to pound as, at first, he couldn't find her. Then suddenly she was there, walking right by him, on the arm of a tall, thickset man in rather an expensive looking suit. Freddy was able to hang back at bit further now as the man was at least six feet five, meaning he was easily head and shoulders above the others in the crowd.

Freddy followed them as they made their way through the crowded streets until they entered the doors of a rather impressive hotel on the front, called the Grand. Freddy had waited outside for half an hour before venturing into the hotel's lobby. Inside was a large entrance hall, with a large curved reception desk in one corner and a rather busy bar area in the other. Freddy picked up a leaflet from a rack by the door and peering over it scanned the bar for Elsie and her new-found friend. They were nowhere to be seen. Cautiously, Freddy approached a bellboy heading for the front door and asked if there were any other communal areas. He was told that, no, there weren't. There was only the bar and the dining room and that was closed for the evening. Freddy thanked the bellboy then followed him out the front door and crossed the road over to a covered bench and waited for Elsie to reappear. At just before 10pm, Elsie emerged from the hotel alone and was practically running off in the direction of her flat. Freddy once again began to follow her. She was clearly in a hurry to get back before Derek did. Freddy smiled to himself. It seemed his mum was still up to the same old tricks with Derek has she'd been pulling on his dad. Maybe it ought to be Derek Collins that he should be having the quiet word with instead of Elsie!

ELSIE

Elsie had the sneaky feeling that someone had been following her all evening. No one in particular had stood out to her until she'd taken the second peek out of Morris's hotel window. There, across the road, sitting on the bench of the tram shelter, was the same guy who'd been there half an hour earlier. He obviously wasn't waiting on a tram as they ran by every fifteen minutes. She'd taken a quick glance across on leaving the Grand and instantly saw the same guy. Elsie had a feeling she knew who it was!

She'd had no time for a detour on her way back to the flat, she was running late as it was. Instead she quickened her pace and headed straight home. There had been no time to turn around, but Elsie just knew her shadow was still there. Elsie climbed the stairs to the door of the flat, never once looking back or down. Once inside, she turned on the kitchen light but made her way through the flat into the front room without turning on any more lights. She resisted the urge to move the net curtain out of the way to see the street outside more clearly. Instead she got as close as she could and peered out. There he was! Standing just inside the arcade opposite, smoking a cigarette. It was Freddy! Elsie wanted to run down and slap his face so hard for being such an interfering little shit! But Derek was due back any time now and she needed to change into her nightclothes and remove her make-up before he arrived home. She also needed to keep an eye on Freddy to make sure that he didn't go talking to Derek.

Elsie kept up her vigil at the window. Removing her make-up and changing into her nightie, keeping Freddy in her sights all the time. Eventually Derek came wobbling down the road. He'd no doubt had too much to drink as usual but thankfully he wasn't a mean drunk. Well, not to Elsie at least. She'd lost count of the number of times he'd got into fights while drunk in their short time here in Blackpool. If Freddy was to confront him now he'd get a good hiding for his trouble. But Freddy had just watched Derek teeter by then had run off in the opposite direction. Elsie looked at the clock on the mantelpiece. It was five to eleven. Elsie suspected that Freddy was staying in a B&B close by. Most of them had eleven o'clock curfews, especially on young men staying alone. A plot began to form in Elsie's mind. By morning it was already in action.

From the kitchen, Elsie heard the 5:30am alarm go off for Derek. She listened as he practically fell out of the bed and then stumbled across to the bathroom, slamming the door behind him. Elsie set about making him a strong black coffee and buttered him a piece of toast. Five minutes later Derek entered the kitchen and slumped down at the table. He wearily lifted his head and looked at Elsie. Suddenly he was as sober as a judge. There across the table from him sat Elsie with a nasty-looking black eye. Elsie knew Derek was staring at her, but she kept her gaze on the cup of tea before her. Slowly she raised her head to look Derek in the eyes. He just stared back. Lost for words. Elsie reached across the table and held his hand.

"Don't fret, sweetheart," she began. "It was an accident. As you turned over in the night you flung your arm over and it clouted me in the eye."

"Are you sure?" asked Derek meekly. Elsie gave Derek one of her best smiles.

"I know you was drunk last night when you came home, darling, but you'd never hurt me, not intentionally anyhow, would you?"

"No, no, I wouldn't. I just don't remember any of it. I'm so sorry, Else."

"No need to apologise. It was an accident and I'll survive. Now, you best hurry else you'll be late for work." Elsie rose from the table and went to Derek. She gave him a hug and passionately kissed him then handed him his lunch for the day and saw him to the door.

"You best phone in sick today, love," suggested Derek. "Don't think they'd want their prize barmaid turning up like she's been fighting with the punters." Derek was obviously trying to make light of it, but she knew deep down he didn't want folk thinking he'd hit her.

"Okay, Derek, if you think it's for the best. I'll get

dressed and slip out to the phone box around nine with my sunglasses on. I'll pop to the butchers and get us a couple of juicy steaks for tea. At little treat for us, as no doubt we'll be staying in tonight."

"Good idea, Elsie, now I've gotta fly. See you around five," and with that Derek was gone. Elsie smiled to herself. Her plan was off to a good start. While Derek had slept peacefully last night she had gotten out of bed and had gone into the kitchen. There she'd wrapped a tea towel around the wooden meat tenderiser, shoved another firmly into her mouth and then had whacked herself in the eye several times with the covered tenderiser. It had hurt like hell but the effect this morning was well worth it. She had the most swollen, blackest eye anyone had ever seen. Now for phase two of her plan.

At quarter to ten, dressed in her work attire and donning sunglasses Elsie set off to work. By the time she reached The Manchester's doors, she was positive that Freddy was hot on her heels. Elsie banged loudly on the doors and was rewarded by a quick response. She pushed pass Norman Fowler, The Manchester's landlord, removing her sunglasses as she went.

"Well, wonders will never cease," proclaimed Norman as Elsie hurled passed him. "What do we owe this honour of you turning up for work early?" Elsie turned to face him, removing her sunglasses as she came face to face with him. Norman took a step back.

"What the hell happened to you?" he asked.

"Derek came home drunk again last night. He was in a foul mood. Started lashing out at me. He's usually a crafty git though and rains blows to my body where no one ever sees but last night…" Elsie started to cry. Norman pulled her into his arms and let her cry on his shoulder.

"I knew he liked a drink, Elsie. Even knew he liked to throw his weight around when he was drunk but I didn't know he was into hitting women."

Elsie cried a few more of her crocodile tears then with a quiver in her voice replied,

"He blames me. Says it's all my fault. Says I bring out the worst in him. Last night I thought he was going to kill me. He was ranting on and on about some young lad he'd seen me with. Said I was making a fool out of him. Said we'd both regret crossing him. I haven't slept all night. He told me not to come to work today. To phone in sick. To stay home, else there'd be hell to pay. I'm so frightened, Norman." Elsie threw herself back into Norman's arms and cried like a baby. Norman gently rubbed her back. He looked up to see his wife standing there.

"It's not what you think, Maureen," Norman began.

"Don't go giving yourself a heart attack, Norman. I heard it all. Couldn't help it with all that wailing and shouting she's doing." Maureen held out her arms to Elsie. "Come here, pet, let's have a good look at ya." Elsie moved away from Norman and slowly she turned to face Maureen. Elsie did look a sight. Her face was streaked from where her mascara had run, and she had the most swollen black eye Maureen had ever seen.

"Best go clean up your face then take yourself home and if you've got any sense you'll pack your bags and put as much distance between you and that bastard Derek before he realises you've gone." Elsie gave Maureen the saddest face she could muster.

"I would, Maureen, but Derek has all the money. I've not got a penny to my name. I'd have buggered off before if I had. Have to hand him my wage packet unopened, I do. Got a friend up in Glasgow be happy to put me up just can't get there." Maureen had a gut feeling that what May was saying wasn't all the God's honest truth, but her big soft heart and her conscience couldn't let her stand by and doing nothing. That nasty black eye hadn't got there by itself and Derek Collins was well known for his explosive temper.

"Go clean yourself up, then come into the office," Maureen said and left the bar area.

"Go on, May, do as Maureen says." Elsie gave Norman a weak smile then scurried off to the ladies' room. Once inside she gave herself a nice fat juicy smile before setting about cleaning her face up.

It only took Elsie a couple of minutes to wipe the mascara from her cheeks, but she waited in a toilet cubicle for ten minutes as she didn't want to appear to have got herself together so quickly. Slowly she made her way into the back office. Maureen was sat at the large desk writing in a ledger when Elsie entered. She quickly closed the book and then removed a rusty old tea caddy from an open drawer on the bottom-right-hand side of the desk, placing it carefully on the top. She wiggled the lid off the caddy then withdrew a small roll of notes from it, held together by a rubber band. She then replaced the lid and in one swift movement had returned the caddy to the drawer and closed it. Maureen held up the roll of notes to Elsie.

"Here, take this, May, and get as far away from here as you can." Elsie reached out to claim the roll but at the last second Maureen snatched it away.

"I can't say that I totally believe you, May. Something with you has never sat quite right with me, you might say. It's like you're always holding something back. What, I have no idea, but I'm going to help you out just this once. But I never want to see you or hear from or about you ever again, do you hear me? Because if I do, lady, that black eye won't be a patch on what I'll do to ya! Do I make myself perfectly clear?" Elsie nodded her head like an errant child. Maureen threw the money down onto the desk and reopened the ledger and began to resume her book work. Elsie retrieved the roll of notes, slipped it into her pocket, donned her sunglasses and left The Manchester pub without a backwards glance. As she made her way to the Grand Hotel, Elsie fingered the roll of money in her pocket and mentally patted herself on the back. Now for phase three, she said to herself as she entered the hotel and stopped to check that Freddy was still hot on her heels.

Morris had been suitably appalled by what Derek had done to his beloved May. He'd quickly agreed to her plan for them to abscond that afternoon and head for his homeland of Ireland. He'd meet her at the train station on Waterloo Road at two o'clock sharp. Elsie was on a roll. Her plan so far was going better than she'd hoped. All she needed to do now was set the scene. She'd begin by knocking a few things around in the flat and by making sure that Freddy was well and truly out of the picture then get as far away as possible from this godforsaken place with good old rich Morris Connolly.

The hairdresser's downstairs was packed out. Fridays were blue rinse and set day and it seemed as if half the population of Blackpool was having its hair done in Betty's today, which was brilliant news for Elsie. With hairdryers going flat out, water gushing in the sinks and the boiler rattling away, not to mention a dozen women or more shouting to be heard over all the noise, no one in the salon heard a thing as Elsie toppled furniture, smashed crockery and broke ornaments. She had planned at first on packing a few things but then decided against it. Instead she set about ransacking her drawers and wardrobe. Retrieving a pair of lightweight summer gloves from the floor, she put them on. Then, opening Derek's bedside drawer, she took out his engraved flick knife and placed it in the pocket of her dress. Before heading out of the bedroom she checked her reflection in the mirror for any signs it was there. But, no, it was beautifully concealed. She crossed over to the front window and she could see Freddy in his all too familiar place now. Elsie smiled wickedly then exited the flat.

There were two entrances into the amusement arcade, the one Freddy had been watching her from and one a little further up the street. Elsie made across the road to the arcade and walked by the first entrance, in which she knew Freddy was hiding, then hotfooted it into the next. Elsie had to be quick now. Freddy was just about to high tail it out of the arcade when Elsie planted her hand on his shoulder. Freddy reeled round, coming face to face with his mother. Elsie reacted quickly. She moved straight in for a full-on cuddle, nestling her head on his shoulder, and whispered in his ear.

"Let's just link arms, son, and head off back to the flat, where we can talk in private, eh?" Freddy nodded his head in agreement and linked arms with his mum and headed off towards her flat. To anyone watching them, they were like a pair of lovers meeting up for a date. No one batted an eyelid at the dark handsome young man leaving with the sexy blonde in sunglasses.

Elsie led Freddy up into the alley that ran behind the hairdressers. She steered him past the gateway to the rear of the salon. Freddy hesitated for a moment but continued to let Elsie guide him further down into the deserted alleyway. They had almost reached the brick wall at the end of the alley when Elsie slammed Freddy up against the decaying rear wall of a derelict house. He slumped against the wall, wondering what his mother was going to say. But Elsie remained silent, just staring at him intensely behind her sunglasses. Freddy broke the silence.

"Always full of the dramatics, eh, Mum?" he began. "You should have been an actress," he mocked. Elsie reached into her pocket and drew out the knife then flicked open the blade. In one swift movement, she had plunged it into the unsuspecting Freddy's stomach. Freddy stared in horror at his mum as he felt the burning incision of the blade penetrate his belly. Before reality had sunk in she had plunged the knife in again, twisting it as she pulled it out. Freddy grabbed the opportunity to fling his arms to his ruptured stomach to staunch the bleeding and fend off any further assaults. His head was spinning, and he could no longer hold himself up. He was sliding down the wall to end up sitting in a ruck on the cold, hard concrete. He was finding it hard to breathe. Using all the strength he could muster, he looked up at his mum.

"Why?" he managed to get out. Elsie stooped down to meet her son's dying gaze.

"Because you just couldn't stop sticking your nose into my affairs," then Elsie laughed at her own joke. Freddy could feel his life's blood draining out of him.

"And this way, sonny, I'm well rid of that arsehole Derek Collins too. So, thanks for that." Elsie straightened up, took one last look at her son, then walked back off to the flat.

Freddy lay in the foetal position on the concrete. He knew his life was over, but he had no sorrow or thoughts for himself, only for little Janie. What chance in life did she have with both her parents being cold-bloodied murderers?

Elsie made it back into the flat unseen. She had an hour before her rendezvous with Morris. She took the flick knife that she'd carefully held away from her dress and used it to slash open her free arm. Blood quickly rose to the surface and dripped out onto the bedroom carpet. With clenched teeth Elsie tossed the knife into the strewn clothing then quickly went to the bathroom to dress her wound and clean herself up. Twenty minutes later Elsie was scurrying down the back stairs and off to meet Morris. She'd bandaged her arm and had washed out Freddy's blood from her gloves. They were now safely ensconced in an old waterproof make-up bag in the bottom of her handbag. Elsie hurried into the busy station and headed straight for the line of public telephone boxes. She dialled Derek's place of work. Putting on a London accent she asked for a message to be given to Derek as soon as possible. The message read "GET HOME ASAP YOUR WIFE IS ABSCONDING WITH HER LOVER". Elsie replaced the receiver then headed back outside the station to wait for Morris. She didn't have to wait long. He was early as usual. Elsie climbed into the passenger seat and Morris drove away from the station heading for the next ferry to cross to Ireland.

DEREK

Derek's first instinct when he had been called into the boss's office and given the message about May absconding with another man was to get back to their flat ASAP. His boss, Mr Saunders, had been happy to let him leave and, as he put it, "Put an end to this nonsense." Once out on the street, Derek set off as fast as he could. His mind was in a whirl. Was it really true? Was Elsie at this very moment hot-tailing it away with another bloke? If so, how could Elsie do this to him? That answer came easy! That night when she'd thrown her case onto the back seat of his car and climbed into the passenger seat, she'd shown NO remorse. NO guilt. NO nothing. It was as if it was just a natural everyday occurrence to her. In all the months they'd been here together, she'd not spoken about the children she'd left behind. She had never shown an ounce of remorse or guilt for what she'd done to them. Derek suddenly found he was no longer in a hurry to get to the flat and stop Elsie from leaving. Just like Harry before him, he found he was happy to let her go. This new-found emotion left Derek craving a drink of the hard stuff. It was late afternoon so no chance of finding a pub open, but he did have the best part of a bottle of Scotch under the passenger seat of his Mini. He licked his lips at the mere thought. The Mini was parked up on a piece of wasteland three streets away from the flat. He felt for the keys in his pocket and caressed them fondly as he formed a plan. He'd take the car and its precious cargo down to a deserted part of the coast he knew and together they'd while away the rest of the day. Then, later in the evening, he'd go back to the flat. Hopefully, by then, Elsie would be long gone and then he'd make the decision on what to do next. Plan formed, Derek headed off to the wasteland and his car. Come 9pm, Derek was parked up on a deserted car park facing the seafront. The bottle of Scotch lay empty on the floor by his feet and he was sleeping like a baby slumped over the steering wheel of the car.

Over in Dublin, at just around the same time, Elsie was taking her first steps on Irish soil. She inhaled deeply and smiled as she exhaled the Irish air from her lungs. Life just kept getting better for her, she thought. She was no longer a wife, a mother of four, an adulteress or even a murderer! Elsie Arnold or May Collins no longer existed to her. Now she was Joanie Allen. Mistress of a very wealthy business man. Kept woman. Lady of leisure. Oh, life was definitely getting better and better.

At the end of the dark alley behind Betty's Hairdressers in Blackpool, Freddy's body lay slumped against the cold wall, lifeless. The blood that had oozed from his stab wounds had long since stopped. It had soaked into his clothes and congealed on the ground, like a dirty deep brown stain. The darkness of the alley and the night engulfed him. Freddy wouldn't be found tonight. No one who cared knew he was dead.

Way across town, Ruby Walters lay crying into her pillow. She'd really thought that this Freddy was the one. Really thought he'd felt the same way about her but, obviously, she had been wrong. Very wrong. She'd waited nearly an hour for him to show up at the tram stop opposite The Manchester. What a fool she had been. He'd never turned up and now she felt so alone. So unwanted. So ashamed. Ruby buried her face deeper into the pillow and began to scream out in anger at Freddy.

Just before one in the morning, Derek woke with a jolt as his head slipped off the steering wheel. His tongue felt like sandpaper and his head was beginning to pound. He groped around in the confines of the car for the bottle of Scotch. He needed another drink. He quickly located the bottle down by his feet, only to find it empty. He threw it into the passenger seat footwell and looked at his wristwatch. It was almost one. Surely Elsie would have buggered off by now, he thought. He hoped there was plenty to drink back at the flat. He started up the Mini. Feeling a little groggy, he opened the window slightly to let in the cool night air. Then, putting the Mini in gear, he sped off back in the direction of the flat. It was only a short journey and the roads were deserted so within fifteen minutes Derek was parking up outside the hairdressers below the flat. He'd probably get either an earful off Betty, the salon owner, for nicking her parking space or a ticket for illegal parking come the morning. But, right now, all he wanted to do was to get in the flat and pour himself a very large Scotch. He practically fell out of the car and stumbled his way round to the back entrance of the salon and up the fire escape to the flat's front door. In his drunken haze, he didn't register that the door was unlocked or that the living room looked like a bomb had dropped. All Derek noticed was the full bottle of Scotch on the drinks trolley and the welcome sight of the comfy couch. He unscrewed the cap off the Scotch and took a long, hard swig then collapsed, bottle in hand onto the couch. Several healthy swigs later, Derek was back in the land of nod, totally unaware of the bloody knife lying on the bedroom floor. For now, Derek was blissfully drunk and blissfully unaware of the horrors to come.

THE TWINS

Saturday, 22nd August 1970

By 8:30am on the Saturday morning, Peter and Paul Taylor were enjoying a hearty cooked breakfast in Cathy's Café on the main drag of Blackpool seafront. Paul had driven them there at breakneck speed in his new MG sports car. Peter, although the definite muscle of the two, had hung onto to the edge of his seat as Paul had hurtled down the M6 motorway at speeds of up to a hundred miles an hour. Paul looked up at his twin brother.

"That breakfast is starting to put some colour back in your cheeks, Pete," Paul teased. Peter looked straight into Paul's eyes and saw the mischief there.

"There were times on that motorway I thought I'd never get to eat again," quipped Peter. Paul started to laugh.

"I was in complete control, Pete. Sterling Moss has got nothing on me," he replied with the laughter still in his voice.

"That well may be, Paul, but I'm not in such a hurry to meet my maker as you appear to be," began Peter. "Now shut up laughing and finish your grub. I'm here to have me a good time."

"Me too, Pete, me too," replied Paul. They finished the rest of their breakfast in silence, promptly paid the bill, then headed off to meet Freddy at the B&B he'd booked them into.

Mrs Davidson hurried to answer the front door of her B&B. Saturdays were always the busiest day. Current guests dragging their feet to check out and new guests hurrying to check in. It was as if the rules of 10am check out and 2pm check in did not exist. The front doorbell sounded again just as her hand reached out to open the door. Mrs Davidson wasn't in a very good mood this morning and the bell ringing in her ear had done nothing to ease her mood at all. She yanked opened the door and immediately yelled at the two young men on her doorstep.

"We have NO VACANCIES and booked rooms are not available until 2pm." With that she went to shut the door, but Peter quickly wedged his foot in the doorway. This only blackened Mrs Davidson's mood even more.

"Take your foot out of my doorway and then kindly remove both of your persons off my property before I call the police," she shouted at them. Peter stood his ground and, keeping his temper in check, began to speak.

"We're here to meet up with Freddy Arnold. He's a

53

guest of yours. Been here since Thursday. Booked an extra room for tonight, for me brother and me. We're Paul and Peter Taylor." Mrs Davidson immediately stepped back and opened the door wide.

"You best come in. We need to talk." She said. The twins entered the hallway. The landlady closed the door behind them and led them into the visitors' lounge on the left and asked them to take a seat. They did as they were asked. Both now curious as to what was going on. Mrs Davidson sat down on a chair opposite the twins. She stared at them silently for a few minutes before she eventually spoke.

"I'd like to apologise for my outburst on your arrival. Saturdays are always a bit fraught. But yesterday's events played heavily on my mind and this morning has brought me no comfort." She paused to take a breath before continuing. "Your friend Freddy has left me concerned for his well-being."

"What?" exclaimed Paul and Peter at the same time.

"Freddy arrived Thursday as you said," continued Mrs Davidson. "I found him to be very polite and he abided by the strict set of rules I ask all my guests to adhere to. He arrived early for both his evening meal Thursday and his breakfast yesterday morning. We chatted a little in the dining room as I cleared away the breakfast things. Before he left for the day, he asked what culinary delights I was serving that evening. I told him, as it was Friday, it would be a nice piece of fish served with new potatoes, veg and parsley sauce. His favourite, he informed me, then he was gone, waving a cheery goodbye as he left." Mrs Davidson reached into her apron pocket and retrieved a handkerchief. She wiped her nose and replaced it where it had come from. The twins eagerly waited for her continue with her story.

"Well, the evening meal came and went. But there was no sign of Freddy. I found this very odd after our conversation at breakfast time, but Blackpool has a way of making people lose track of time, so I assumed that was what had happened to Freddy. I close the door here at 11pm sharp. There's no need for decent folk to be out after that. I noticed Freddy's room key was still on the hook in reception as I locked up for the evening. I then decided to check on the room he was staying in. I knocked a couple of times on the door and when I didn't get a reply I let myself in. The room was as it had been left by the maids earlier in the day. With a heavy heart, I retired to my quarters. I spent a restless night worrying about this polite young man. I have a bad feeling about why he's never returned and you two turning up expecting to meet him here as only heightened that feeling." Paul and Peter were now both worried about Freddy. If what this landlady was saying was true, it was just so out of character for Freddy. He was a stickler for timekeeping. He was never late for anything and he most certainly wouldn't have stopped out all night! Unlike themselves, who would have thought nothing of pulling a bird and bunking down with her for the night. Freddy just wasn't like that. It was Paul who spoke first.

"Mrs Davidson did Freddy mention any names or places to you?" she just shook her head. She clearly had picked up on their own concerns.

"Freddy rang us yesterday morning at home. We'd left

for work, but he left a message with our mum. He'd said to let us know that he'd found his mum and he'd be seeing her later today and to tell us he had a date with Ruby that evening."

"He found his mum: whatever does that mean?" enquired Mrs Davidson.

"It's a long story, Mrs Davidson, but can you phone the police and ask them to meet us at the flat above the hairdressers on the corner of Windsor Street please?" The twins rose and headed for the B&B's front door. Mrs Davidson came after them.

"Ring the police?"

"YES!" shouted Peter a little too loudly. "Sorry, but we think Freddy may be in a spot of bother and best go there ready armed, in case of any trouble." The twins practically flew out of the front door. Across the road, parked up, was Freddy's car. The twins quickly crossed over and peered inside. No sleeping Freddy. Not that for one minute they thought he would be, but they had hoped against hope.

Remembering the telephone conversation they had had with Freddy on the Thursday evening when he had relayed the day's events to them, they managed to navigate their way to Windsor Street. The hairdressers below the flat Elsie was renting was already a hive of activity. Paul and Peter walked passed the salon window and turned the corner and made for the rear entrance to the flat above. They cautiously entered the rear alleyway and made their way to the back gate of the hairdressers. Although it was fast approaching ten o'clock on a bright sunny morning the alley seemed cold and uninviting. The twins stopped outside the open gate and strained their eyes to see down to the bottom of the alleyway. A gust of wind separated the overgrown shrubbery at the end of the alleyway, allowing a ray of sunlight to make its way through, only to bounce off a shiny surface then disappear from view once again. But the glint of reflected light had not gone unnoticed by Peter. There was something or someone down the end of the alleyway and he was going to face whatever it was head-on. Paul waited patiently by the open gate, ready to back up his brother if need be. Peter slowly edged down the alleyway. It felt almost like dusk down here. Then the wind got up again and for a split second the end of the alleyway was bathed in the warm sunlight.

Peter screamed out, "FREDDY, FREDDY," as he ran to where he'd seen his best friend slumped against the wall. He threw himself to his knees alongside Freddy and instantly sensed his lifelong friend was dead. He let out a gut-wrenching scream that brought Paul hurrying to his side. He too fell to his knees at the sight of poor dead Freddy. Then, like two lost infants, they cradled each other and sobbed their hearts out.

Derek was woken from his drunken reverie by a couple of policemen yanking him to his feet. His head was pounding and the entire flat seem to be a blur of police uniforms, swaying in and out of focus. He tried to make sense of it all, but the Scotch had scrambled his brain and his stomach was busy doing somersaults.

"In here," called out a strange voice from the bedroom. He tried once again to focus, to get his brain to work, but this time his somersaulting stomach won out. He threw up all over the policeman to his right. Both coppers quickly released him, cursing at him as he fell back onto the couch. Derek hung his head between his legs and threw up again. He stayed like that. Sitting on the edge of the couch with his head between his legs. A pair of shiny brown brogues appeared in his line of vision. He kept his head down. Sitting like this helped. The fog slowly began to clear.

"Somebody get this piece of scum some black coffee. I want him sobered up, cuffed and locked up in a cell by lunchtime, do you all hear?" roared out Detective Inspector Jack Wilde. A chorus of "yes, sir" rang out around the flat.

"We also need to locate Mrs Elsie Arnold. Better known round these parts as May Collins. I want to know all there is to know about Derek here and his absent partner. I want to know all their movements since the time the deceased arrived here in Blackpool. I want no stone left unturned, do you hear?"

"Yes, sir" they all chorused once again. Inspector Jack Wilde had a gut feeling that all was not as it seemed here. Somethings just weren't adding up. Hopefully they'd find this Elsie and then everything would come together. But, for now, he no option but to arrest Derek Collins for the murder of Frederick Arnold.

"Can someone arrange for the victim's father, Harry Arnold, to be informed and transported up here, please? I'd like to interview him myself."

"I'll get right on it, sir," said PC Jones. DI Jack Wilde thanked the PC then took a stroll out of the flat and down into the back yard. The sight of that poor young lad dead in the alleyway had really struck a nerve with him. His own son, Trevor, would be turning sixteen in a few weeks. This lad was only a few years older. Such a waste of life. He vowed there and then in that small cobbled backyard that he wouldn't rest until Freddy and his family had justice. And he didn't entirely believe that the blame lay with Derek!

HARRY & JACK

As soon as the two men climbed out of their car and crossed the garage forecourt towards Harry, he knew they were cops. He picked up an oily rag off the workbench and began to wipe the oil from his hands with it.

"Mr Arnold? Mr Harry Arnold?" asked the taller of the two plain clothes policemen.

"That's me," began Harry. "What can I do for you?" The shorter of the men spoke this time.

"I'm Detective Inspector Mike Jarvis and my colleague here is PC Alan Beddows. We'd like a quiet word with you in private, if you don't mind. Perhaps in your office, Mr Arnold?"

"What's this all about? I'm a busy man, Inspector."

DI Jarvis butted in. "It's about your son Freddy," he began.

"Let me stop you right there," started Harry. "Freddy's in Manchester, seeing a lady friend, has been since

Thursday, so don't be thinking you can go accusing him of stuff. I'm first to admit he went a bit of the rails for a short time after his mum left but he's back to the good lad he always was now."

"I really think we should talk in private, Mr Arnold. I understand your concerns, but I can assure you we are not here to frame your son up for anything." Harry looked right into the eyes of the DI. There appeared to be some hint of sadness in them. Harry suddenly had a feeling that these two policemen were about to rock his world once again. Without saying a word, he walked off to his office.

PC Beddows was the last to enter and he silently closed the door behind him. Harry was now seated behind his desk and DI Jarvis was seated opposite him. DI Mike Jarvis took a deep breath. He hated this part of the job. He knew Harry Arnold had been through the wringer over the past few months and now he was about to land an even bigger blow to this poor man.

"I'm sorry to have to inform you of this, Harry, but I'm here to let you know that your son Freddy has been found murdered in Blackpool." Suddenly Harry to laugh.

"I think you'll find you're mistaken," began Harry. "I've already told you. Freddy's in Manchester has been since Thursday seeing a bird. You've got the wrong bloke."

"I wish I could say that was true, Harry, but I'm afraid your son has already been formally identified by both the Taylor twins. It was them who found the body." Harry jumped to his feet, banging his fists down on the desk.

"The Taylor twins? What the fuck is going on here? Freddy told me he was going to Manchester to meet up with a girl called May he'd met a few weeks back on a trip to Rhyl with those fucking good-for-nothing twins." He slumped back down into his chair. Did he really know his son anymore? DI Jarvis let the outburst go and waited for a few minutes before he spoke again.

"It seems Freddy had a tip-off from some friend of your daughter, Anne, that your wife Elsie was living and working in Blackpool. She was going under the name of May Collins and was working at The Manchester pub. Freddy had gone up to confront her. The twins had wanted to go with him, but he refused their offer but had agreed for them to join him there this morning. He had telephoned twice while he was there. Once on the Thursday evening to let them know he'd located his mum and to give them the name and address of the B&B he was staying in and that of his mum's. He rang again Friday morning and left a message with their mum. He said he was going to talk to his mum that afternoon and then he had a date in the evening with a young girl called Ruby. He went on to say he'd meet them the next morning at the B&B." DI Jarvis paused to let Harry take in what he was saying.

"The twins travelled up to Blackpool early this morning. When they arrived at the B&B, the landlady, a Mrs Davidson, said she was worried about the young man as she hadn't seen him since he'd left after breakfast on the Friday morning. The twins told her to ring the police and get them to meet them at the address they gave her. Paul and Peter Taylor then ran round to the flat Elsie was renting. They found Freddy's body slumped up against a wall at the end of the alleyway that led to the flat's entrance." DI Mike Jarvis stopped talking again. Harry Arnold had silent tears rolling down his cheeks and they were landing on a car parts catalogue left open on the desk before him. With his head bent, he looked like a defeated man. DI Jarvis had no desire to add to this man's misery, but he still need to finish what he had to say.

"On their arrival at the flat, the police found Derek Collins passed out on the couch. There'd obviously been some altercation in the living room as it was turned upside down. On further inspection of the flat a flick knife with DC etched into the handle was recovered in the bedroom. It had blood all over it. The room had been ransacked but there was no sign of your wife Elsie Arnold. We're still trying to track down her whereabouts. Derek Collins has been arrested for the murder of your son Harry. A Detective Inspector Jack Wilde has requested that we come here to inform you of this tragedy and asked that we accompany you up to Blackpool, where he'd like to talk to you about matters leading up to this event." Harry looked up at the DI. The tears still blurred his vision, but he had heard every last word that had been spoken to him. He felt sorry for the poor copper. What an awful job he'd been sent to do! What on earth had possessed Freddy to go chasing after that WHORE of a mother of his? And where was the BITCH now? Taking care of herself somewhere safe, no doubt, if he knew her! What part had she played in the death of her own son? The thought frightened him, but it didn't mean he couldn't believe her incapable of such an atrocity. Harry was only too happy to go to Blackpool and help solve his son's murder but first there were things he needed to do.

A couple of hours later, Harry was sitting in the back of the unmarked police car heading towards Blackpool. He'd left the garage in the capable hands of Frank Aston, his lifelong friend. His elder sister Mary was taking care of his children Anne, Charlie and Janie. He felt such a heel leaving them right now, but they had all understood his reasons. They'd only asked that he bring Freddy back home where he belonged.

"Almost there, Harry," spoke PC Beddows, who was sat in the back with him. Harry just nodded his head. He already knew that. He'd brought the kids here along with Elsie many times for short breaks and fun-filled days out. It had always been Freddy's favourite seaside destination. Anne preferred Borth, Charlie loved Barmouth and little Janie just loved beaches. All the Bs, they'd sing out in unison. Harry doubted they'd ever return to Blackpool after this. All the memories of the thrills at the funfair. The splashing in the sea and laughing at the clowns in the tower would all now be overshadowed by Freddy's brutal and untimely death here. Harry already wanted to leave before he had even arrived but that wasn't an option for him.

The first two faces to greet Harry at the police station in Blackpool were those of Paul and Peter Taylor. Harry was shocked by their appearance. Their sharp suits were all crumbled and covered in stains. Harry didn't want to hazard a guess from what! Their hair, normally groomed to perfection, was just a tangled mess, sprouting from their scalps. But the most striking difference was the looks on their faces and body posture. Gone were the identical cocky, self-assured expressions and puffed-out chests. Now they looked like two lost, frightened souls who wouldn't say boo to a goose. They rose from their seats in the waiting room and were obviously bracing themselves for the usual dressing-down Harry bestowed upon them. But Harry felt nothing but compassion for these two boys and hurried over to them and gave them both a fatherly embrace.

"We're so, so sorry, Mr Arnold," spluttered out Peter. "We should have insisted we came with him. He'd still be with us if we had. It's all our fault," he tailed off.

"He's right," said Paul, as he placed a protective arm around his twin. "We should never have let him come alone." Harry smiled at the twins. He knew they could be right tearaways at times but as far as his Freddy went they'd always been diamonds. Freddy being a gentle soul had always been plagued by bully boys, but the twins had always run to his rescue. It must be hitting them hard to know that this time they hadn't stopped the bully. Hadn't protected their favourite buddy. Harry gently touched Paul and Peter on the shoulder.

"You found him, though, for me. You made sure he was found. Freddy wouldn't blame you for his death and neither do I. No one was to know what evil lay in store for our Freddy. But now we can help him. We can make sure the person who did this to Freddy gets his just deserts. That they're made to pay for what they've done. So, no matter what happens, we have to open up. We have to answer all the questions asked of us truthfully and honestly. No matter what the consequences are to ourselves. We must help the police one hundred per cent. Do you understand me, boys? The police need to know everything!"

"We understand, Mr Arnold," answered Paul for them both. Harry hugged the boys once more then was beckoned down a long corridor to meet the man in charge of the investigation.

Harry immediately took to Detective Inspector Jack Wilde. He seemed like a man who would stop at nothing to find the truth, the whole truth and nothing but the truth. After formally introducing himself, he'd gone on to bring Harry up to speed on the events so far. He'd then accompanied Harry to the local morgue to see Freddy. He'd stayed only for a few moments with Harry, then he had discreetly left Harry alone with his son. DI Jack Wilde had then waited outside until Harry had finally joined him.

It was already late in the day and Jack didn't want to keep Harry holed up in the police interview room all night. So together they strolled to a quiet restaurant that Jack knew served good food and over dinner Harry told Detective Inspector Wilde all about his doomed marriage to Elsie. DI Jack Wilde had been an avid listener. His gut feeling about something not being right about this case loomed large again in his stomach. He also had a sneaky feeling that Harry also thought that Elsie was perhaps more than an innocent victim in all of this. There was still no sign of her, but some useful information had come to light from both The Manchester public house staff and its owners. DI Wilde escorted Harry back to Mrs Davidson's B&B. She'd been only too happy to let Harry have the room Freddy had already paid for and the twins were already tucked up in their room for the night. As Jack made his way back to the station he was already forming a plan of action for the following day.

Early the next morning a break in the case came from the unlikely source of Mrs Taylor, the twins' mother. She'd phoned up the B&B her boys were staying in to check that they were all right. However, she got talking to Mrs Davidson and out came the conversation she'd had with Freddy on the phone. When Freddy had mentioned he was going to talk to his mum, she'd asked what on earth he was up to. Freddy had told her he'd gone up to Blackpool to check out if the information about her being there was true. He'd not only found out it was her and she was shacked up with this Derek bloke but that, while he was following her, he'd caught her up to her old tricks with some swanky bloke staying at the Grand Hotel on the front. Mrs Davidson had immediately told Mrs Taylor to contact the police and relay the conversation with Freddy to them; it could prove to be very important. It was just the break Detective Inspector Jack Wilde needed. Armed with two officers in uniform and photographs of both Elsie and Freddy, Jack descended on the Grand Hotel.

It hadn't taken long to establish that both Elsie and Freddy had been recent visitors to the Grand. The young girl on reception not only remembered Elsie but also that she'd been a frequent guest of a Mr Morris Connolly. She'd handed over Mr Connolly's home address and the time of him checking out. She'd added that he wasn't due to leave for another three days but a call had been taken on the Friday morning for him and he'd checked out by 1:30pm that same day. No, she hadn't taken the call. Mary Stokes had. It was her day off today, but she was happy to give them her home address as well if that would help. However, she'd not seen Freddy in the hotel. That didn't matter though. A bellboy had confirmed he'd spoken to Freddy on the Thursday evening. Something about, "other areas to eat, drink or sit". He'd informed him that there weren't, and he'd left. He hadn't seen him since. By Monday afternoon, the address given to the Grand Hotel as Mr Morris Connolly's home address was found to be bogus. Oh! A Mr Morris Connolly lived there all right, but he was a seventy-year-old farmer who had never in his life travelled further than the local farmers' market. Right now, the police artist was drawing up sketches of the said 'Mr Morris Connolly' from both the receptionists at the Grand. DI Jack Wilde had a team of officers knocking door to door with a photograph of Elsie in the vain hope that someone would recognise her and remember seeing her on the Friday. He still had a feeling that she had more to do with the demise of her son than just simply running away with a lover. But, unfortunately, that wasn't a crime he could charge her with when he eventually tracked her down. And track her down he would!

As for Derek Collins's tale of events, there was nothing of any significance to prove his innocence but a whole stack of it to prove his guilt. Unless he had a major breakthrough in the next day or so, Derek Collins was going to be found guilty of the murder of Frederick Arnold. And, still, it didn't rest easy with DI Jack Wilde. Too many questions were being left unanswered. Where was Elsie? Why hadn't she come forward if she had nothing to hide? He didn't believe for one minute she was dead. Murdered by Derek? It didn't fit! Why hide her body and not Freddy's? And who really was this Morris Connolly fellow? Why had he given a false name and address to the hotel? Yes, there were far too many unanswered questions for Jack and he wouldn't stop looking until they'd all been answered.

BEA

Monday, 21st September 1970

Derek Collins stared at the cold, grey walls of his cell in Strangeways Prison, Manchester. He was waiting for the courts to decide his fate on the murder of Frederick George Arnold. A murder he hadn't committed but he knew he'd be sentenced for. Without Elsie being found, he was damned. And he knew it. Derek knew that today Freddy's family would lay him to rest. He offered up a prayer for the poor young man. He suspected his own mother had stabbed him. He even suspected that Detective Inspector Jack Wilde had his own suspicions. But suspicions were of no help to Derek. He needed hard evidence and that was something he greatly lacked. Derek lay down on his bunk and for the umpteenth time tried to think of a way of finding the elusive Elsie and getting out of this nightmare she'd left him in.

In their local family church, Harry listened as the Reverend Stokes spoke so elegantly and knowledgably about his son. He talked of Freddy's christening in this very church. Of his time spent in Sunday School and his brief venture into the choir. Reverend Stokes spoke of a sensitive young man, who'd patiently taught his younger brother Charlie to ride a bike. Of how he'd walk Anne home from the Girl Guides on the dark winter nights. The times he'd spent down the local park, pushing little Janie on the swings. And how until his untimely death he'd worked side by side with his father at the family garage. Reverend Stokes finally wound up his eulogy with how greatly missed this young man would be by everyone who had ever met him.

"Time is a great healer," he finished off, "but no amount of time could ever fill the void that has been left by the sudden and so unnecessary death of young Freddy. Amen." Harry, holding tightly onto Janie's hand, led the procession behind Freddy's coffin out of the church and across the graveyard, to what was to be Freddy's last resting place. As they gathered around the graveside, Harry looked out across the sea of familiar faces, searching for one particular face. Finally, he found her! The black veil covering her face didn't fool him. It was her! She'd actually come! Bea had come to his rescue!

Beatrice Evesham had stood right at the back of the church during the funeral of the nephew she'd never got to meet. With her veiled face, her presence had gone unnoticed by her so-called family. Except for Harry, of course! Harry had recognised her straightaway at the graveside. Oh!

How her heart ached for her younger brother. He'd just been about to celebrate his tenth birthday, in 1943, when she'd been thrown out of the family home. The war was full on with Germany. Every able-bodied man and woman was doing their bit for the war effort. Bea's father, George, had shut up his small garage and gone off to keep the tanks rolling across enemy lines. If he'd been home, she'd never have been cast out. He would have seen through Mary's lies and would have gone on to welcome Arthur into their home and family. But, he hadn't been there to save her. But luckily, Bea had other allies in her camp. Allies that had helped make her forced exile bearable. Allies that had tried to tell George the truth on his return from the war. But war had changed George. He'd left as a strong-willed, determined man, only to return as a mere shadow of his former self. All the fight was gone from him. He'd just accepted the lies fed to him. He just let Ethel and Mary walk all over him.

Patricia Aston had remained her best friend and link to her home. Trish was the elder sister of Frank, Harry's best friend. In those first few dark weeks, months, years, Trish had, along with Irene, been her lifeline. Bea used to write to Trish, enclosing a message for Harry. Trish would pass on the message to Harry when he'd call round for her brother Frank. There'd always be a PS at the end of Trish's letter to Bea with a return message from Harry. Trish had continued to be their go-between until Harry left home. After that, they'd written directly to each other without the rest of the family knowing. Harry had pleaded with her over the years to come home. To clear her name. But Bea had refused. She had a new life. A wonderful life and even when Arthur passed away she had still refused to come home, as Bea hadn't been up for 'the battle', as she'd called it, with Mary and her mother. But now, now was different. Harry needed her to get through this dreadful period in his family's life. Now, it was time to return the favour, so to speak. So, two days ago, she'd made the journey home! Trish and her husband, Ron, had been letting her hide out at their home.

"It's the least we can do," they'd both said. "After all, you and Arthur gave us the money to buy this house back in 1955 when we got married. Bea had smiled at that. Back then they'd fought against the very idea, but she and Arthur had won out.

"Let's call it a loan," Arthur had said. "A no-interest loan, with no time limits and only one restriction. You pay us back the exact amount when we ask and not before." And that had been that. Over the years, they'd offered both Arthur and Bea the money, but they'd always refused it. "We'll ask when we need it," they'd always replied. Finally, they'd stopped asking and accepted that they'd never be asked to repay the money. But every now and then it was brought up in jest, just like it had when Bea had asked if they'd take her in, prior to Freddy's funeral.

Bea had returned to Patricia's after the funeral. She'd waited there patiently, for most of the mourners to leave the wake back at Harry's, before making her entrance. Now, she was standing just inside the living room, veil still in place. Harry somehow sensed she was there and rushed over and held her in a warm embrace. The chatter stopped. Tension filled the room. Who was this woman Harry had run to embrace? It couldn't possibly be Elsie, could it? Noticing how quiet the room had gone, Harry released Bea and slowly she raised the veil from her face. Instantly, Mary set about her.

"How dare you show your face here," she screamed. "You have no right to be here. We don't need your sort round here. This is NOT YOUR FAMILY. Just FUCK OFF back into whatever hole you crawled out of." Bea had come prepared for this and was determined to stand her ground.

"Still shouting out the odds according to your rules, I see, Mary," began Bea smiling. "Still stamping your feet if you don't get your own way," she added. "Well, I'm back, Mary. In fact, if truth be told, I should never have been made to leave. Thrown out by my own mother because you DIDN'T GET YOUR OWN WAY. Poor little spoilt Mary had mummy throw the naughty girl out."

"You stole my man, Beatrice Arnold. You and your sluttish ways. Came onto him like a bad rash, you did. Arthur didn't stand a chance against your wicked ways."

Bea just laughed out loud.

"I stole your man?" she chuckled. "Arthur was never YOUR man, Mary. Arthur thought you was a vicious, back-stabbing cow. He'd say, you'd never guess in a million years we were related, let alone sisters."

"That doesn't surprise me," butted in Mary. "You with your boobs hung out for all the world to see. Fluttering your eyelashes, face caked in make-up, reeking of cheap perfume. While I showed respect for myself. I didn't go around flaunting my wares for all the world to see." Mary became even more angry by Bea laughing even louder than before.

"What's so funny, Bea?" she snarled.

"You! You stupid cow. You walked around in Dad's overalls from the garage like you owned the place. Treating people like dirt, with that venomous tongue of yours. You never had a kind word for anyone. But you couldn't handle it when someone stood up to you, could you, Mary? You'd run off crying to mummy when someone said something hurtful to you. Then Mummy would give whoever had upset her precious Mary a right tongue lashing, wouldn't she? Even going so far as to cast aside her other daughter. And what for, Mary? Hey! Did it send Arthur flying into your arms? No, it didn't? Instead he lost interest in the farm. Handed it over to the war effort and signed up for active duty. People relied on him, Mary. He wasn't just their boss. He not only paid them good wages but made sure families were well taken care of while their menfolk fought on the front line."

"Yes, Bea. Those families, ours included, lost out because of you. Arthur was just a good time to you, but he meant a roof over most people's head and food on their table to others. Lots of families went hungry when the government took over. There were no more food parcels for them."

"No, Mary, it wasn't my fault, it was yours," intervened Bea. "That day mum threw me out on the street, I didn't go running to Arthur. I went to see Aunt Vi. She gave me some money and an address of an old friend of hers that would take me in. I set off that very same day, for

Llandudno. For three years I lived and worked alongside Irene Stevenson, in her small haberdashery. Then one day Arthur appeared in the shop doorway. He told me how he tried to convince mum that I'd done nothing wrong. That he had no interest in Mary, that he never had and that he never would. But she refused to believe him. Said I'd stolen him from her lovely Mary. She was so blinded by your lies she'd been unable to see the truth. Even when it was right there in front of her. So, Arthur had handed over the farm to the government, donned a uniform and went off to fight for his country. He was captured and held in a German prison camp till the war was over. On his return to England, he was handed back the farm but couldn't face running it. Couldn't face living in the same area as YOU or our mother. So, he sold it and purchased a little flat over a small general store in New Quay, Wales. He threw himself into the business in an attempt to put all the horror of war and losing me out of his mind. But he just couldn't forget about me. Then, one day a customer asked him what it was that troubled him so. He showed him an old photograph of me. One that Harry had given to him the day that he'd left for war. The customer recognised me immediately. I was the young lass living and working with his sister-in-law in Llandudno. So, there he was. Arthur Evesham. I couldn't believe my eyes. He asked me to marry him that very same day and I said yes! So, you see, Mary, IT WAS YOU! You and mum, who drove not just me away but Arthur too. You two, who caused people you knew to lose out, not me."

Mary sneered at her younger sister.

"So, if all this is true, where's your precious Arthur now? See he's not here to back up YOUR LIES!"

"He's dead, Mary. My lovely, sweet Arthur is dead, while you evil bitches roam this earth spewing your hatred. It makes me sick." Bea spat out. Mary, thinking, once again only of herself, decided to turn her hatred onto Harry. The few remaining mourners looked on in horror.

"Harry," she screamed, "if you think for one minute this WHORE is staying in our family home, you're wrong. Once mum and dad find out you've welcomed their good-for-nothing daughter back into their home, you'll be out on your ear just as she was. And what will become of you and the kids then, hey? Harry? Answer me that?"

"It's MY house now, Mary, along with the garage. Dad and mum signed it over to me, as you well know. So, there'll be no throwing out of anyone unless I say so. And guess what, Mary? I'm throwing you out."

"We'll see about that," Mary shouted over her shoulder, as she shoved her way past Bea. "Just you wait till mum and dad hear what I have to tell them." Mary slammed the front door as hard as she could behind her.

"Still throwing her dummy out of the pram and telling lies, I see!" quirked Bea.

"Oh, yes!" replied Harry, then everyone in the room burst into laughter. At some point in their lives they'd all been a victim of Mary's vicious tongue and to see her put in her place was definitely something to laugh about on such a sombre day.

GEORGE

George Arnold was enjoying a large whiskey, sitting in his favourite armchair by the fireside. His wife, Ethel, was on the sofa, her knitting needles going ten to the dozen. George took a large gulp of whiskey and felt the warmth of it trickle down his throat. He stared at the framed photograph on the mantelpiece. It had been taken earlier that year. George had happened to pop round on that Sunday afternoon. Harry, Freddy, Anne, Charlie and Janie were all in the back garden enjoying the early May sunshine. George had been quickly followed in by the Taylor twins. Peter had a fancy new camera and was eager to test it out. So he'd had them all stand together so he could take a group shot of the family. Two weeks later, Peter had presented both George and Harry with identical framed photographs from that day. They'd all been smiling directly at the camera. It showed such a happy family. George wiped the tears from his eyes. Today it was such a sad family. Today he'd had to bury his grandson. George took another swig of whisky and this time drained his glass.

"Don't think you're getting another," chirped up his wife. George looked across at her. His cold, bitter wife. What had he ever seen in her? He remembered she had once been a beauty, but she'd never been a warm, loving person. Ethel was more of a glass-half-empty girl, while George had been more of a glass-half-full type of person (well, until the war he had). Chalk and cheese, his old dad used to say about them.

"No good drinking yourself into a stupor," screeched Ethel. "It won't solve anything. Freddy's gone. We have to put it behind us. Move on. Think of the living," she remarked. George, after fifty years of marriage, was still shocked by how heartless his wife could be. The only person she ever showed any compassion to was their miserable daughter Mary. She was definitely cut from the same cloth as her mother. Almost as Mary entered his head, she appeared in their living room doorway. Her face was bright red and sheer hatred oozed from every fibre of her body.

"You'll never guess who's had the nerve to turn up like butter wouldn't melt in her mouth at your grandson's wake?" Mary didn't wait for a reply, she just continued to rant and rave. "Only, that WHORE BEA! That's who! And guess who welcomed her with open arms? Bloody Harry did! And he stood there and let that WHORE talk to me like I was something that she'd scrapped off her shoe! I told them! I said, wait till mum and dad here about this! You'll all be out on your ear! How dare Harry invite that

WHORE into your home!" Finally, Mary ran out of breath. Ethel threw her knitting down on the sofa beside her and got to her feet.

"We'll see about that," she began. "Come on, George, we'll go sort this out right now." George didn't move. He just glared, first at his daughter, then at his wife.

"I said get up, George. GET UP THIS INSTANCE," yelled Ethel at her husband. The anger in George rose like he had never known before. He slammed down his whisky glass so hard on the wooden coffee table that it shattered on impact.

"WHAT DO YOU THINK YOU ARE PLAYING AT?" insisted Ethel. "YOU BEST GET CLEAR THAT UP NOW AND DON'T YOU DARE BLEED ON MY CARPET," she shouted at him. George felt all the years of suppressed anger for his wife rising to the surface. After all these years, George was finally laying the ghosts of the war to rest and George of old was now rising to the surface like a phoenix from the ashes.

"SHUT UP, WOMAN," he roared at Ethel. "SHUT UP AND SIT BACK DOWN. AS FOR YOU, MARY!" he shouted, turning to her. "YOU CAN BUGGER OFF HOME AND FOR ONCE KEEP YOUR NOSE OUT OF OTHER PEOPLE'S BUSINESS." All indignant, Mary addressed her mother.

"Are you going to allow him to speak to you and me like that, Mother?" she asked.

"I'll speak to you both how I see fit," shouted George. "Now get out of my house before I throw you out."

"I'm going," yelled Mary at her father. "But don't

expect me to come crawling back, because I won't," and she turned and left the room.

"THANK GOD FOR THAT!" shouted George after her. The next thing he heard was the front door slamming shut. George turned back to look at his wife. She was white from the shock of her husband answering her back.

"Twenty-seven years ago, you and that vicious daughter of yours drove Bea from, not just her home, but her family, her friends, her job and from the man she so innocently fell in love with. You cast her out like a leper while I was away fighting for king and country. All these years I've lived with the guilt of not being here to defend an innocent child. Our child. Because, Ethel, she was just a child. Barely sixteen she was. And why was she cast out like an old shoe? Because she fell in love with a man who her elder sister was besotted by. A man that could barely tolerate the sight of our Mary. Who wouldn't have noticed her if she was the last woman on earth!"

"Arthur would have noticed Mary and he would have married our Mary if that harlot Beatrice hadn't forced her way into his affections," replied Ethel. George let a harrowing laugh.

"For Christ's sake, Ethel! Mary worked on Arthur's farm for five long years before our Bea ever set foot on it. In all those years, he never looked twice at Mary. He never asked her on a date. The only things he ever asked our Mary to do were work-related tasks. He had NO INTEREST in Mary. Yet, the first day, our Bea goes to work there, Arthur asked her if she cared to join him for dinner that very same evening. The first day, Ethel." George wrapped his handkerchief around his bleeding hand as he spoke. "Bea did nothing wrong, Ethel. Everyone knew that, apart from you and Mary. So you both told lies. Made out Bea had stolen Arthur from Mary. You pair didn't even stop your vicious lies after Bea was long gone." George let out a muffled laughed. Then the memories came flooding back and his smile was replaced by a look of sadness.

"I came back from the war a broken man. I'd seen things no man should ever see. Me! A mere mechanic, faced with the atrocities of war. Home was all I thought about. You, Mary, Bea, Harry and the garage. It kept me going. Then what do I find when I finally get home? My lovely Bea has been hounded from her home by her own mother and sister. Nobody wanted to tell me what had happened. I only had your version of events to go on. I tried to find Arthur but again nobody seemed to know or care. I should have fought harder for Bea, but war had taken all the fight out of me. When I asked Patricia Aston, she would only say that Bea was safe. She'd promised Bea she'd say no more. I'd resigned myself to never seeing or ever knowing what had really happened while I was gone. I let you lead the way. I just wasn't interested anymore."

"You'd never had much backbone, George Arnold. You were weak before the war came along and you were weaker still when you came back. If I hadn't pushed you'd have had us out on the street." Ethel started to rant.

"It was you that made me weak, Ethel. Everything with you was always a battle. You had to have everything your way or there was hell to pay. Mary is the same and Bea paid the price for getting in her way. Well! No more!

Enough is enough. I know what really happened back then. I know Arthur came to see you. He came to right Mary's wrong, but you'd not listen. You took Mary's side as always. Because darling Mary must always have what she wants. But Mary didn't get her own way, did she? Oh, Bea was gone all right but that didn't get Mary Arthur, did it? NO! Because he left soon after. Two lives you ruined that day, along with mine, didn't you?"

"You know nothing of what happened that day. You're just guessing because your darling Bea couldn't be to blame, could she? Dad's little girl could do no wrong."

"I'm not guessing, Ethel. I know. It was Bea's birthday and I was very down. Harry gave me the letters to read he'd been receiving from Bea since she'd left. Harry had always known the truth, but he made me swear not to reveal what I'd learnt."

"If Harry knew the truth, then why didn't he confront us? Why let us be part of his life? Eh! Answer me that if you can." Ethel spat the words out at her husband. George just stared at her. She was so caught up in her own lies, her own sense of truth that it almost scared him.

"Bea asked him not to," George answered calmly. "Just as she asked Patricia not to. Bea had made a good life for herself, she didn't need you or Mary poking your nasty noses in. She wanted to be left alone with her Arthur. And who could blame her? Not me. So, I kept shtum. For over ten years, now, Harry's kept me informed on how Bea's doing. And all the time my hatred of you and Mary has festered away inside me. I've waited so long for this day. The day when Bea would finally return. Well, that day has arrived. Bea's come back of her own accord to help Harry. She's come back knowing that she'll have a war on her hands with you and Mary. But this time Bea's got an army to fight you both with. She's got me, she's got Harry and by the time we've finished spreading the word you'll be the ones without a friend in the world."

Now it was Ethel's turn to laugh.

"Big talk from such a little man," she began. "And just how do you think you can help her, George? You've said yourself, you are weak where I'm concerned. Do you really think you can stand up against me, George? You couldn't stand up to me even with help from of your precious Beatrice and your devious son Harry behind you." George headed for the front door. Then turned to face his wife one last time.

"Oh! That's where you're so wrong, Ethel. It's you that's going to need all the help you can get because, dearest Ethel, I WANT A DIVORCE! I want this bungalow sold and I want a life without you in it! And right now I'm going to Harry's to ask Bea if she can ever forgive her father for his failings. After that, I'm going to see about bedding down at Frank's for the night. I'll be back tomorrow for my things and you'd best not be here if you know what's good for ya." Now it was George's turn to slam the front door shut as hard as he could.

Harry had been expecting a visit from his mother, not his father. So, when he opened the front door and found his father standing there with the biggest grin on his face he'd ever seen, Harry thought his father had gone mad. Even more so when he began to speak.

"I've sent our Mary packing and I've had a few words with your mother too. In fact, son, I've told her I want the bungalow sold and a divorce. I've waited a long time to put that old bat in her place. So, when Mary stormed in, shouting the odds about our Bea being back. Well! Son, I let rip, I can tell ya. Now! Where's our Bea? I've got some serious apologising to do." Harry could hardly believe what his father was saying. Stunned, he stood aside to let George pass, then shut the door and followed his dad into the living room. Immediately on seeing Bea, George began to regale his story and apologises to his youngest daughter. Bea listened carefully as her father told her how, after many years, Harry had broken his silence and had shown him Bea's letters. How, ever since that day, he had hidden the loathing he felt for wife and Mary. Until today. Her return had set him free, he said. Free to begin a new life before it really was too late for him. Bea told George that she had never blamed him for what had happened and neither had Arthur. As far as she was concerned, there was nothing to forgive him for. They'd held onto each other, almost afraid to move apart in case the spell of happiness that had been cast upon them was broken. They'd both missed not having the other around. Finally, George left for Frank's, with a spring in his step and a renewed zest for life. But there was one more stop to make before Frank's.

George stood by the fresh mound of earth covering his grandson's coffin and began to speak.

"You would have loved Bea, Freddy. I'm only sorry that you never got to meet her. Even more sorry that it took your death to bring her back to us. I've no doubt your Aunt Mary and Gran filled your head with tales of her wanton ways. Well, she wasn't like that, Freddy. She was a gentle child. Warm and loving. Funny too. I used to wonder where all that good nature of hers came from. It certainly wasn't from your gran. Then I'd remember. I used to laugh a lot before I meet Ethel. You look at the world through rose-tinted glasses, she used to say. I think she stole those lovely glasses from me, along with my desire to laugh. But I've got a new pair now, Freddy and for the first time in a long time I can see a better future. My only regret is that you're not here to share it. But I know you're up there, watching over us now. I best be off now, lad, but I'll be back. I'll be here so often that you'll be sick of the sight of me. Love you, kiddo."

JANIE & BEA

Janie lay in her bed and thought what an odd day it had been. At six and three quarters, she'd never been to a funeral before and she certainly didn't want to go to one again. She missed Freddy so much; it just didn't seem fair that he was dead, especially when there were really old people, like miserable old Mr Forbes who lived next to the green, still alive. It just didn't make sense. Janie didn't like the thought of Freddy being in a coffin down in that deep dark hole. It was all wrong. Today had been all wrong. Everything was changing again. Just when she seemed to get used to things, they changed! First her mum had gone. Change! Then Freddy had gone. Change! Then this Bea had arrived. Change! Now grandad was leaving granny. Change! Would it ever stop? Why did things have to keep changing? She hadn't wanted her mum to leave or Freddy to die. Had she done something really bad to make all these things happen? She didn't think she had. And now, not only was her head hurting but she was crying again, and she couldn't make either of them stop.

"Janie's crying, Dad," said Charlie as he entered the living room. "I could hear her as I passed her bedroom door." Harry got up to go see to his daughter but Bea stopped him.

"Let me go see to her, Harry, please," asked Bea. "Give us a chance to get to know one another, hey?"

"Okay, Bea, thanks." Bea patted her brother's shoulder and headed upstairs to Janie's room. She knocked gently on the door before entering. Janie was hiding under the covers but Bea could still hear Janie's suppressed sobs. She perched on the edge of the bed and began to tenderly stroke the mound beneath the covers.

"Let them all out, sweetheart," Bea began. "You'll feel so much better when you've let them all out, believe me. I've cried many tears over the loss of loved ones over the years. I've also got angry and screamed and shouted at the unfairness of it all. It didn't change anything. None of it did. But, boy, did I feel better afterwards." Janie began to peek over the covers. Her tears were silently ebbing away.

"You told Aunt Mary that Arthur was dead. Was he one of your loved ones?" she asked. Bea smiled down at the little puffy-eyed girl.

"He was. Arthur was my husband, Janie. I loved him very much."

"Was he murdered like Freddy was?"

"No, sweetheart. Arthur was taken very poorly one day. He had a tumour on his brain that wouldn't stop growing and there was nothing anyone could do to stop it. He was in lots of pain before he died but he never complained; he was very brave. I wasn't so brave. I cried lots and lots. I shouted and screamed a lot too. I was very angry at the world, at everyone and everything for a very long time. But then I realised that Arthur wouldn't want me to be so sad. To be so angry and upset all the time. He'd want me to be happy. To live the life, we'd planned. So, I stopped crying and I did what he'd have wanted me to do. I started living again for the both of us."

"So, you were brave in the end?"

"Oh, yes, sweetheart, I was. I still am. And together we can make you brave too."

"Freddy would want me to be brave, wouldn't he?" enquired Janie.

"Of course he would. You've got to live enough for you and Freddy now."

"I can do that?" perked up Janie.

"Of course you can, sweetheart." Bea brushed aside a curl from Janie's cheek. "You just have to believe in yourself and Freddy."

"Oh, I do believe, I do. It's just I don't want things to keep changing. I don't like it."

"You've gone through some bad changes that's all, Janie. Not all changes are bad. Some are very good. I can see some good changes coming your way, I really can."

"Can you, really."

"Oh, yes, Janie. Now you get some sleep and we'll talk about these new changes in the morning over the lovely breakfast I'm going to cook us all, okay?"

"Okay, Aunt Bea. Night, night." Janie snuggled back down under the covers.

"Night, night, sweetheart, sleep tight."

"And I won't let the bed bugs bite," chorused Janie from beneath the sheets.

Janie woke the next morning to the smell of bacon cooking. She quickly slipped on her dressing gown and slippers and headed downstairs to the kitchen. Sitting round the table was Anne and Charlie, while Bea was busy frying eggs on the stove. Janie plonked herself down beside Charlie.

"I like my bacon crispy and my eggs runny," she exclaimed.

"I've already told Aunt Bea," began Charlie. "I've even told her you don't like the skin or cores on your tomatoes too." Janie beamed at Charlie. He was only three years older than her but he was so much wiser, she thought. Bea placed the cooked breakfast down in front of Janie. It was perfect.

"Thank you," Janie said politely to Bea.

"You're very welcome," she replied.

"She's not going to have time to eat that before school," scoffed Anne.

"Your father has informed the schools that none of you will be in today," began Bea.

"Why ever not?" cut in Anne. Bea shrugged off Anne's butting in. Harry had already warned her that Anne would be a problem. So she continued her answer without any sign of annoyance in her voice.

"He's holding a family meeting later this morning to discuss with you all the future of this family and—"

Again Anne butted in.

"Have Aunt Mary and Gran been told to come?" Bea was beginning to get a little ruffled now.

"They are not invited, Anne. It only concerns those living h—"

"Aunt Mary and Gran have always been invited. I don't see why today should be any different, just because you—"

This time it was mild-mannered Charlie's turn to cut in.

"Anne, let Aunt Bea explain, will you?"

"Well, I don't—"

"Your father, Anne," Bea began, "has invited me to live here." Anne was poised to butt in again but Bea quickly put her off with a raised finger to her lips. "I've agreed to be here during school term time, but I'll be spending the school holidays at my cottage in Talybont, Wales. During term time, I will take over the day-to-day running of this house and you children. In the holidays, you will be given the choice of staying here or joining me by the sea."

"I thought you'd told Aunt Mary that you lived in New Quay with Arthur. Or was that just another one of your lies?" spat out Anne. Bea inhaled deeply. Harry was right. She was going to have her work cut out with Anne. She obviously had the same mindset as both her Aunt Mary and Gran.

"When we were first married, we did live in New Quay. Together we ran the shop. But a couple of years later we bought a derelict cottage overlooking the sea in Talybont. There Arthur would paint and I'd sew."

"SEE, Anne, Aunt Bea wasn't lying. So, did you sell

the shop with the flat?" continued Charlie. Then both he and Janie poked their tongues out at Anne and started to giggle. Bea smiled at their antics.

"No, we didn't, Charlie. In fact, the same couple still live in the flat and run the shop who took over when we left."

"Did you give it to them?" asked Janie.

"No," giggled Bea now. "They rent it from us, well, me now. I offered them to buy me out after Arthur died but they just wanted to continue to rent, so that's what we settled on."

"Aunt Bea?" Janie asked with her mouth full of bacon. "Do you not have any children?"

Charlie nudged Janie.

"That's rude, Janie." said Charlie. Bea gave them both a big smile.

"No, sweetheart, I've never had a child. Oh, Arthur and I wanted one more than anything else in the world. For many years we wondered why it wasn't happening to us, then, finally, I fell pregnant. For two glorious months we were the happiest people on earth. Then Arthur fell ill, very suddenly. The brain tumour took hold very quickly and within weeks he was gone. The shock of it all and the grief from losing my Arthur took its toll and I was rushed into hospital, where later I lost our baby." The smiles fell from both Janie's and Charlie's faces at the sad news, but Anne waded in with a horrible remark.

"Well, I'd say it was for the best. That baby could have been born with some dreadful disease from that brain tumour her dad had."

"ANNE BEATRICE ARNOLD, you take that back," shouted Harry from the doorway. He'd come in through the back door as Bea was explaining about not having any children and was mortified by what Anne had just said.

"No!" replied Anne. "It's true, it could have been born—"

"STOP RIGHT NOW, YOUNG LADY, AND APOLOGISE NOW FOR SUCH A CALLOUS REMARK," roared Harry at his eldest daughter. Anne just dug her heels in.

"NO, I WON'T, I'VE DONE NOTHING WRONG," she replied, all indignant. Harry could feel his blood reaching boiling point.

"I SAID, TAKE IT BACK AND APOLOGISE NOW," he shouted at Anne. Anne visibly shook but still refused to apologise.

"I'm not apologising for speaking the truth," began Anne. "I'm only saying what everyone was probably thinking at the time."

"My baby was perfect in every way," cut in Bea. "It was my grief that caused the miscarriage, nothing else. Every day I live with the guilt of that. The guilt that I killed my baby, our baby. Arthur's brain tumour wasn't contagious or hereditary. I caused the death of our baby. I couldn't keep anything down. I couldn't provide the nourishment she needed to grow. To survive. So, you see, Anne, it wasn't for the best. It was the worst possible thing that could have happened. In such a short space of time I'd lost the love of my life and our child. If I'd been able to eat properly, been able to stop myself from vomiting, to stop the pain in my heart and the tears from constantly running down my face, I could have saved her. But I couldn't. So the pain grew worse until I could no longer bear it. I took an overdose. I wanted to die. I was happy to die. I wanted to be with my Arthur and our unborn child. But God had other plans for me. I was found before it was too late. I was nursed back to health by the same wonderful lady who'd taken me in all those years before. She made me strong again. Gave me the strength to carry on. To ignore the rants of vicious, jealous people. Because that's all those sorts of remarks are."

"I'm not jealous of you," spat out Anne. "I'm not jealous of an old whore like you! I'm—"

"Get out of this house right now, Anne, and don't come back until you've learnt to have a civil tongue in your head," shouted Harry.

"It's okay, Harry, there's really no need," began Bea.

"Oh, there is. Things are changing round here, believe me. I've let things slide since Elsie left and poor young Freddy's death only made that worse. I let Mary and our mother have too much control over my home and family these past few months but not anymore.

"And you think letting a whore look after your house and kids is a better idea?" raged Anne.

"OUT! GET OUT NOW, BEFORE I SLAP YOU SO HARD, GIRL, THAT YOU'LL NOT KNOW WHAT DAY OF THE WEEK IT IS," yelled Harry. Bea came to stand between Anne and Harry. She had no desire to see anyone get slapped and poor little Janie looked about to burst into tears.

"Why don't you go to your room, Anne? Give everyone

time to calm down and gather their thoughts." But Anne was having none of it. Bea's interference only incensed her all the more.

"Oh, shut up, you old hag. I don't have to listen to the likes of you," Anne snarled at Bea. Janie at this point began to cry. "And you can shut up as well, you ginger-haired cow." She screamed at Janie. Suddenly Anne felt the full force of her father's hand as it made contact with her left cheek. The whole left side of her face felt like it was on fire. Anne glared at Harry. Her father had never raised a hand to her before. Oh, she'd had more than her fair share of beltings off her mother, but never her father. He'd never hit any of his children and had often chided her mother for being quick to lash out, and now he'd hit her. The shock was now being replaced by pure hatred, not for Harry but for Bea and Janie. They were to blame for this.

"This is all your fault, whore," she screamed at Bea. "Dad's never laid a finger on us before today. See what happens, Dad, when you let people in who don't belong in this family? You forget about me, Charlie, Aunt Mary and Gran. Instead you take sides with your whore of a sister and some other man's kid."

The sound of Harry's hand contacting Anne's cheek for a second time echoed around the kitchen.

"Now get out of my house, Anne, and stay out. You're evil. You've let them old hags brainwash you. Well, now you can go stay with them. I've washed my hands of you and your vicious tongue. Now, get out before I really lose my temper." Anne stared at her father, defiant to the end.

"You can't just throw me out, in the eyes of the law I'm

still a minor." The cockiness in her voice belied her fifteen years. Harry eyed his daughter coldly then walked out into the hallway and picked up the receiver of the telephone and began to dial.

"Who do you think you're phoning?" asked Anne, with the cockiness still in her voice. Harry answered his daughter calmly, as he continued to dial.

"Social services to have you taken into care."

"You can't do that," responded Anne, with a quiver in her voice now.

"As you said, Anne. You're a minor, I can't throw you out, but I can place you into care." Anne came hurling into the hallway and cut the call off.

"You're not sticking me in some godforsaken children's home to rot. I'm off to Aunt Mary's." And with that she headed straight out of the front door, slamming it behind her. Harry replaced the receiver back on its cradle and walked back into the kitchen and sat down at the table. Janie's eyes were all swollen, but she'd stopped crying. She looked so lost, so confused by what had taken place.

"Come sit on your dad's knee, pumpkin," Harry said while holding his arms out to Janie. Janie immediately scampered round onto Harry's knee and curled herself into his open arms.

"What did Anne mean by I'm someone else's kid?" she asked. Harry felt his heart ache for this poor little child.

"Nothing, pumpkin. Anne was just angry, and she lashed out at Aunt Bea and you. You're my little pumpkin and Aunt Bea isn't a whore or an old hag. Anne was just being spiteful."

"She wasn't spiteful about Charlie though?"

"No, she wasn't, pumpkin. She wanted to keep Charlie on her side, that's why. Pay no attention to her."

"But why's she so angry, Daddy? Aunt Bea had made us a lovely breakfast and had said we could go live with her by the sea in the summer holidays." Harry brushed away the tiny red curls from her forehead and planted a tender kiss there.

"Anne has been listening to all the lies that Aunt Mary and your gran have spread about your Aunt Bea. Unfortunately, Anne believes them, not us. So, she doesn't want Aunt Bea to stay and look after us. She wants me to send Bea away and let Mary take care of us."

"I want Aunt Bea to stay," chirped up Charlie. "Aunt Mary makes us eat that horrible lumpy porridge and she's always clipping me round my ear. I'll be either deaf or brain-damaged if she continues to look after us." Harry smiled at Charlie.

"She pulls that hard brush through my hair every morning, cursing my curls," added Janie.

"So, Bea," asked Harry. "Are you going to make horrid porridge, clip ears and try to straighten out curls?"

Bea smiled at the three of them.

"I only make smooth, milky porridge. I wash ears, not clip them, and I absolutely love your curls, Janie, so there'll be NO straightening of them while I'm in charge. However, I do expect you to eat your greens, say please and thank you and, lastly but most importantly, I expect you both to be normal, happy children."

"Hurray," cheered Charlie and Janie in unison.

"So, that's settled then. Aunt Bea stays."

"YES, YES, YES," yelled out both children. Then Janie climbed down off Harry's knee and went and gave Bea a big hug.

"I'm going to like this change," announced Janie.

ELSIE

June 1971

Elsie re-read the small column in the national newspaper, for the umpteenth time.

BLACKPOOL MUDERER JAILED

Kenneth Harlow was yesterday sentenced to life imprisonment for the murder of Frederick Arnold last August in the seaside resort of Blackpool. Harlow was residing there under the name of Derek Collins. One of the many aliases used by the accused. He had been sought by the police up and down the country, for numerous accounts of GBH and similar offences. Judge Fairbourne recommended that he serve at least 15 years for the senseless murder of a young man whose only crime was in trying to make contact with his absent mother.

Mrs Elsie Arnold has not been seen or heard of since that fateful day. Detective Inspector Jack Wilde said that all lines of enquires to locate her had been fruitless. The Inspector had gone on to say "he would not rest until Mrs Arnold had been found." The Arnold family were not in court for the sentencing.

Elsie hadn't known that Derek was really Kenneth Harlow until the case came to court. In fact, she hadn't known about his suspect past at all. As always in a rush to get out of one relationship, she'd just hurtled straight into another without stopping to find out who she was really getting involved with. And history had repeated itself yet again for Elsie. Morris Connolly was the not the respectable businessman he'd led her to believe back in Blackpool. Morris Connolly, just like Derek, had several aliases! To his wife and children, he was Douglas Moore. To acquaintances he was Seamus O'Brien. To Elsie, Morris Connolly. And to his IRA counterparts, Paddy Adams. And they were just the ones she was privy to. All Elsie's dreams of a good life with Morris had been shattered within weeks of landing in Ireland with him. She was not to be his adored mistress, lavished with expensive gifts and doted upon. No, Elsie was more like his prisoner! She was kept in a small farmhouse in the middle of nowhere with a constant bodyguard. When Morris arrived, he was usually closely followed by several other men. Elsie had seen all of their faces appear on both the local and national news in connection with recent bombings and shootings. While they locked themselves away in the front living room, Elsie was banished to the kitchen to prepare them all food. Once their meeting and the food was finished they'd leave. Morris would stay on a little longer to quench his sexual appetite. As time passed, his idea of sexual fun was becoming more and more brutal. After he was finished with her, he'd leave. Elsie then was left clear instructions to clean the place up and have it at the ready for further visits.

Morris and his friends had been the previous evening. The farmhouse was a mess and Elsie's back, red raw from the lashing from Morris's latest toy, a cat-o'-nine-tails. The only thing Elsie could focus on now was the brand-new passport sitting in the dresser drawer. Morris had shown it to her after everyone else had left for the evening. He had then told her of his plan to set England alight. Elsie was part of that plan. Together they'd travel to London. Not as a married couple but as a businessman with his secretary on a business trip. Once in London the plan was to plant as many nail bombs around the capitol as they could. Elsie was to travel with Burt, her bodyguard, to Belfast at the end of the week, today being Wednesday, where she'd be taken to a safe house. Once there Burt would return to the farmhouse. Elsie would be there for three days. During this time, she was to buy suitable clothing for her role as a secretary. Her blonde locks were to be dyed a deep brown and spectacles were to be purchased. Everything about her was to be forgettable. There should be nothing about her that would draw attention to either herself or Morris. Instead of her usual Marilyn Monroe image, she was to go more for the plain-Jane look. Morris himself would be collecting her on the Monday to travel to London.

Elsie had no desire to go back to England, especially on some IRA bombing spree. She had too much to lose. If she were recognised or turned in to the police she'd be done for. She knew that this Detective Inspector Jack Wilde suspected her of being in some way involved in Freddy's murder and she also knew he'd do his damn best to prove it. She had no intention of ending her days in Holloway Prison. Elsie also knew that Morris kept a stash of money behind the bath panel in the bathroom he'd had installed before she'd arrived. She'd woken up one night, just after New Year, to hear him cursing in the bathroom and a knocking sound. She'd waited a couple of days to check out what Morris had been doing in the bathroom. So, armed with her portable transistor radio and a book, Elsie had told Burt she was going to take a long soak in a hot bath. With the taps running and the radio blasting out the latest tunes, Elsie had managed to prise open the bath panel enough to peek in. Using the small torch she'd concealed in her toiletry bag, she'd peered into the gloom. In neatly stacked piles around the legs of the bathtub and under its belly were wads of notes, of all denominations. A small fortune lay concealed there. Ever since then, Elsie had made regular checks on the money. It was still there. That money, along with her newly acquired passport, was her way out. She'd pack a large amount of that money into her travel bag just before Burt took her to Belfast. As soon as he was gone she'd head into town and straight to the local travel agents. There she'd book the first available flight out to Spain, or anywhere in Europe failing that. She'd then dye her hair as Morris had requested and buy not secretary's clothing but holiday attire. Come Monday morning, with any luck, she'd be sitting by a hotel pool drinking sangria when Morris came to collect her.

JACK

March 1976

Recently promoted Detective Chief Inspector Jack Wilde made his way into the interview rooms of Wandsworth Prison. He'd been given clearance to interview an IRA man who had recently been captured after a foiled attempt at bombing a city-centre pub. Jack had no interest in the man's IRA activity, only in his apparent dealings with the elusive Elsie Arnold. DCI Jack Wilde had never stopped looking for Elsie and finally he was on the verge of getting a genuine lead on her. Jack took his seat at the table and waited for the prisoner to arrive.

Douglas Moore entered the room, screaming and shouting at the prison guards. Jack found this big man laughable. Despite being caught planting a bomb in a busy pub, being identified by another captured

IRA member as one of their hotshots and having had numerous passports, licences and guns found in several of his properties, he was still shouting out his innocence. Jack lit a cigarette and offered the now-seated Douglas Moore one. He gave Jack a curious look then accepted the proffered cigarette. Jack lit the cigarette and Douglas inhaled deeply, letting the smoke curl from his lips.

"So, what can I do for you?" asked Moore.

"I'm here to ask after an old flame of yours," replied Jack. Moore laughed out loud.

"You expect a man like me to remember some bird I've poked. You're having me on, mate, surely?" Jack smiled at Moore and took a drag on his cigarette. He'd met too many 'hard men' to feel intimidated by this one.

"Oh, I'm sure you'll remember this one. You picked her up on my turf in Blackpool. She used to visit you at the Grand Hotel. You and she went AWOL the day her son got stabbed to death in the alley at the back of her flat." Jack stared Moore right in the eyes as he spoke. "You went under the name of Morris Connolly then. A passport was found in that name in your hotel room. You fit the description of him perfectly." Jack continued to stare straight into Moore's eyes. They were darting all over the place, but the expression on his face gave away the truth. He'd remembered Elsie and he obviously wasn't best pleased with her.

"I'm gathering from the look of pure rage on your face you remember our Elsie Arnold, or, should I say, your May Collins. Like you, Moore, she liked to change her name." Moore let out a deep sigh and pursed his lips before spitting on the floor. Then he leaned back in his chair and grinned.

"So, what if I did know this Elsie woman? What's it to you? Or, more importantly, what's it worth to me?" Jack had been expecting this. Moore wasn't going to get any deal from either him or anyone in the entire judicial service, but he wasn't to know that.

"Well, Moore, that depends on how useful your information is to us." Douglas Moore didn't like the vibes he was getting off this DCI. He'd come across a lot of coppers in his time and this one was one of those rare breeds. They were like a dog with a bone. They just never gave up. Just kept digging and digging until they got what they wanted. This DCI Jack Wilde could cause him a lot of grief if he didn't tell him what he wanted to know, he realised that. He'd keep after him and Douglas didn't need any more grief bestowed upon him. The police hadn't found all his money or even knew the half of the crimes he'd committed but this DCI Wilde would find out. He was sure of it and he couldn't have that. Besides, May had ripped him off and now maybe it was time to repay that debt.

"I want protection while I'm in here," began Douglas. "I'll do my time, but I want to walk out of here not be taken out in a wooden box because some screw turned a blind eye to me being done over." Jack was a little surprised by how quickly Moore had agreed to a deal but still he took his time in replying. Best not appear too keen agreeing on a deal that would never happen.

"I'm sure we can reach to that," replied Jack. Douglas

stubbed out his cigarette and reached for the newly opened packet on the table. Jack placed his hand over the cigarettes.

"You need to talk before you smoke," Jack informed Douglas. Douglas moved his hand away from the packet and began to regale his story. DCI Jack Wilde listened intently as Moore informed him of how May had robbed him of a sizeable chunk of money then had fled the country on the forged passport he'd had done for her in the name of Joanie Allen. He said he'd traced her back in '72 to a resort on the Costa del Sol but by the time he'd got there she'd vanished into thin air. There'd been various sightings of someone answering to her description over the past few years but nothing solid. He did, however, believe that she was still in Spain. DCI Jack Wilde left Wandsworth Prison a happy man. At long last he had something to go on with Elsie Arnold. He felt a holiday to the Costa del Sol was just what he needed!

ANNE

April 1976

Anne took a deep breath and then swung open the door to her father's office at the garage. On seeing Harry, seated at his desk with a look of total confusion on his face, Anne launched into her prepared speech.

"I'm getting married next month to Mr Eric Holmes. As you are my father and tradition states the father of the bride pays for the wedding, I'm here to collect a cheque from you for the sum of one thousand pounds." Harry leaned back in his chair and began to laugh.

"I'm not joking, Harry. I want that cheque. I need that money. It's rightfully mine." Anne's words only made Harry laugh even more. Anne crossed the short distance from the doorway to her father's desk and slammed both her fists down onto it.

"Don't you dare laugh at me," she spat out. "I'm your only daughter and you cast me out for your whore of a sister and a spoilt little brat that's not even yours, so you owe me big time." Harry immediately stopped laughing and had to stop himself from doing what he'd done on their last encounter. Slapping her! Instead, he crossed his arms and starred back at his eldest daughter wondering where he had gone wrong! Anne straightened herself back up. She hadn't meant to say those things, but she didn't like being laughed at. And besides, she'd only spoken the truth, hadn't she? Finally, Harry spoke.

"As long as you insist on spewing out these dreadful lies, you'll not get a penny out of me, Anne. It's been almost six years since we lost Freddy and yet you proceeded to rip our family apart. I've tried to make amends over the years. I also know that Bea has tried on numerous occasions to talk with you. I've lost count of the times that Janie has come home crying after seeing you. And, well, Charlie…"

"Charlie's never been to see me. In fact, he just downright ignores me."

"Can you blame him, Anne?"

"I'm his sister…"

"And so is Janie, Anne, so is Janie."

"That's not true, now, is it?" began Anne.

"JANIE IS MY DAUGHTER, Anne, just as you are," roared Harry.

"Not according to Aunt Mary and gran she isn't. There's never been a carrot-head in our family despite what you say."

"Not on your gran's side of the family, no, but on

grandad's there was." Anne really didn't want to pursue this but it was obvious that her dad wasn't going to let it go. She just wanted her money, not a fight. But she wasn't about to back down.

"Well, he's a liar too, seems to be a family trait among the men in our family," Anne added.

"It seems you've inherited the bitter and twisted trait from your gran's side of the family," responded Harry. Anne wanted with all her heart to say she was sorry. Sorry for calling Bea a whore. Sorry for saying Janie wasn't her dad's child, but between her own stubborn pride and the constant onslaught of nastiness towards them all from her aunt and gran, she just couldn't seem to back down. Instead, she was turning into the same bitter, twisted person as them. That's why she needed this money to marry Eric.

Eric was twenty years older than her. He was as dull as dishwater and had no looks to speak of, but he was kind to her. He was her ticket out of all this mess. He'd promised to take her far away from her money-grabbing aunt and gran and that alone was why she'd agreed to marry him. It was also the reason why she was here asking for money. Eric had invested every last dime he had on a grocery shop with a small two-bedroomed flat above it, in a place called Heanor in Derbyshire. Anne couldn't wait to leave this all behind her. But, now, here she was, losing every last chance of getting her hands on the money and still wading in with more insults.

"At least we're loyal, unlike Bea!" Anne began. "Seems she's took off. Find a better proposition, did she? Someone with something better to offer come up? Should I check that she hasn't tried to make off with Eric?" Anne threw in for good measure. It was Harry's turn to slam his fists down on the desk this time, making Anne jump back in fright.

"Like I said before, Anne, you spend too much time listening to the foul lies that spew out of those evil women's mouths. Bea has gone to America to take custody of Arthur's thirteen-year-old niece, who tragically lost both her parents in a car accident back in March. As soon as the papers are signed she'll be returning to England with Megan and they shall both be living here with me, Charlie and Janie. And, so help me God, if any one of you cause that poor child any harm at all, I'll not be responsible for my actions, do you hear?" yelled Harry. Anne nodded her head in acknowledgement.

"Good. Now, on the subject of this money which you say is, 'rightfully yours', you can have it on one condition. You stop these vicious lies and apologise to Janie and to Bea on her return. Otherwise, you don't get a penny out of me." Anne knew it was not only the smart thing to do but also the right thing to do, but once again her stubbornness and pride won over.

"Go to hell," she screamed at Harry then before he could see the tears welling up in her eyes she turned and ran out of his office like a bat out of hell. Anne ran as fast and as far away from her father's garage as she could before she collapsed to her knees crying her heart out. She'd blown it. What would Eric say? What would Aunt Mary and Gran have to say? What had she done? There would be no big white wedding now. Slowly the tears began to subside. After all, what did it matter what her aunt and gran had to say? Once she was married to Eric she'd be gone. And Eric wasn't the one insisting on a big wedding. Why? It wasn't even her idea. It was her aunt and gran's. Eric had just wanted a quiet registry office wedding. Well, they could still do that, couldn't they? She'd been squirrelling money away since she'd first arrived at Aunt Mary's so now she had a nice little nest egg of her own. It would be more than enough to pay for a registry wedding and still have some left over for some nice new things for their little flat. Anne blew her nose on her hankie then checked out her face in the small compact mirror in her handbag. Her eyes were a little puffy and red, but Eric wouldn't care or even notice. Getting to her feet and dusting herself off, Anne set off for Eric's. She had a new plan to discuss with him.

ELSIE

June 1976

Elsie lay on the top deck of the luxury yacht, three miles off the coast of Marbella reading a trashy romance novel and sipping sangria. Below decks, her 'lover', Tommy Jones, was in bed with her 'son', Carl Adams. The life she was leading would make a far more interesting story, she thought.

Elsie put down the book and lit up a cigarette and cast her mind back to when she'd first meet Carl Banks, as he was known then. They were both tending bar in Torremolinos and had hit it off immediately. A lot of the customers assumed one of two things about them. They were either lovers or mother and son. Together they'd had fun acting out both roles. Life had been starting to look up again for Elsie, then a big, burly Irishman had shown up asking questions about a Joanie Allen. Luckily for Elsie, Carl had been the one he'd asked, and Carl had told him that she had been working there but had left a few weeks back with another man and he hadn't seen or heard from her since. That very same evening, Elsie and Carl had packed their bags and left together for pastures new. Up until eighteen months ago, they had been working their way along the Costa del Sol, under various names and guises, in a variety of different jobs. Then they really landed on their feet. Elsie had been working in a swanky five-star hotel as a waitress when in walked Tommy Jones. Elsie was instantly attracted to him. At over six feet tall, with a well-toned, tanned body and a mass of blonde hair, he was every woman's dream. Elsie was known now as Joyce Adams and long gone were her blonde locks. Instead, she sported the short-tussled redhead look. It suited her well. At almost forty she still looked good. It hadn't taken her long to catch the eye of Tommy. But Tommy was no wide boy. He'd soon got the measure of Elsie and more importantly of her 'son', Carl. Carl, like Tommy, preferred the pleasures of men rather than women. But Tommy was an East End face and known hard man. If word got out that he was a 'gay', not only would his reputation be in tatters but also all his businesses. And Tommy couldn't have that! He liked his lifestyle. He liked being a Face. He liked that people respected him and feared him. But most of all he liked all the trappings that his money brought him. So, to the outside world, Tommy Jones was a womaniser. Elsie, however, had spent enough time around Carl and his friends to spot a 'gay' at a hundred paces.

Within days of their first meeting in the hotel restaurant an agreement had been arranged. Eighteen months on, Elsie was the respected wife of Tommy Jones and Carl was her son from a previous marriage. Together they lived in a huge six-bedroomed villa high in the hills overlooking the Mediterranean. Elsie had returned to the English coastline several times since they'd met but had never stepped foot on English soil once. Instead, she'd stay on their yacht and Tommy brought his business associates out to the yacht to be entertained by the glamorous Mrs Tommy Jones. At these times, Carl would go ashore and spend the evening cavorting with a string of girls. Carl enjoyed girls but he still preferred boys. But in order to keep up the pretence and the lifestyle he'd grown accustomed to, he was only too happy to bed a few gorgeous girls every now and then. Elsie lay back on the sun lounger and stared at the clear blue sky above her. She watched as a jet plane left a white trail across the skyline. More tourists thought Elsie as she drifted off to sleep.

High above in the sky, DCI Jack Wilde was sitting in that jet plane. He was looking forward to his nice little break in the sun. He was even entertaining thoughts of finally coming face to face with the elusive Elsie Arnold.

BEA, HARRY, JANIE & MEGAN

August 1976

Harry parked his car in front of the garage and headed for the path running along the right-hand side of Bea's cottage. From the front, it looked more like a small bungalow but once you headed down the pathway you soon became aware that it was so much bigger. The cottage was built on an incline and its sloping gardens stretched all the way down to the beach. At the back, you saw that the cottage was actually on two levels, with the lower level branching out to the left. The normally immaculate tiered garden was looking very sorry for itself. This summer was turning out to be the hottest and longest summer ever on record and water usage was restricted all over the UK. Gardens everywhere were becoming dry, arid areas rather than colourful blooming displays of flowers.

Harry walked down the brick pathway to where Bea was seated on the lower patio, wearing one of her enormous sunhats. Janie and Megan were across the beach, splashing around in the sea. Their laughter carried easily across the sand towards Harry and Bea.

"Hello, stranger," began Bea as she rose from her lounger to give her younger brother a hug. "There's beer and lemonade in the cool box just inside the sun house," she finished as she returned to her seat. Harry crossed the patio and entered the sun house. The shade it offered from the blazing sun was very welcome and he quickly found the cold beer and took a long swig, quenching his thirst. He then sat on the bench outside the sun house that offered a modicum of shade from the sun.

"Girls look like they're having fun," remarked Harry.

"Janie's been a godsend for Megan," began Bea. "She's found someone she can talk to in Janie. Janie listens and never passes comment, just offers a reassuring smile and a hug. She's older than her years in some ways but such a little girl in so many others."

"Janie's been through a lot herself, Bea," replied Harry. "She's experienced both the pain of losing someone she loves and the hurt those same loved ones can cause."

"I sometimes forget how much heartache Janie's been through, Harry. She never complains or acts up. She just seems to have her cry then deals with it. She's a strong little soul."

"She is, Bea, she is." Harry took another swig of his beer. "Is everything sorted with Megan now? I mean about the car accident? Is she definitely here for good now?"

"I had the final paperwork three days ago; there's no need for either Megan or me to return to the States, unless of course we choose to."

"What actually happened, Bea, or should I just mind my own business?" asked Harry. Bea looked over at Harry. He was about to welcome Megan into his home and his life for the foreseeable future. He had a right to know the truth behind what had gone on. Besides, Megan wanted him to know, so that he'd understand why she wouldn't be totally comfortable in either his or Charlie's company, for the time being at least, anyway.

"There was no car accident, Harry. I lied. We all lied to protect Megan. She was being sexually assaulted by her own father. Drew had told Megan that he would kill both her and her mother if she told a soul about their 'special times', as he called them. Amy, her mother, was working nights as a nurse at their local hospital. It seems the stress of her job had her turning to alcohol more and more. That fateful night Amy had been too drunk to go to work. Drew was angry with her and they got into a fight. He'd beaten her until she lost consciousness, then he'd gone into Megan's room and began to viciously rape her. Amy came to, to the sound of her daughter's screams. She took the handgun Drew owned from his bedside cabinet and shot him five times before turning the gun on herself. She blew her brains out right in front of Megan. The emergencies were on the scene within minutes of a neighbour making the call, on hearing gunshots coming from the house. Megan had to have emergency surgery on her womb due to the severity of the vicious sexual assault she'd been subjected to. With everything that Megan had gone through, those close to her decided a cover up story needed to put in place. A tragic car accident was decided upon. I'd like it to remain that way, please, Harry." Harry was deeply upset by what Bea had told him; he couldn't do anything but nod his head in response. A tear trickled down his face. Megan wanted me to tell you, so you'd understand why she may act oddly towards you at times or just simply not want to be alone with either you or Charlie. She doesn't want you to think she's ungrateful for all that you're doing for her. She just wants to put it all behind her and start afresh. She's only a month older than Janie. She shouldn't have been subjected to such atrocities. She just wants to be a normal little girl." The heat had dried the tears on Harry's face. He finished off his beer and then helped himself to another before he'd finally composed himself enough to speak.

"I'll not tell a soul, Bea. I promise." Bea smiled up at her brother.

"I know you won't. I also know that Megan has told Janie the truth too and that she'll never repeat it to another living soul either. Megan knows it as well. Now, the girls have spotted you, Harry, so slap a smile on your face and tell me what's been going on back home."

***

31st December 1976

Bea sat alone in the darkened lounge of her brother's house. It was just after 1am. This time tomorrow another year would be over and a new one would just be beginning. Bea prayed that it would be a quiet, uneventful year. This last one had been such a struggle at times. Thankfully, Megan had settled into school and her new home nicely. She still woke up most nights in a cold sweat, though, the shootings and assaults invading her sleep. But she no longer sought comfort from Bea. Instead, she'd climb into Janie's bed. Janie would just budge over and go back to sleep. They'd become inseparable. It filled Bea's heart with so much love for them both. Two little girls, helping each other carve a path through a world that had shown them so much hurt and pain. They were going to be a force to be reckoned with as they got older, these two.

It had been a rollercoaster for Harry as well. Harry had had an unexpected visit from DCI Jack Wilde about Elsie. Seems he'd flown out to the Costa del Sol after a tip-off she was working out there. He'd managed to locate a bar she'd worked at in Torremolinos. From there she'd changed her name several times and had appeared to have hooked up with a young homosexual guy. He'd traced them both down as far as Fuengirola, but both his time and luck had run out there. He'd keep Harry informed on any new information he was able to find out. Between the news from DCI Wilde and Anne's outburst Harry had been through the mill emotionally.

Three weeks after bursting into Harry's office demanding money, Anne had married Eric in a registry office with two strangers off the street acting as their witnesses, much to the annoyance of her aunt and gran. Immediately afterwards they'd left to start a new life in Derbyshire. Harry had received a birthday card out of the blue from them both in the July. Then, two months later, Harry, Charlie, Janie, George and Bea had all received letters of apology from Anne. She said, "Eric had made her see the error of her ways". Anne had also told them she'd sent a letter to her aunt and gran, informing them that they were wrong about Bea and Janie and telling them to stop spreading their hateful lies around and she no longer wanted anything to do with them. Harry had promptly sent them off a cheque for a thousand pounds as a belated wedding present from them all. A big family reunion at the cottage in Talybont was planned for the coming summer. Anne wrote a letter addressed to them, including Megan, every fortnight telling of her new life as both a wife and greengrocer. Janie made sure everyone in the house wrote a little something back.

The clock in the hall chimed 2am and Bea rose from her chair. It was going to be a very long busy day and she needed to get some much-needed sleep. In the dark, she silently made her way upstairs to bed and lay her head on her pillow. Her last thoughts as she drifted off to sleep were the same as always. Of her darling Arthur.

DEREK

October 1978

Derek Collins's legs were shaking so hard that he actually thought he was going to collapse in a heap on the visiting room floor. When Harry Arnold had requested a visiting order to see him, he'd happily obliged, but now seeing him sat at a table across the visiting room he'd suddenly become a physical wreck. He'd caused this man so much hurt, yet he'd never once spoken badly about him. Derek took a deep breath, then took the final few steps to the table. Once there, he quickly pulled out the chair opposite Harry and practically fell onto it. His legs had finally given way and now butterflies were churning up a storm in his stomach. Derek slowly lifted his gaze from the tabletop to meet Harry's and was surprised to find him smiling.

"I've not come to berate you," began Harry. "I've come

to say I hope your appeal next week is successful and, in the light of what DCI Jack Wilde has told me, you'll be a free man in no time at all". Now it was Harry's turn to feel the flutter of butterflies. What he was about to say he'd never really voiced before, but deep down inside had always known to be true!

"Elsie killed Freddy. That can be the ONLY reason for her to hide away like she has. Innocent people don't hide in the shadows. They step out into the light. You stepped out into the light, Derek. In all this time, you've never wavered. You knew Elsie was alive and out there somewhere. She'd set you up, didn't she?" Derek felt his own butterflies being settled at Harry's words.

Derek looked Harry straight in the eyes as he spoke.

"I believe she did, too. From the moment, I first set eyes on Elsie, she lied to me. Oh! I know I was no saint, Mr Arnold, I'd been in trouble all my life. But Elsie, well, she's in a different league. I mean, I know, I've done time in the past for GBH when my temper got the better of me. But, they weren't harmless kids, Mr Arnold. They were grown men, out looking for trouble. But Freddy, well, he was just a kid. He was no real threat to me. If he'd come looking for a fight I'd have given a good hiding, I'll admit that. But I wouldn't have killed him. I most certainly wouldn't have stabbed him, Mr Arnold. A bust lip and black eye would have been all it would have taken. Then I'd have packed up me and Elsie and moved on, nothing more. Like I told 'um. I never carried a knife. My fists have always been my weapons, Mr Arnold. Elsie gave me that knife as a present. I had no interest it in. I said my thanks then slung it in the bedside drawer and forgot about it. Why she saw fit to buy me a knife, I've no idea. But, as I've lain in my cell all this time, I've come to the same conclusion as you, Mr Arnold. Elsie used that knife to stab Freddy. To stab Freddy and frame me. If she wanted out, why not stab me? Why kill your own son and set up your lover? There's just no reason on earth that justifies killing your own flesh and blood. But she was they only one who knew about that knife, Mr Arnold. She's the only one who knows why she did it." In his haste to get it all out, Derek had forgotten how much his words must be hurting this poor man.

"I'm so sorry, Mr Arnold, I just got carried away." Harry held up his hand to stop Derek from speaking. Although tears were running down his cheeks he still managed to smile at Derek.

"There's no need to apologise to me, Derek. Elsie twisted you round her little finger, just like she'd twisted me and countless others round it. You weren't the first affair she'd had. Christ! You weren't even the first she'd planned on doing a runner with. I'd just got tired of getting her to stay. Tired of all the lies. Tired of being taken for a fool. Freddy came to me that night you pair took off to get me to stop her. I told him it was time to let her go. I told him everything she'd put me through. Freddy didn't go to Blackpool to make her come home. Freddy went to tell her to never, ever come back. So why she chose to stick a knife in him and let you take the blame, as you've said, only she knows. This Douglas Moore chap has confessed to fleeing Blackpool with her. His story has checked out. DCI Wilde has found evidence of her on the Costa del Sol and, although progress is slow, I believe he'll track her down eventually and she'll be made to pay for her crimes."

"Do you really believe he'll find her?" asked Derek. Harry smiled across at Derek.

"DCI Jack Wilde always believed you was innocent, but the evidence against you was so strong at the time. He's put a lot of time into finding Elsie, both on and off duty. He wants justice for Freddy. For me and my family. And he wants justice for you too, Derek. He's a fair man. He's asking to speak in defence of you at your appeal hearing. His evidence, along with Douglas Moore's statement, will ensure you are freed. I've also written a letter in your defence to the board. But can I ask one thing of you now, Derek? Once you're released, don't go looking for Elsie. Don't let her ruin any more of your life. She's not worth it. Trust in DCI Wilde to bring her in. Stripping Elsie of her freedom is the worst thing that could happen to her, believe me. She got locked in an out-building once and she went ballistic. Spending the rest of her life behind bars in a poky cell will kill her."

Derek looked at the man before him with such respect and admiration. He'd stolen his wife. He'd been jailed for murdering his son. Now here he was, telling him to not waste the life he was helping to get him back. Why Elsie had chosen to cause this man so much grief was beyond him. He prayed that Harry Arnold would live to get the justice he so truly deserved. The bell signalling visiting was over interrupted his thoughts.

Harry rose from his chair and waited for Derek to do

the same, then he extended his hand out to him. Derek quickly shook the offered hand before a guard came to escort him back to his cell block.

"I won't go looking, Mr Arnold, I promise," shouted Derek over his shoulder.

"Go looking for what?" enquired the prison guard.

"Trouble," replied Derek. "Trouble."

HARRY

Harry left Strangeways Prison with a heavy heart, not because he'd just visited Derek Collins but with what he was going to have to tell his family before word was leaked to the press. He drove home wishing the drive would take ten times longer. With every mile that took him closer to home, the heavier his heart felt. What he had to tell his children would change their lives yet again. And he feared for poor young Janie. Janie was such a forgiving child. Eager to please, happy to help and so full of love. He could not imagine what it would do to her if she learnt the real truth. The truth that both her biological parents were murderers! He prayed for all he was worth that she'd never find out and that by some miracle she'd not inherited the killer gene. Harry drove on, his resolve set to make sure that Janie turned into the beautiful, caring adult she was so clearly meant to be.

Bea had made sure that Charlie, Janie, Megan, and

Harry and Bea's father, George, were all seated in the lounge for Harry's return. He'd rung her from a phone booth expressing how important it was for them all to be there to hear what he had to say. Only Bea knew that he'd gone to visit Derek, but she had no idea what it was about. All she really knew was that some detective kept calling both the house and the garage more and more frequently. At last Harry entered the lounge, silence fell across the room. Whatever he was about to impart on them, they could tell from his face it was serious. Harry crossed the room and slumped down into his favourite armchair.

"Tea?" asked Bea. Harry shook his head.

"After, Bea, after," Harry began. Then he wiped his hands over his face and through his hair before addressing his family.

"I don't know any other way of telling you this so I'm just going to come straight out with it, so here goes. For a while now, I've been having talks with DCI Jack Wilde. He's the detective who dealt with our Freddy's murder. He's never stopped looking for Elsie, as he's always believed she had something to do with Freddy's demise. Well, a couple of years ago, a known IRA man was captured by the police in London. On his presence was a passport in the name of Morris Connolly. He also disappeared the day Freddy was murdered. DCI Wilde went and interviewed him. He admitted to fleeing Blackpool the day Freddy was murdered, for Ireland with Elsie. He said after getting her a new passport and identity she robbed him of thousands of pounds and fled to Spain. DCI Wilde investigated Connolly's story and it all checked out. Elsie fled to the Costa del Sol under the name of Joanie Allen."

"That's her best friend's name," piped up George.

"Yeah, Dad, you're right, it was."

"So, have they found mum?" asked Charlie.

"Not yet, son, not yet."

"So why has this detective been contacting you, then, Harry?" asked Bea.

"Because next week Derek Collins, as we came to know him, will have his appeal heard to quash his conviction, and it will be. He'll be a free man."

"They can't do that, can they?" enquired George.

"They can, and they will, Dad, and rightly so."

"But he killed our Freddy, Dad, how can they—" burst in Janie.

"BECAUSE he's innocent, Janie."

"So, did this Connolly bloke kill Freddy then?" asked Charlie.

Bea sensed where this was heading and her heart went out to Harry. She needed to help him out.

"No, Charlie, it wasn't him, was it, Harry?"

Harry shook his head. Suddenly the penny dropped and everyone looked at each other to see if they had reached the same conclusion. Finally, George spat it out.

"ELSIE. It was Elsie, wasn't it?" Harry just nodded at first.

"It seems that way. There's no other reason for her not to come forward. Connolly picked her up at the train station in Blackpool the afternoon of Freddy's murder. He said she had no luggage and was sporting a bandage on her arm. He also said it was the first time he'd ever known her to be jumpy. Investigations show that the call made to Derek's workplace was from the train station. Next week, Derek will be freed from prison and a warrant for Elsie's arrest will be made public. First Connolly, then Wilde traced her to Spain so a televised appeal for her will be made here as well as there in the hope someone comes forward with information on her whereabouts. I'm sorry, kids, but it's going to get rough for us all. The press will have a field day over this. As of Thursday next week we'll be having around-the-clock police protection. Just when we thought this nightmare was over, its starting all over again." Harry held his head in his hands and openly began to cry. Janie and Charlie rushed to their father's side to comfort him as they shed their own tears. Megan, unsure what to do, stayed rooted to the spot, while George gently rubbed his daughter's shoulder.

"We'll get through this, for Freddy's sake," said George. "He deserves justice and I for one hope to live to see the day that evil woman is made to pay for what she has done to not just Freddy but this whole family." They all nodded in agreement. As hard at it was going to be coming to terms with it all, they'd face up to it for Freddy's sake. He deserved that.

An hour later, Harry replaced the phone receiver back on its cradle. Telling Anne over the phone her mother was a murderer wasn't the easiest of things but there was no way he could get up to see her in person before everything came out. He was just glad that she had Eric to lean on.

Under his breath, he cursed Elsie for every wrong doing she had bestowed on her family. He, like his father, hoped to live long enough to see her brought to justice. In fact, he wouldn't rest until she was caught.

ELSIE

November 1978

Elsie had just finished washing up the last of the pots from their meal. The percolator was happily spitting out its last few drops of freshly made coffee and Elsie was feeling very contented. She and Tommy had enjoyed a rare day alone. Usually, Carl or other hangers-on, as she referred to them, were with them. But yesterday evening Tommy had ordered everyone to stay away for a couple of days so that he could enjoy some alone time with his wife. They'd started the day browsing around the shops and then done some haggling in the market place before returning to their villa for a swim in the pool and finishing off the rest of the afternoon sunbathing on the terrace. After they'd both showered and changed, Tommy had cooked their meal of steak and chips. It had been a lovely day, then Tommy shouted from the living room.

"Come quick, Joyce, you're not going to believe what's on the TV." Elsie knew better than to not go when Tommy called so she walked out of the kitchen and into the living room, drying her hands on a tea towel as she went.

"What's not to be belie—" began Elsie until, suddenly, she was stopped in her tracks as her glaze fell upon the TV set in the corner of the room. There, in full technicolour, was a picture of her with Freddy. It had been taken the summer before she'd run off with Derek, on the forecourt of the garage. His arm was draped across her shoulder and they were both beaming at the camera. Then suddenly it was replaced by a close-up photograph of her taken that same summer. Elsie felt the colour drain from her face. Her ears were consumed by a large buzzing sound and the room was spinning round her, then everything went black.

"Damn, scared the life out of ya, did that, eh? Joyce?" Tommy said as she opened her eyes. He'd obviously laid her down on the couch and was seated beside her, leaning right over her.

"There was me thinking I was the big bad criminal in this family and it turns out it was you instead," Tommy boomed out in laughter. "Got the whole of England, Ireland and Spain looking for you, they have. Quite a big shot murderer by all accounts, Joyce, aren't ya? They say you're wanted in connection with the murder of your own son." Tommy stopped talking and handed her a glass of brandy.

"Sit up and get this down your neck," he offered. Elsie

pushed herself up into a sitting position then, taking the glass, drank down its contents in one go. Tommy took the empty glass from her and placed it on the table.

"So, what are you gonna do, Joyce? I mean, I can't have the filth snooping round my affairs, can I? Got too much to lose, as you well know. I should kill you for this, Joyce. I mean, how could you bring so much trouble to my door and think you could get away with it? I'm not some mug you can have over, you should know that. You've put me in a nasty dilemma, Joyce. Your face is as familiar round here as mine is. People are going to know it's you the filth are looking for. I can't be dragged into this, Joyce. If I kill ya, like I ought to, then the police are going to come after me. So, I'm afraid, Joyce, that's not a viable option. So instead I suggest you take your lying, scheming, murdering self out of my sight as quickly as possible. Do you understand me?" Tommy roared at her. Joyce flinched under the full force of Tommy's words, but she was not by any means about to skulk off into the distance. Pulling herself up fully she raised her defiant chin and looked straight into the face of Tommy Jones.

"I'll go, Tommy, but not without your help and financial support until the day I die. I mean what would do your reputation more harm? Me been found out as a murderer or you being a bona fide SHIRTLIFTER?" The sound of Tommy's fist connecting with her right cheek was most definitely bone crunching and the searing pain kicked in instantly. But still Elsie wasn't beaten.

"I may well be a murderer and I may well be running away from a life sentence but I'm not ashamed of who I am or what I've become. If I get caught I'll hold my head high and take what's coming to me but what about you? Mr Big Shot Tommy Jones? What will happen to you and your precious empire of crime? Who's gonna be afraid of a QUEER, a NANCYBOY? Eh? Not those goons who you mug off, that's for sure. Because, so help me God, I'll shout it from every roof top that you're sleeping with Carl not me. After all, like you said, you can't really kill me; too many people think I'm your wife. I've got nothing to lose, Tommy, but you sure as hell have if you don't get me safely out of here and keep me in the splendour I've become accustomed to." Tommy drew back his fist to pummel this piece of shite before him, but her words stopped him from doing so.

"Go ahead, Tommy, hit me some more. I'll only end up in hospital somewhere and the police will put two and two together," she spat out. Tommy lowered his fist and then let out a hearty laugh.

"Okay, Joyce, you win for now. I'll get you a safe passage out of Spain and I'll even stump up the money to keep you there but one day, one day, Joyce, the heat will die down from the filth then I'll know just where to find you. Then I'll chop you up into little pieces and send you back to the family you shitted on." And with that Tommy rose from the couch and left the room to make the necessary arrangements for Joyce to disappear.

TOMMY

Tommy Jones slammed his office door shut behind him and snatched up the headset of his private-line telephone and dialled Barney Brown. Barney was his right-hand man, the only other living person, apart from his dear old mum, that he trusted. Barney picked up on the fourth ring.

"Boss," was all he said.

"Joyce wants to take the yacht out, do a spot of night fishing. Said to ask Carl if he wants to join us. Meet at the marina in, say, half an hour?"

"Course, Boss. Any live bait needed?"

"Nah, frozen will do." With that, Tommy hung up. Barney would know what was expected of him now. Elsie was in the bathroom, pressing a cold flannel to her cheek, when Tommy found her.

"You've got an hour to get yourself and your belongings together before I come back for you. I'm off to set up your safe passage outta here, so make sure you're ready to go when I get back." He ordered her. Then he headed off to the marina.

Barney was already aboard the yacht when Tommy arrived. Tommy quickly filled him in on what needed to be arranged then returned to the villa. Elsie was out by the pool waiting for him. Tommy strode inside and quickly packed an overnight bag. As he exited the villa and opened the boot of his car, Elsie quickly gathered up her bags and scurried after him. Tommy didn't offer to load her bags in the boot; instead, he just slid behind the steering wheel and revved the engine. Elsie threw the bags in the boot and slammed it shut, then scrambled into the passenger seat. Before she'd even closed the door, Tommy was pulling out of the driveway. Tommy drove to the marina in silence. He just wanted rid of this woman as quickly as he possibly could, but it rankled him that he couldn't just slit her throat and be done with her.

Tommy didn't help Elsie load her bags onto the yacht either and he stopped Barney from doing so as well. Once they were safely aboard, Barney went ashore and Tommy steered the yacht out of the marina and out to sea. Elsie watched from below decks, as the Spanish coast disappeared from view.

"Joyce," Tommy called. "In the safe is all you need. Passports, cash and the account details set up in the name of Marianne Thomas-Smythe. Everything you need to know about accessing the funds are there as well. There's a pretty penny in there so it should keep you going for a good while. That, along with the money you've no doubt been squirrelling away, should see you all right." Elsie winched at the mention of her hidden cash but made her way into Tommy's cabin and opened the safe he kept in there. Altogether, there were nine passports. Elsie quickly sorted out the ones she'd be needing then gathered the cash and a large brown envelope with the name Marianne Thomas-Smthye on. A quick peek inside revealed all that Tommy had said it would. She placed the items into her handbag and joined Tommy at the helm.

It was pitch back now but Elsie could hear the faint sound of an engine in the distance. She couldn't see it but the noise was definitely getting louder and closer to them. It was almost alongside them before the small powerboat became visible to her. Tommy had already killed the yacht's engine and was letting it drift towards the approaching boat. As it drew near, it too killed its engine and the man threw a rope for Tommy to catch. He deftly secured the powerboat alongside and then helped the man aboard.

"Fahd," Tommy greeted the man.

"It is an honour," began Fahd, "to be of service to you, Señor Jones." Tommy turned to face Elsie.

"This is the lady I need you to escort to safety, Fahd. Her name is Miss Adams. She is very dear to me and I need you to keep her safe and answer only to her, do you understand Fahd?"

"Oh, yes, Señor Jones. Fahd will take great care of Señora Adams." With that Fahd bowed to Elsie, then offered out his hand.

"Come, quick, Señora Adams. I will have you safely ashore before the sun begins to awaken." Elsie, grabbing her handbag, stepped towards Fahd.

"My bags," she began.

"Once you're safely aboard Fahd's boat I'll toss them across. Now, get a move on, Joyce, time is not on our side." Fahd had by now alighted from the yacht to his boat and was holding out his hand for Elsie to take. Clutching her handbag even tighter than before she stepped to the edge of the deck and reached for Fahd's hand. He quickly grabbed her hand and in one easy pull he'd hauled her aboard the powerboat. Tommy rapidly began to toss her remaining bags onto the floor of the boat. They fell onto the deck around Elsie's feet. Tommy then cast off the powerboat and gave it a gentle nudge away from the yacht. Fahd powered up the engine and without another word whisked Elsie off into the night.

Tommy stayed up on deck until the engine of the powerboat could no longer be heard then he headed down to his cabin. Putting on a pair of gloves he removed one of the passports from the safe then, from his jacket pocket, he took out a second passport and placed both passports inside a plastic bag. To this, he added a bundle of notes then sealed the bag up. He next removed the remaining passports, placing them in his jacket pocket before leaving the safe open and making his way to the back of the yacht on its lower deck. Before long the sound of another boat approaching could be heard. This time it was just a small dinghy, manned by Barney and containing two other passengers, a man and a woman. Tommy and Barney loaded them into the yacht's dinghy, then Tommy handed them over the sealed plastic bag.

"You both know what do?" asked Tommy. The pair

nodded obediently. Tommy beamed at them.

"If all goes well, you will both be handsomely rewarded on your return to Marbella." Again, the pair nodded. Then Barney cast them off. The man started up the outboard motor and gently pulled away before setting off at full speed in the opposite direction to the one Fahd had taken. As they waited for the sound of the engine to be swallowed up into the silence of the dark night, Tommy handed over the contents of his jacket pocket to Barney. Barney pocketed the passports, then, checking the dinghy was long gone, opened the storage trunk on the deck. It normally stored the fishing gear but tonight it held the chained-up, dead body of Carl Adams. Together, Tommy and Barney hauled Carl overboard, where he instantly sank without a trace. While Barney retrieved the fishing gear from the galley, Tommy quickly doused the inside of the trunk with disinfectant then hosed it out. Barney replaced the fishing equipment in the chest, then followed Tommy into the living area of the yacht. As Tommy reached for a glass from the bar, Barney slugged him from behind with a whiskey bottle that he had hidden by the door earlier. Tommy crashed to the floor. Barney knelt beside his fallen boss and with his gloved hands checked for a pulse. He found it pulsating away strongly. With that, Barney returned to his dinghy and headed back for the shores of Marbella.

JANIE

Within hours of Derek Collins's release from prison, Janie's family home had been besieged by reporters. She understood better than anyone their need for a story, as she had designs on becoming a journalist herself, but the way they had hounded her and her family was beyond belief and days on from the TV appeal for her mum had aired they were still encamped on their doorstep.

"Do you think they'll give up?" Janie asked Megan.

"Eventually," she responded. Megan had been in this situation before. After all, her mum had killed her dad.

"Eventually isn't good enough," announced Charlie from the girls' bedroom door. "I say we make a stand and go out and face them. What do you say, Janie?" The thought had crossed Janie's mind. Perhaps if they did go out and give them a statement they'd go away. Janie turned to face her older brother.

"I'm willing to give it a go, but do you think Dad and Aunt Bea will let us?"

"Don't see why not. I mean, it is our choice. Let's go downstairs and see what they say. Janie started to cross the room when she noticed that Megan hadn't made to get up.

"Come on, Megan. United front and all that."

"I'm not so sure it's me they want to see," Megan responded.

"They're raking it up every day about your parents, Megan," began Charlie. "We need to show them how much it hurts. We're not responsible for what our parents have done. So why should we be held prisoners in our own home?"

"He's right, Megan. It's affecting all our lives. We may as well put our side of the story." Megan couldn't argue with that, so she followed Charlie and Janie downstairs to confront both the adults and the media.

Neither Harry or Bea was keen on their idea but finally relented to go along with it as long as they had a prepared statement to read out. Janie had volunteered to read it out, with Charlie and Megan standing either side of her for support. Harry reluctantly opened the front door and was immediately greeted by the flash of cameras going off and questions being hurled at him. He calmly raised his hands in the air to quell the noise and flashes so that he could be heard.

"Charlie, Janie and Megan are going to come out in a moment and Janie will read you a statement they, together, have prepared. They will not be answering any questions but ask that you listen carefully to what they have to say."

Harry then stepped aside to allow the three of them to exit the front door and to stand side by side on the front step. The camera flashes went off like fireworks, lighting up the entire front of the house. Janie, Charlie and Megan waited patiently for the flashes to subside before Janie finally spoke.

"The events of the past few weeks have just been the last in a long line of dreadful things, we, as children have had to deal with. From our mother deserting us, to the horrendous murder of our brother Freddy. As a family, we are pleased that the man known to us as Derek Collins has been acquitted and freed from prison. However, finding out our own mother murdered our beloved Freddy has shaken us to the core. Megan joined our family to put the horrors of her own parents' demise behind her. Now, you all see fit to plaster your newspapers and our TV screens with the dreadful events that led Megan here, to our home. So today, we stand before you and ask that you leave us in peace to come to terms with these new revelations. We ask that you focus your attentions on helping to track down the woman that has caused her children, her husband, her family so much pain and heartache. Let us go about our daily lives as normally as we possibly can under the circumstances. If you allow us our privacy, we promise that once Elsie Arnold is arrested we'll willingly, as a family, sit down and give a collective interview. Thank you for listening to us." As Janie and the rest of her family turned to re-enter the house a round of applause erupted from the reporters and camera men. They all smiled and waved then re-entered the house, with Harry closing the front door behind them. Janie collapsed onto the bottom step of the stairs from the stress of it all. Charlie meanwhile was peeking through the letterbox and watched in amazement as press began to leave. He turned to Janie in excitement.

"We did it, sis. We did it," he screamed out. "They're packing up and leaving."

"It's true," joined in Bea from the living room. "They're going." Harry, Janie, Megan and Charlie all joined Bea in the lounge and watched from behind the lacy net curtains as one by one the line of vans and cars were packed up and driven off.

"Who'd have thought?" said Harry.

"I told you it was worth a try, Dad," announced Charlie. Harry ruffled his son's hair.

"That you did, son, that you did."

JACK

Dec 1978

DCI Jack Wilde wondered into The Manor restaurant and took a seat at a table right by the staff-only door and waited to be served. He browsed at the menu on the table while he waited. He'd been on the road from Blackpool down to the East End of London for most of the day and he was feeling both thirsty and hungry. Eventually, a spotty youth with greasy hair ambled over to his table.

"What can I get you?" he asked without making eye contact. Jack placed the menu down on the table.

"A pint of your best bitter, a medium steak with chips and all the trimmings and a word in Tommy Jones's ear if you please, sonny." Jack placed his police badge on the table as he spoke. The spotty youth shot up straight and stared open-mouthed at Jack.

"Pick your jaw off the floor, laddie and go do as I asked," ordered Jack. With a new-found speed, the waiter hurled through the staff-only door. Jack leaned back in his chair, closed his eyes and waited for a response.

The aroma of the steak being placed on the table in front of him roused DCI Jack Wilde from the catnap he'd been enjoying. To his surprise there was also a pint of beer on the table. When he looked up from the table he expected to see the spotty youth hovering over him but instead found the man himself, Tommy Jones.

"Mind if I join you while you eat?" he enquired.

Jack gestured to the empty chair opposite him.

"Be my guest," he replied. Tommy sat down and watched as the DCI added condiments to his food and cut off a large piece of the steak, admired it, then placed it in his mouth. Jack savoured the taste of the meat in his mouth before swallowing it, then rinsing it down with a hearty swig of the beer.

"I'm assuming you didn't ask to see me so I could watch you eat?" Tommy smiled.

"You brought out the food. Didn't you expect me to eat it?" Jack returned the smile.

"I guess I thought what you had to say to me was far more important," returned Tommy.

"Oh! It is! Believe me. But I hate to talk business on an empty stomach, and right now my stomach is doing all the talking, if you get my drift." Tommy decided he liked this copper. There was an honesty about him, which was a very rare thing in his opinion.

"In that case, eat, DCI Jack Wilde," replied Tommy,

reading the name from the ID card in the detective's wallet containing his police badge. "I shall return when you have finished your meal." Tommy then rose from the table and walked over to the bar area at the front of the restaurant. Jack cut into his steak again.

As soon as the spotty youth had cleared away his plate, Tommy rejoined Jack at his table.

"Dessert? Or has your stomach been quietened?" he asked. Jack wiped his mouth with his napkin then laid it on the table.

"Never been a dessert man, so I guess we'd best get down to business. I'm here regarding a certain Elsie Arnold or, as you'd know her, Joyce Adams." Tommy went to speak but Jack held up his hand to prevent him. "I have no interest in your version of events, Mr Jones, nor do I have any interest in, let's say, your business dealings. My only interest is in catching this sorry excuse for a human being."

"I don't know where—" began Tommy, but once again Jack held up his hand.

"I believe you helped her escape that night. I believe that Elsie, Joyce, call her what you like, has some sort of hold over you, Mr Jones. I mean, why else would you let her get away?"

"She and that so-called son of hers clobbered me one on the yacht and took off in the dinghy with my money," protested Tommy.

"So, you claim, Mr Jones, but the thing is I don't believe you."

"I was found drifting out at sea with an almighty gash

on the back of me head and the dinghy was recovered on the beach of some fishing port along the Portuguese coast. So how would I know where the lying bitch is?"

"Because you set the whole thing up, didn't you?"

"And why would I do that? Eh?"

"'Cause like I said she's got something over you. What that is, I don't know, neither do I care. I just want this evil woman caught."

"I'm sorry but I can't help you," said Tommy as he began to rise from his chair. Like lightening, DCI Wilde was up out of his chair and knocking Tommy back into his seat. Tommy was surprised by the swiftness of the detective, along with his actual strength and the amount of front he had to assault, him, Tommy Jones, in his own restaurant. This copper really had a hard on for Joyce, so it seemed. Jack sat back down in his chair.

"Let me tell you a little about Elsie Arnold, Tommy. She's a user, a liar and a murderer. She killed her own flesh and blood for no other reason than to set up the bloke she left her husband and four kids for. And why did she set him up? So she could fuck off with some other unsuspecting bloke who seemed like he could give her more. Only thing is she didn't know he was a key IRA man. He was planning on using her to help him bomb London. But Elsie was no fool. She took the passport he'd got her and his money and headed off to sunny Spain. She thought she'd got away scot-free until a burly Irishman showed up at the bar she and Carl worked at looking for her. So now her and this Carl team up as a mother and son double-act, working their way along the coast, ripping people off. Mainly men,

I might add. Then they stumble upon you, don't they Tommy? And eureka. They think they've hit the jackpot. And they had until a certain Douglas Moore, a known IRA bigwig, is caught. He's only the fella Elsie mugged off. He was only too happy to help me find her. The IRA are still looking for her, Tommy. They don't let things like that slide. And, well, if you're protecting her, well, what can I say?" Jack paused to let what he'd said sink in. "But, like I said, Tommy. I'm not interested in you, or Carl, or Douglas Moore and the IRA. I'm only interested in Elsie. And I will do everything in my power to catch her. So, if that means ruffling a few feathers here and there, or even turning a blind eye every now and then, I will. So, I'll ask again. Do you know where she is?"

Tommy hadn't realised that Joyce was wanted by the IRA. The Irish weren't the wisest of people to cross, never mind the ones wrapped up in all that religious shite. This put a whole new spin on things. But before he went shooting his mouth off he needed to check out a few things first. He had a lot more than this DCI Jack Wilde knew about to lose if Joyce began shouting her mouth off.

"Just say I knew how to find Joyce. And just say she did have something on me that I'd rather not be made, shall, we say, public. How do you intend on not dragging me into this?" Jack smiled.

"Elsie Arnold is a proven liar. A cheat and someone not to be trusted. She could say that you've murdered, raped, robbed, beaten and threatened half of London and no one would believe her. She's the most hated woman in the UK, Tommy. She stuck a knife into her eldest son and left him to bleed out in a back alley so that she could run away with a man whose sole purpose in life is to blow innocent people to pieces. Do you really think that whatever she said would be taken seriously? People would just think she was trying to buy her way out of a hefty prison sentence. People want to see her hung out to dry. To face the family whose lives she's tried so hard to ruin. No one cares about what she has to say. The press is likening her to Myra Hindley. So, I ask again, Tommy, can you help me bring her in?"

"Let me check out a few things. See if what you say is true."

JANIE

June 1980

"I see Pathetic Pete, the pressman, is sat in his old banger across the road. What's Murderous Mummy done now?" proclaimed Janie, as she entered the front door of the family home and made her way into the kitchen at the back of the house, where her Aunt Bea was preparing tea.

"Oh Janie!" began Bea. "You don't half give folk some funny names. What do you call me behind my back?" she asked. Janie helped herself to a freshly baked cookie off a tray that was cooling on the side.

"Busy Bea, Beautiful Bea or Bossy Bea," replied Janie. "Depending on what mood you're in," she added with mischief in her voice. Bea threw the tea towel she was holding at Janie.

"Who said you could have one those cookies?"

"Who said I couldn't?" Janie replied in a playful manner, tossing the tea towel back at her aunt. "And you still haven't answered my question about Elsie, have you?" Bea poured herself a cup of tea then sat down at the kitchen table. She took a sip before speaking.

"DCI Wilde called in, about ten minutes after you and Megan left for your exams this morning. Some Moroccan villain was captured last week and he's looking at the death penalty. He's trying to bargain it down to a life sentence using information about your mum. He says Tommy Jones paid him to transport Elsie off his yacht and over to Morocco and to help keep her safe until he managed to get over there. But then Elsie had paid him even more to help her disappear. He says he knows what name she's living under and where she's living. He demanded to speak to the English policeman who's in charge of her case. He seems to think that DCI Wilde can help get him out of this death penalty and even out of prison itself. So DCI Jack Wilde called in to let us know what was going on, on his way to the airport." Janie had sat down opposite Bea at the table.

"Typical Elsie," said Janie. "Today, Megan and me officially left school. It was supposed to be our day, but NO! BLOODY ELSIE steals the limelight yet again." Bea reached across the table and took hold of her niece's hand and gently stroked it.

"It's still yours and Megan's day, sweetheart. It'll only be Elsie's if you let it be. Megan will be back any minute now, then you can both go get ready for the disco tonight at the Town Hall and dance all your cares away. Then you can go give 'Pathetic Pete', as you call him, a photograph for his paper, of the pair of you, looking like you haven't a care in the world." Janie looked up Bea and smiled. She always seemed to know the right thing to say. She and Megan had been looking forward to tonight for so long now. It was what had got them through all those hours of revision and exams for the past month. Tonight, the Town Hall DJs would be Peter and Paul Taylor. They had been her elder brother Freddy's best friends and had called their set up FREDDY'S FUNK MACHINE, in honour of him. Whenever they did a disco, Janie and Megan not only got in free but the twins did northern soul, mod and Motown sets for them. Janie decided there and then that there was no way she was going to allow her Murderous Mummy to spoil their long-awaited night.

"You're right, as always," began Janie. "I'm not going to skulk in the shadows. That's HER job. I've done nothing wrong. Tonight belongs to me and Megan."

"Too right it does," shouted Megan as she closed the front door behind her. "School is officially over and I for one intend to celebrate. Now why is Pathetic Pete on our doorstep again?" she asked, as she entered the kitchen.

"Murderous Mummy," both Janie and Bea chorused together, then burst out laughing. Megan didn't care what Elsie had been up to. The smile on her aunt's and cousins' faces was enough to let her know it wasn't anything too serious.

***

Janie and Megan were centre stage on the dance floor. A classic northern soul tune was being played and they glided and twirled effortlessly around the floor, their feet moving in time to the beat and their circle skirts spinning out, then falling with a whoosh and a slap as they suddenly stopped twirling around. A crowd had gathered on the fringes of the dance floor to watch them. As the tune faded out and another, more familiar one took its place, a few of the onlookers ventured onto the dance floor, imitating Janie and Megan's dance steps. Both slowed down their movements in order to let them see the steps more clearly. Gradually more and more people filed onto the floor to embrace this new mode of dancing. Janie and Megan beamed across at each other, then, in unison, they began to spin around rapidly, the material of their skirts rising out at their sides, swaying, up and down, until suddenly they both halted at the same moment, causing their skirts to wrap around them in an almighty flap. Moments later the record ended. The northern soul set was over for now. As they left the dance floor, people clapped and cheered. Paul spoke over the intro of the next song.

"That was Janie and Megan dancing along to some northern soul tunes. Now for a few chart toppers, starting with Adam and the Ants."

Janie and Megan made their way to bar area for a drink. As it was a sixteen and overs disco, only soft drinks were being sold. They bought two lemonades then sat down at a table away from the main area.

"Wow, how fab was that?" remarked Janie.

"Fantastic fab," replied Megan. "Did you see how many people were watching us?"

"I know. It was like something out of a film," giggled Janie. Megan nodded in agreement.

"That guy you like was watching you," Janie told Megan. "The one who comes into the garage on his scooter for petrol all the time."

"Nooooo!" exclaimed Megan.

"Yeessss," came the reply from behind them. Both girls looked over their shoulders to see who was butting into their conversation, uninvited. Janie started to laugh but Megan turned a bright red. It was the guy they'd been talking about.

"I got a good look at your knickers, too," he remarked. Megan turned even redder. He smiled at Megan.

"I'm David Evans, by the way, pleased to meet you." And he offered his hand for Megan to shake. In a trance, Megan took his hand but, instead of shaking it, he bent over and kissed the back of it. Megan blushed even more. Janie held up her glass of lemonade for her.

"You'd best take a drink of this Megan before you overheat and your cheeks explode," she teased. But Megan didn't care. The gorgeous guy on the scooter had just kissed the back of her hand. She was in seventh heaven. Janie stood up from the table.

"Watch my drink, Megan, please, while I pop to the loo, will ya?" Megan just nodded, not taking her eyes off David Evans for a second.

Janie didn't need the loo – it was just an excuse to leave the pair of them alone – so she made her way back to the main dance area. She stood out of view of Megan but to the side of the dance floor and watched others dancing their hearts out. After a few more tunes had played, 'Going Underground' by The Jam blasted out from the speakers. Janie edged onto the dance floor. She and Megan loved The Jam. She began to sing along to herself as she danced along to the beat when someone whispered in her ear.

"Thought you was a Saturday girl, working in Woolworths," he remarked. Janie turned to see who had spoken. It was a guy who came into their local Woolworths branch, where she had a part-time job. Every Saturday, like clockwork, he came in and browsed the record section.

"As a rule," she replied, "I am, but tonight I'm Going Underground to join the Modern World." Janie was using The Jam references as a reply to his use of the lyrics from the 'Saturday's Kids' record by the band.

"Touché," he said with a smile on his face. Janie hadn't noticed before how dark his brown eyes were. He wasn't drop-dead gorgeous but there was something about him that Janie realised she quite fancied. She returned his smile then continued to dance along to the beat. As the record came to an end she found herself face to face with him.

"Can I get you a drink?" he offered.

"I've already got one, thanks. My friend Megan is watching it for me." He smirked.

"I think your friend Megan is more interested in watching my mate Dave than your glass of lemonade." Janie stared at him open-mouthed. "I'm Josef Wojtaski, by the way,"

Janie smiled at him. "No point in telling you who I am, is there?"

Josef shook his head. "I didn't think so,"

Janie responded. "But I have to ask," she continued mischievously, "are you and this Dave Evans stalkers?" He immediately started to laugh out loud. Janie thought he was better looking with a smile on his face. It was the kind of smile that lit up his entire face.

"I can see where you're coming from but no. Dave's been smitten by Megan since she served him a few months back at the garage. He's new to the area but well, I knew who you both were due to Freddy."

"Oh!" began Janie and started to walk off. Josef grabbed at her arm.

"Once again, I can see where you're coming from, but Freddy was a mate of my cousin, Gab. He'd often come round to our house with the twins. Go ask them if you don't believe me." Janie stared into his eyes. He looked and sounded sincere enough, but she couldn't recall a friend called Gab. As if reading her mind, he spoke again.

"All Gab's friends called him Taz. As in WojTAZek." Janie smiled. She remembered a Taz.

"He's hyper, dad always said."

"That's our Gab. Everything must be done at double speed. His dad says he'll meet himself coming back one of these days." They both laughed. 'The Queen of Clubs' by KC and the Sunshine Band began to play.

"Dance?" asked Josef. Janie just smiled and headed onto the dance floor.

***

The girls' Saturday shift seemed to drag on forever. Dave and Josef had walked them home after the disco last night and had asked them to join them at a nearby club that evening to see a band called UB40. They'd agreed immediately. They both liked the band's music, but it could have been anyone playing and they'd have still accepted the offer. Bea and Harry hadn't been keen on the idea but by lunchtime had both changed their minds after the boys had called in at the garage to introduce themselves and ask for their permission.

Suddenly, athetic Pete the reporter sitting outside their home didn't seem to matter anymore. They were finally starting to have lives of their own.

JACK

May 1982

DCI Jack Wilde tilted his head towards the morning sun to warm his face. All around him the small fishing village busied itself away. He'd first come here at the end of November 1978 after the missing dinghy from Tommy Jones's yacht had been spotted on the beach by a local fisherman. Praia dos Olhos de Agua in the Algarve region of Portugal had since become like a second home to him. He was due to retire at the end of the year and had decided on buying a home in the area. Unfortunately, Olhos de Agua hadn't got a suitable place for him to buy. He wanted a two-bedroomed apartment with a place to paint and sell his work. Jack had never married. He had a son, Trevor, but he'd never married his mother and she had never wanted to marry him either. Trevor was twenty-eight years old and living in Australia along with his mother. They'd never been that close as Jack was married to his job. He'd always been too wrapped up in police work to make a proper go of any relationship and he'd seen too many of his colleagues dragged through the divorce courts to want to venture down that road. Any free time he got he spent sketching and painting. Somehow, it helped clear his mind of all the atrocities he came across in his job. The clear blue waters and endless blue sky of the Algarve were far more inviting to sketch than the grey skies of Blackpool and the dirty brown North Sea. So far, he had three properties to view. One in Vilamoura marina this morning, then two in Albufeira in the afternoon. Jack glanced at his watch. It was just after 9am. The agent would be here in a few minutes. It was time to drink up and move.

The first property in Vilamoura was a disappointment. It had all the required rooms but they were way too small. The first one he'd visited in Albufeira was no better either. He just hoped this next one was better. From the outside, it looked very promising. It was a small shop, just off the main square. At the rear of the shop was a light, spacious storeroom, ideal for using as his studio. There was also a small kitchenette and toilet set right at the back. The entrance to the apartment was reached via a door to the side of the shop. There was a small hallway, then straight ahead the staircase. Upstairs, above the shop, the only bedroom was located with a good-sized bathroom next door. At the rear of the property there was a large open-plan kitchen/dining/living room. Jack had already fallen in love with the place despite the lack of a second bedroom. The large balcony that led off from the main room had sealed the deal. The view was spectacular. It overlooked the large plaza with sea views in the distance. He stood taking in the vista when suddenly a woman walking across the open plaza caught his attention.

She was of slender build with auburn hair. She carried herself like someone who had perhaps modelled in the past. There seem to be an aura about her despite her years. She was definitely someone you'd never forget meeting. But Jack had never met this woman before... although he'd spent a long time looking for her!

HARRY

June 1982

Harry stood at the arrivals entrance of Manchester Airport awaiting the arrival of DCI Jack Wilde. He'd been badgered by the gathered press for the first half an hour but had just remained tight-lipped. He wasn't there to speak to anyone. He was there purely to check it was Elsie, as the woman DCI Jack Wilde had had extradited had been furiously claiming it was a case of mistaken identity.

Flashbulbs and calls of, "over here, Jack" alerted Harry that finally the waiting was over. The noise from the waiting reporters was overwhelming but the second that Harry caught his first glimpse of Jack and his ward the noise ebbed away. There, in all her splendour, was Elsie. She didn't look like a murderess or a captured fugitive.

Instead she looked like she'd just walked out of some high-class beauty salon. Her suit bore no creases. Not a hair was out of place and, as always, her make-up was immaculate. Elsie Arnold looked every inch like a movie star. As Elsie passed by Harry she just stared straight ahead as if he didn't exist. DCI Wilde, however, made eye contact with him and Harry gave him a slight nod to say it was her. Then both Jack and Elsie were gone from his sight and once again the noise of the reporters roared around him. Once again, they were aiming both questions and cameras at him, but Harry just silently turned away and headed for the exit. Sitting outside waiting for Harry was an unmarked police car ready to take him to Blackpool Police Station. Harry climbed into the front passenger seat and the car pulled away.

Detective Sergeant Alan Beddows was behind the wheel. He'd been one of the officers sent to inform Harry of Freddy's murder. He waited until they were out of the airport perimeter and on the motorway to Blackpool before he spoke.

"Is it her?" he asked. Harry just nodded yes.

"Want to stop for a cuppa on the way?"

"No, thanks. Let's just get this over with, then you can buy me a stiff drink at the pub after."

"Deal," replied DC Beddows and he pressed his foot down harder on the accelerator.

Harry had had to wait for just over two hours before he was allowed into the identifying room. Nine other women, similar in stature, age and looks to Elsie stood in the line-up. Elsie stood third from the right. From behind the one-way mirror, Harry never took his eyes off her. She didn't seem bothered by it all. You'd never know by just looking at her that she'd cold-bloodedly stuck a knife into her eldest child and left him alone in an alleyway to bleed to death. There was no emotion on her face. Harry could feel the warm, salty tears beginning to slide down his face, but he did nothing to hide them. He welcomed the tears. They'd been a long time coming, waiting for this moment when Elsie would be made to pay for what she'd done to Freddy, to his family. DCI Jack Wilde placed a hand on his shoulder.

"Do you see Mrs Elsie Arnold in the line-up?" he formally asked.

"YES," replied Harry as loud and as clear as he could. "She's third from the right."

"Are you certain it's suspect number THREE."

"Positive. Elsie Arnold is suspect number THREE." Harry spoke clearly as he'd been instructed. His response was being taped and so he wanted to make sure there was no doubt in anybody's mind that he'd picked Elsie out of the line-up.

"Thank you, Harry, that'll be all," concluded Jack and Harry was led from the room. Thirty minutes later Jack joined him in a small room just off from the viewing room. He took a seat opposite Harry.

"Stubborn old cow she is, Harry. Even after you'd formally identified her, she still insisted she was Ruby Walters not Elsie Arnold. Soon changed her mind though when I told her we'd be only too happy to drag Morris Connolly aka Douglas Moore and Tommy Jones up here. Now she's screaming the place down demanding protection from them." He laughed. Harry smiled too. It was just like Elsie to put herself first.

"Has she admitted to killing Freddy?"

"Not yet! Now she's finally admitted to being Elsie she wants a lawyer and apart from the screaming for protection she's remaining tight-lipped.

"Is there one on their way?" enquired Harry. Jack just beamed.

"Duty lawyer is with her now, but we've already arrested her for falsifying documents and perverting the cause of justice. So, I'm afraid it's going to be a night in here for her. And seeing as how she's refusing to talk, we might as well get us a drink and a bite to eat. Mrs Davidson has cooked us both a roast dinner and has a room for you to stay in at her B&B for as long as you want. Oh! And no payment required. She insisted." Harry got to his feet.

"Let's go find DC Beddows and get that drink first." Jack stood and headed towards the door then turned to face Harry.

"The calm-before-the-storm-drink, I like to call it. You do know it's going to get rough from here on in for both you and your family, don't you?"

"It involves Elsie, so of course it'll be rough. But we'll survive just as long as Freddy gets justice. Now let's go have that drink as we don't want Mrs Davidson's dinner to go to ruin."

TOMMY

The television was full of images and videos of Elsie Arnold being led through Manchester Airport by DCI Jack Wilde. Of course, it was headline news. After the acquittal and release of Derek Collins the manhunt had hit global scales for the woman who had murdered her son in cold blood. But Tommy Jones couldn't care less about that! His main concern was what Elsie Arnold, or Joyce Adams, as he'd known her, was blabbing about him! Barney had warned him time and time again about letting Joyce know too much about his criminal activities, but he'd not listened. But that wasn't the worst of it! Joyce knew, had even helped cover up and embraced, his homosexuality. He still missed Carl, but Joyce had left him no choice but to end his life. Tommy loved that boy, though he'd never told Carl or anyone else for that matter. It had taken his demise to realise it but by then it was too late. Tommy banged his fist down on his desk. Christ! He hated Joyce with every ounce of his beginning. He should have killed her that night, not Carl. Carl would have still been here by his side, loyal and dependable.

"FUCKING WHORE," he screamed at the telly, as another shot of her passing through the airport graced his television screen.

"YOU'LL PAY FOR WHAT YOU'VE DONE TO ME WITH YOUR LIFE, ELSIE ARNOLD," he yelled at the television. "Once you hit prison you're toast!"

DOUGLAS

In the common room of Wandsworth Prison, Douglas Moore sat at a table staring at the same news report as Tommy Jones was watching. May, aka Elsie, still was a good-looking woman, he thought. He remembered how other men used to stare at her with longing in their eyes. How he'd felt privileged to be the one she'd chosen. She had been a vision to behold and yet acted like a common whore in the bedroom. Not that he'd minded. He did after all have a penchant for the sadistic in that area. Even now, the memories of her lying naked and inviting on top of the bed were beginning to send his pulse racing. Douglas shook his head, as if to shake the lurid memories from his mind. This woman had stolen from him, he reminded himself. She'd made him look a fool in front of his associates and men. NO ONE made a fool out of him and got away with it. But, somehow, she had. His men had manged to track her down but somehow she'd always managed to stay one step ahead. But not any longer. Now she was just like him. Cornered like a rat in some godforsaken stinking prison. And NO ONE, NO ONE was safe in prison. Why! Even he'd been got at and bore the scar right down his left cheek to prove it. It had only been a warning from the IRA to keep his mouth closed but he'd bled like a pig. There had been no need for them to worry. Douglas Moore was no grass. His silence had paid off. He might end his days inside, but he'd have as many home comforts as the place could afford, along with protection and the status of top dog. Elsie FUCKING Arnold would have no such luxuries. Elsie Arnold was on borrowed time and he knew exactly who was going to do the dirty work for him. Tommy Jones was and then he'd wipe out him too!

DEREK

Derek Collins had been sat across from Blackpool Police Station since he'd learnt that Elsie was on a plane bound for Manchester Airport. He was quite comfortable in his window seat at the Pump & Truncheon on Bonny Street opposite the station. The landlord knew him from old and when Derek had asked him if he could keep an eye out for Elsie from his establishment he'd been only too happy to help. As a retired copper, he'd understood the need for Derek to see Elsie with his own two eyes, the need to check it was actually her they'd nabbed, but that hadn't stopped him from frisking him first for any concealed weapons.

Derek hadn't minded. He'd no desire to kill Elsie. He'd been to prison. He'd served time and it had been no picnic. Prison would bring a slow, suffering death to Elsie without his help. He just wanted to see her. There were rumours flying around that it wasn't her that was being flown in but some innocent woman. Derek doubted that very much. DCI Jack Wilde was too shrewd a man to get it wrong a second time. Wilde had never really believed that Derek had murdered Freddy in the first place. If it hadn't been for him, Derek would probably still be rotting away in some prison cell while Elsie was living the life of Riley out in the free world. No, DCI Jack Wilde was bringing Elsie home, he was sure of it.

Derek took a sip of his now-cold tea and was just about to head off to the loo when cars started to pull up outside the station. DCI Jack Wilde exited the car first and then in full view of the waiting press he hauled Elsie out of the back of the car, showing her off as his prize. Derek stopped dead in his tracks, his gaze held by the beauty before him. Derek broke down and cried.

ELSIE

"Shall we begin?" said DCI Jack Wilde as he sat himself down opposite Elsie and her appointed lawyer Glenn McCartney, his finger poised to hit the record button on the interview tape machine.

"Can we speak off the record first?" enquired Glenn. Jack leaned back in his chair, placing his hands in his lap, indicating he was listening. Glenn nodded Elsie to begin. Elsie hadn't taken her eyes off the DCI since he had entered the room. He was a good-looking chap, she'd give him that, but there was coldness to his eyes. He wasn't a man to make promises that he couldn't keep or someone she could play for a fool, that was for certain. All her pleas, of being an innocent mistaken identity, had held no sway with him. It was as if he could look deep into her soul and see her for exactly what she was and that terrified her more than anything. Here was a man that she couldn't cajole into seeing or doing things her way. She was going to have to play it straight with him, if she wanted to stay alive, even if that life was spent behind bars.

"Say I was to just up and plead guilty. Save my family from going through a trial and let slip a few names, dates, etcetera about a couple of people your lot are interested in. Could you guarantee me protection in prison?" Elsie asked.

"Nope! I can make sure you're given a cell of your own at a maximum-security prison, that you have as little interaction with other prisoners as possible, but I can't guarantee your safety. No one can." Elsie pondered over his reply for a few minutes, still keeping her gaze firmly on him. Glenn went to speak but she held up her hand to silence him.

"Could I be placed in solitary long term?"

DCI Wilde leant forwards and placed his hands on the table. "I thought you hated confined spaces, Elsie. What's brought around this need to be locked up all alone suddenly?" Elsie could see the small beginnings of a smile flickering at the corners of his mouth. She too leant forward and placed her hands on the table.

"Shall we say the desire to remain in one piece and breathing. After all, even murderers get parole." Elsie let a smile caress her lips for a fleeting moment. The DCI made no movement.

"Have to be pretty big information to wangle that, Elsie."

"Morris, or, should I say, Douglas, talked in his sleep and had me wait on him and his IRA cronies at least once a week. Now, Tommy Jones didn't share his bed with me, Detective Chief Inspector, but he did share his dirty dealings with me. I know more than enough for you to bust half of the IRA and put Tommy away for a very long time. So, solitary confinement to me sounds a blast compared to what they've all got planned for me. So, do we have a deal or not?" Jack Wilde rose from his seat and headed towards the door. As he knocked for it to be opened he turned back to face Elsie.

"I need to make a few phone calls before I promise anything. I'll have one of my officers bring in some refreshments while you wait." And with that he exited out the now-open door.

Elsie sat back in her chair. She hadn't expected an immediate response from the DCI. In fact, if he'd have agreed straight away, she'd have had to rethink her whole analysis of him. This dimwit of a lawyer they'd assigned her had advised her to just cough up to the murder and hope they'd go easy on her. Once they'd agreed to her terms then she'd get a better lawyer to represent her, but he'd have to do for now. As if on cue, he spoke.

"They won't agree to your demands, Mrs Arnold; I can assure you of that. He's just left you here to sweat it out, that's all." Elsie turned on the lawyer with a vengeance.

"Are you stupid or something? Don't you know who the fuck I'm offering information on?" she spat out. "I've fucked two of the nastiest, evil bastards this country has ever had the pleasure of knowing and you think they're going to let me live?"

"I-I-I don't know who you're on about," stammered Glenn.

"Call yourself a defence lawyer and you've no fucking idea who Tommy Jones and Douglas Moore are? You must be fucking kidding me, right?" Elsie watched the lawyer squirm in his seat.

"I've not come across them," he replied. His answer made Elsie laugh out loud.

"You've never come across either of them. Christ, do you walk around in a fucking dream or something? I mean, I know Blackpool is no hotspot for terrorism or gang lords but Jesus H. Christ that pair of bastards has been plastered across the front pages of newspapers for years and they are seen on the telly more times than the fucking Queen. Where the fuck have you been?" Elsie could see the sweat beads forming on Glenn McCartney's brow. She watched in amazement as he straightened his shoulders and puffed out his chest.

"I'm not a fan of television, if you must know, and I only read the Times. I don't pay any mind to those gutter press tabloids you are obviously referring to. As I practise in family law, the firm thought as this was primarily a family matter I'd be best suited to your needs." With that he stood, brushed imaginary crumbs from his suit and made for the door.

"I shall assume you no longer require my services so I shall ask to be excused and see that you get someone more suited to your needs." Glenn made to knock on the door, but it flung open and caught him square on in the face. He broke into childish crying immediately, making Elsie almost wet her pants in laughter. The police officer who had flung open the door to make way for the tea tray nearly crapped himself when he realised what he'd done to the lawyer.

Elsie called out before returning to fits of laughter,

"I need the fucking loo before I piss myself." The other officer plonked the tea tray down on the table, then grabbing Elsie roughly by the arm escorted her to the loo. By the time she returned to the room, DCI Wilde was pouring himself a cup of tea and Glenn McCartney was nowhere to be seen.

"He's being treated by the duty doctor and another lawyer is being sent to represent you as we speak," he informed Elsie.

"And our deal?" she asked as she sat back down at the table. Jack placed a cup of tea in front of her.

"Solitary it'll be if the information you give us is worth our trouble." Elsie smiled and sipped the weak tea.

"Oh, it's good, very good. So, let's make sure the next sap of a lawyer you palm me off with is up to the job."

"We're not palming you off with anyone, Elsie. Mr Ivan Harris has volunteered his services. He's a royal pain in the ass. Likes to litter our streets with criminals, he does. Coppers have a nickname for him, it's Ivan the Terrible. It seems, Mrs Arnold, that he's taken an interest in you. Perhaps he thinks he can get you off on a lighter sentence. Mr Harris likes the fame, the notoriety defending the bad guys gets him. You're worth a lot of media attention to him. So, think carefully before you let him in on what you know. It's a friendly warning, Elsie. Harris isn't here for your good just purely his own." Elsie listened carefully to what the DCI was telling her. Glenn McCartney might be a wet blanket but what she really didn't need was someone out to feather their nest at her expense, especially not with Douglas and Tommy waiting to top her at the drop of a hat. Elsie nodded to let the DCI know she'd taken on board what he'd said. She'd learnt from some of the best how to suss out a grass and who to trust. DCI Jack Wilde might well be trying to put her behind bars but at least he was upfront and honest about it.

"When he arrives, how about you follow my lead, eh? I need you alive and kicking for more than one reason. I want Harry and your children to get the justice they deserve but I also want to wipe a few more bits of scum off our streets. I retire at the end of the year and I want to do so with a clear conscience and a sense that I served the law-abiding people of this country well. If that means keeping a murderess alive and well inside a prison and an egotistic lawyer in his place, then so be it. I've no qualms about belittling Ivan Harris or seeing you live out your days on your lonesome in a cell. So, what's it to be?"

"It seems like I have no choice but to do as you suggest," Elsie quipped. She'd already decided that she was going to have to put her trust in this man and get what she wanted sorted ASAP if he was due to retire in a few months. So, it may as well begin now.

BEA

August 1982

Bea stole at peek at the kitchen clock. In just under an hour the whole family would be gathered for the traditional Saturday afternoon tea. Usually, the table would be overflowing with home-made cakes and scones. There would be a variety of sandwiches and a big bowl of freshly made trifle, but there hadn't been of late. Home-made cakes had been replaced with ones purchased from the local bakery. Jelly and ice-cream replaced elaborate fruit trifles. The only things that remained the same was the selection of sandwiches on offer. Bea hadn't had the energy to do more than what was already asked of her.

She hadn't just suddenly started feeling tired; it had been a gradual thing that had started sometime around the beginning of the year. She'd just had her fiftieth birthday and had assumed that she was just entering the menopause. What with the heavy irregular bleeding, sweating, headaches, forgetfulness and just generally feeling out of sorts, they were all classic signs of it. But gradually the symptoms had got worse and she'd had to admit defeat and visit the local doctors' surgery. A rather grumpy male doctor had confirmed she was probably right and in the throes of menopause and dismissed her. But Bea hadn't felt reassured by him and so had made an appointment to see a different doctor at the practice.

Dr William Walsh wasn't so convinced and decided that both urine and blood samples needed to be taken for several different tests. He'd logged her weight and height and after finding that her temperature was slightly raised, along with her blood pressure, he had them sent with an urgent request. Three days later, Bea had been called back to see him. There were irregular findings in her samples, she was told, and that he'd like to admit her to hospital for a few days for various tests to be done on her. At the time, so much had been going on. Both the girls had been in the midsts of their A level exams. Harry and Charlie had been overseeing the renovations for a new showroom, so they could start selling cars alongside the day-to-day business of MOTs, repairs and selling fuel. Anne and Eric's first child had been due to be born in a matter of weeks and DCI Wilde had brought Elsie back home from Portugal. There had been way too much going on for her to spring this on them, so instead she'd lied. Bea had told them that she fancied a few days away at the cottage. Time alone to recharge her batteries and they had gone along with it. She'd spent those two dreadful days being poked and prodded by what seemed like half of the hospital staff. There'd been X-rays taken and scans done, along with numerous blood tests and her temperature and blood pressure taken every hour. On her release, she'd felt more exhausted than ever before. Then the surgery had rung to say her results were back, and an appointment had been for her the following day. She'd wanted to ask Harry to come with her then, but he'd been away at Anne's with Megan and Janie crooning over his new grandson, Frederick Eric Holmes. They'd wanted her to go but she'd fobbed them off with the need to stay behind and look after Charlie. So she'd gone alone to see Dr Walsh. That had been three weeks ago, and she'd kept her dreadful secret to herself but two days ago, for the first time since Arthur had been diagnosed with his brain tumour, Bea had been scared. With an appointment at the hospital cancer unit looming, she'd finally told Harry what had been going on.

Initially, Harry had been shocked, but it had closely been followed by a dressing-down for not telling him sooner and then he'd held her as though his life depended on it. After that he'd popped over to the garage to say he was taking the day off then had bundled Bea into his car and taken her to her hospital appointment. The consultant had been very honest and had almost immediately told her the prognosis wasn't looking good. She had cervical cancer. It was aggressive and had already begun spreading to other areas of her body. She needed to start a course of chemotherapy straight away and then they'd give her a hysterectomy. A bed had been booked for her and she was to return the following Monday at 8am sharp to begin her treatment. Bea had left the hospital in a daze. Harry had driven in silence while Bea had just relaxed back into the passenger seat, eyes closed, trying so desperately to get her head around everything that she had been told. Then she'd realised that the car had stopped and Harry had turned off the engine. On opening her eyes, she'd found they weren't outside the family home but parked overlooking the river.

"We used to come as kids, remember?" Harry had begun. Bea had smiled at the memory. "Mum would make up a picnic of sandwiches and boiled eggs, with a flask of tea for her and dad and weak squash for us kids. Of course, there was always home-made Victoria sponge cake with oodles of jam in the middle."

"Always raspberry jam," Bea had offered, remembering how the seeds used to stick in her teeth afterwards.

"We used to skim stones, trying to reach the other side of the embankment. We'd even venture into the river itself if it wasn't too deep. Mum used to shout and scream at us to get out before we drowned but dad would just wade in and join us," Harry had recalled.

"Happy days," Bea had remarked as she had remembered it all.

"Very," Harry had added, before going on to say. "But they didn't last. Mary turned everyone's world upside down in a blink of an eye. Gone was our happy little family, torn apart, and for what? To appease Mary's bruised ego?" Bea had then placed her hand in Harry's. He had given it a gentle squeeze. Then he'd continued to remind her of past events.

"Losing Freddy meant I got you back, Bea. You've held this battered family together. You're still trying to hold us all together despite feeling so unwell. How could we have been so blind not to notice? Not to see that it wasn't just an age thing? It's like I… we've let you down all over again. If only we'd taken more notice, more care maybe we… I could have stopped…" Bea had shifted in her seat and had taken both her brother's hands in her own.

"This isn't your fault or anyone else's, Harry," she'd begun. "You heard what the consultant said. It's an aggressive cancer. It had taken hold long before I even knew. No one is to blame. No one is at fault. I just got unlucky, that's all. Monday, I'll start the chemo then they'll do the operation. They'll know more then. I know it doesn't look too good at the moment but we need to stay positive. I NEED YOU to stay positive for me. I NEED YOU to hold my hand and help me through this."

"I don't know if I can…" Harry had mumbled through his tears.

"YOU HELPED ME through the worst time in my life when everyone else was against me. YOU HELPED ME, all those years ago, to carry on. Just like you helped me beat Mary at skimming stones. You were only little, but you sure had a knack for making those stones skip across the water. You've been helping me all my life, Harry; you just didn't know it, so please, I beg of you, don't stop now," she had pleaded with her younger brother.

"I promise, Bea, I won't," he'd sniffled. Bea had let go of his hands and had given him a handkerchief from her bag.

"You're a big boy now, Harry," she'd reminded him.

"So, blow your nose and stop those tears. Let's get through the next few days as a family, eh?" And so they had. As though nothing had happened. But today, once the food had been eaten and all the dishes washed, dried and put away, the truth would come out and their entire world would be thrown into turmoil.

AFTERNOON TEA

Saturday afternoon tea had started like any other. Janie and Megan were last to be seated as usual, flying in the kitchen door, clad in their Woolworths uniforms and full of their Saturday evenings plans. Once they'd seated themselves at the table, Bea had begun to pour the tea, while Harry had begun to pass round the plates of sandwiches.

In just over an hour, it was as if the whole affair hadn't taken place. With the dishes washed and put away, the usual routine meant a scramble for the bathroom to wash and change for the 'Big Saturday Night' out, but Harry had ordered them all to go directly into the living room as he and Bea had something to tell them.

"Can't it wait?" Charlie had protested. "I'm due to pick Shelly up in an hour and God help me if I'm late. You know what a little cow she can be at times."

"You mean ALL THE TIME," giggled Janie.

"Just cause she's a stickler for timekeeping and—"

"Wearing too much make-up and showing half the town her bust…" interrupted Megan.

"Oh! and belittling you, Charlie," added Janie.

"Just cause she takes pride in her appearance and wants me to do the same, doesn't mean—"

"Enough," bellowed Harry. "I don't give a flying fig if Shelly is kept waiting or who thinks what of her, so can we all stop jabbering on and get on with the reason why we're here?" Immediately, Charlie, Janie and Megan fell silent. Harry hardly ever raised his voice to them. The last time they'd heard him shout was when Elsie had been arrested and they'd talked about how hanging was too good for her. Whatever could it be now that had caused this annoyance in him? But then, surprisingly, Harry had sat down in his chair and Bea began to speak.

"There's no easy way to say this but I've received some bad news, kids." Charlie opened his mouth to speak but Bea held her hand up to halt him.

"I've been feeling a little under the weather for a while now and eventually I went to see the doctor." This time it was Janie who went to interrupt but again Bea held her hand up. "Please let me finish; it's hard enough as it is." Bea took a deep breath. "On Wednesday, Harry and I went to see a specialist. A cancer specialist to be exact. I've got cancer and, as of Monday, I'm going into hospital to start a course of chemotherapy. Once that is over, I'll be home for a short while then I'll have to go back in for a hysterectomy." Bea stopped speaking and the room fell silent.

"And then what?" asked Megan.

"We don't know," lied Harry.

"What do you mean you don't know?" shouted Charlie. "You're supposed to say, that's it! IT'S ALL OVER! AUNT BEA IS GOING TO GET BETTER! WE'LL LIVE HAPPILY EVER AFTER!" With each sentence, Charlie's voice grew louder. Bea went and sat by Charlie and placed her arm around his shoulders.

"I wish I could say that, Charlie, more than anything else in the world, but I can't." Bea let the tears flow freely down her face.

"We'll just have to wait and see what the outcome of the chemo and hysterectomy is first. But I'm in good hands. I just need you all to be strong for me. To be positive for me. To look after, each other for me. Can you all promise to do that?" Charlie, Janie and Megan all nodded in agreement as the same silent tears streaked down their faces. Suddenly being late to pick up Shelly didn't matter anymore. The 'Big Saturday Night' out was forgotten. All that mattered was staying in their cosy living room, as a family, coming to terms with what the road ahead had in store for them.

Janie questioned whether her trip around Europe with Josef in the New Year was wise. Megan wondered if she should defer from starting university for a year. Charlie realised in that short space of time how shallow Shelly was and how deadly keeping secrets could be!

Harry sat back and watched as his remarkable sister, children and niece accepted things and agreed to keep family life as normal as was physically possible. While Bea answered each question, each query as honestly as she thought was necessary at the time, at the back of her mind she kept asking God, "how much more are you going to put these poor children through?" For surely, in their such short lives, hadn't they witnessed enough? Then she offered up a silent prayer, for him to show mercy on them all.

JANIE

Christmas Eve 1982

Janie lifted the black eye-mask from her eyes and slowly opened them to adjust to the winter sunlight streaming in through her bedroom window. Mrs Broadhurst, the assistant manageress at Woolworths, had driven her home a little after 10am as the onset of a migraine had started to take hold when she'd been serving on the record counter. Once Janie had assured her that she'd be fine, despite the house being empty, Mrs Broadhurst left to return to the store. Janie had then taken her prescribed migraine tablets, donned her eye-mask to block out any light and had slipped beneath her bed covers and fallen almost immediately into a deep, dreamless sleep. Janie had woken with the remnants of a headache and the familiar horrid, metallic taste in her mouth that the migraine tablets always left behind. With her eyes now adjusted to the light, she cast a glance at her bedside clock: 2:43pm, the digital display flashed at her. She'd slept for around four hours solid. Janie silently and slowly rose from her bed and headed downstairs towards the kitchen to get a glass of milk to erase the nasty metallic taste from her mouth. As she rounded the bottom of the stairs she heard her father's raised voice coming from behind the closed living room door. Janie edged forwards, careful not to make a sound.

"You can't just swan off to the cottage and expect us all to carry on as if nothing's happening." He was shouting, but then her Aunt Bea's voice cut in on her father's, louder and with a real anger to it.

"Of course, I can, it's my life and I'll bloody well end it the way I choose, not how you and some doctor tells me."

"If you don't want the chemo again, I'll understand, but you can't just slope off and die without telling anyone," Harry was shouting back at her. Janie stood transfixed the other side of the closed living room door, hardly believing what she was hearing coming from the other side.

"They're young, Harry." Bea had lowered her voice with a soft pleading to it. "Don't you think they've been through enough without watching me die?" That was it! Janie could contain herself no longer. With tears clouding her eyes she burst through the living room door. Bea, whose back was to the door, swung round and on seeing Janie standing there with tears streaming down her face, she collapsed into the closest chair and began to sob herself.

Harry didn't know who to comfort first but as Janie seemed to be in some sort of shock he quickly made the decision to take her in his arms first but as he crossed the room, arms out stretched to embrace her, suddenly Janie began screaming at Bea like a banshee.

"YOU LIED TO US. YOU BOTH LIED TO US," Janie screamed at her aunt and father. "You told us that the chemo and operation had been a success. That the cancer was gone. How could you tell us such a blatant lie? Don't you think we deserve to know the truth, to make our own minds up?" As Janie ranted away Bea wiped the tears from her eyes, stood up and made towards her niece but Janie backed away.

"Don't you come near me," she screamed at Bea. "YOU'RE NOTHING BUT A LIAR." Bea saw that the door had slid closed behind Janie so she kept walking towards her. In one quick movement, she was on Janie, clasping her shoulders in a tight grip.

"I didn't want you to have to carry my burden, Janie. I wanted you to go off on your travels with Josef as planned, for Megan to return to university after the Christmas holidays and for Charlie to continue to flourish at the garage. I've lied to you because I love you all and don't want you all to have to watch me being eaten up by this cancer. I want you all to remember me as I am. Not some bag of bones being gnawed away at by this vile thing inside of me. Can't you understand that, Janie? I want to die with dignity. I want to die where my Arthur took his last breath. I want to die looking out to sea, knowing that you are all somewhere, unaware of what is happening to me but now you know and it's breaking my heart."

Janie looked deep into the eyes of the woman who had come to their rescue. Who had shielded them all from harm. Had kept them safe and warm while the wolves were at the door trying to get a reaction to all the atrocities her mother had bestowed on them. Who had taken Megan under her wing and had brought her away from the horrors she'd borne at the hands of her father and the guilt she'd carried at the knowledge that her mother had taken both her father's and her own life to release Megan from the hell she'd been living in. Bea had suffered enough of her own heartache at the hands of her family and the loss of her beloved Arthur, yet she'd returned to face them to help Janie and her family. Now Bea was going to die and the pain in her heart and chest made breathing so hard. Tears were cascading down her face; her nose was running and the snot slipping into her mouth as she gasped to get air into her lungs, but it didn't matter. All that mattered was Bea. Her beautiful Aunt Bea. Janie collapsed into Bea's arms and they held each until their sobbing subsided and their tears ran dry. Harry looked on, shedding silent tears of his own.

Eventually Janie pulled away from Bea and wiped her nose with her sleeve.

"I'm coming with you, Bea. I'm going to the cottage with you. I'm going to be by your side until the very end. I'm going to make you tell me everything there is to know about you. And I'm going to promise that when the time comes I'm going to sit you in your favourite chair looking out to sea. You were there for us, now let me be there for you."

"But your trip with Josef—" Bea began.

"Europe, Asia, America, the rest of the world will be there next month, next year, next century but, my busy Bea, my beautiful Bea, you won't. The trip, Josef can wait; this can't."

"But, Janie, I don't want you to see me wasting away."

"You told me you'd never desert me all that time ago when I was afraid that you'd leave just like mum did. You promised you wouldn't and I promised never to leave you. Do you remember?" Bea nodded her head smiling at the memory. "You taught me never to make a promise I couldn't keep. So, don't ask me now to break it, please. Let me do this for you. Let me take care of you like you've taken care of me, of Charlie, of Megan, of dad. Please don't deny me this, Aunt Bea, I beg of you." Bea held Janie close to her then held her at arm's length.

"I taught you too well, I think," began Bea. "Now it's come back to bite me in the bum, as your grandad George would say. So how can I refuse your offer? But it comes with one condition," warned Bea. "You mustn't tell a soul about any of this until after Christmas is over. Can you promise me that? You as well, Harry?" Bea shouted over her shoulder at her brother. "Let me have this last Christmas Day with the rest of the family unaware of what's happening. Can you both be brave enough to do that one small thing for me? I'll promise to tell everyone the truth after we've had the annual Boxing Day party. I know it's a big ask but I beg of you both, please let me have this Christmas without pity. With the rest of the family and our friends believing I'm cured. I want our last

Christmas together to be a happy one, not one marred by sadness. Can you promise me that? Please say you can." Harry walked over to his sister and daughter and pulled them both into his big, strong arms.

"We'll make sure it's a Christmas to remember, Bea. "We promise, Janie, don't we?" Janie gave Bea a big smile.

"This is my brave face, Aunt Bea," she joked. "I'm going to wear it until Christmas is over. It's my gift to you." The three of them hung on to each other for dear life, afraid to let go, afraid of what the New Year had in store for them all.

ELSIE

Christmas day 1982

"Move it, Arnold," bellowed Prison Officer Lewis, as she swung open Elsie's cell door. Elsie slid off her bunk and with her towel under one arm and her toiletry bag in the other she headed out of her cell, along the landing, down the stairs and into the shower block. Elsie came to a halt outside the entrance to the showers. Steam was causing a fog like blanket inside.

"Move yourself, Arnold." PO Lewis yelled at her. "I've got better things to be getting on with than babysitting you." And with that shoved Elsie in the back into the shower's entrance. Elsie turned to face the prison officer.

"Aren't you were supposed to check the block's empty first," enquired Elsie. Lecherous Lesbian Lewis, as she was known among the inmates, gave Elsie a sickly grin.

"It's Christmas Day, I thought I'd let you have a little dignity, by way of a Christmas present, you might say." Lewis let out a shrill laugh. Instantly, Elsie knew that trouble lay inside the showers for her and Lewis was party to it.

"Go on, Arnold, get in there before I have to give you a fucking beating for disobeying an officer." She spat out at Elsie. Elsie adjusted the rolled-up towel under her arm and tentatively edged forwards into the steamed-up shower block. Usually, Elsie would head to the right-hand side of the block, but her instincts told her to head left instead. Once she turned the corner and was out of view from PO Lewis she placed her toiletry bag on the floor, throwing her towel into it. Left in her hand now was a shard of metal protruding from a makeshift handle of rolled paper and Sellotape. She held it in a vice-like grip as she slunk further into the corner of the shower block. Elsie pressed her back hard up against the shower's tiled wall and waited.

Eventually a clothed figure came into Elsie's view and was heading towards the bank of steaming showers on the far wall. Elsie could see a glint of a blade as it caught in dim light of one of the overhead caged bulbs. She took a deep breath then lunged herself at the back of her would-be attacker.

With the element of surprise Elsie managed to plunge her makeshift knife into the side of the other woman before she'd realised what was going on. As Elsie drew back to take another stab at her, the woman turned and caught Elsie across the side of her left cheek with her knife. Elsie stepped back in shock and the attacker went on to press home her advantage, but Elsie just managed to sidestep the blade coming towards her. Instead of plunging into her stomach it swiped the side of her loose-fitting prison shirt and snagged there, before falling to the tiled shower floor. Elsie quickly used the attacker's force against her and slammed her own blade into the advancing abdomen of the woman hurtling towards her. She let out a gut-wrenching squeal as she collapsed to the floor. Immediately Elsie could hear Lewis calling out.

"Brownlow, have you got her?" she called out into the steam.

"Help," gurgled Brownlow from the floor. Elsie kicked the fallen knife out of her attacker's reach then, quickly retrieving her towel, she flung it out on the floor, holding onto the one end and stooping down low. Lewis rounded the corner.

"Brownlow, where are you? What's going on?" she whispered once again into the steam of the shower room.

"Over here," croaked Brownlow. Lewis took a step forwards, her right foot falling onto the towel. As she lifted her left foot, Elsie pulled on the towel with all her might. Lewis let out several screams as both of her feet left the ground and she came crashing down on the cold, hard tiles of the shower block floor. Elsie gathered up her own home-made knife and crawled across to the large drain over by the running showers. She prised off the grate in the far corner then stuffed her knife down the drainpipe and let the water do the rest of the work for her. Replacing the grate, Elsie got to her feet and ran past the two women laid out on the floor, speeding out of the showers, and pulled the alarm cord outside the shower block. Exhausted, Elsie slumped to the floor, her hands held tightly over her ears to protect them from the shrill sound of the ringing alarm bells and waited for the cavalry to arrive.

***

27th December 1982

Governor Johnson placed a chair by Elsie's bedside and sat down. Elsie turned her head to face him. He smiled at her. Elsie would normally have smiled back at such a good-looking bloke but the stitches on her left check were starting to heal and that meant they were not only driving her mad with the itchiness but they'd pulled the skin all round them incredibly tight.

"Eight stitches, they say. I'm afraid they're going to leave a permanent scar, Mrs Arnold." Elsie just nodded in agreement.

"Anyway, I'm not here to talk scars but about the events of two days ago. It seems Prison Officer Lewis had connections to an old friend of yours, a Mr Tommy Jones. Her brother owed a lot of money to one of his associates. The brother offered him access to you via his sister in lieu of his debts being wiped out. Tommy agreed, with an added bonus to Lewis for getting the job done and a few quid bunged to Brownlow's family. Brownlow confessed all, once she realised that Prison Officer Lewis was placing all the blame at her door. Brownlow has five children back home and only a few months left of her sentence to serve. She coughed up everything she knew to get a favourable hearing and a lower sentence should you press charges." Elsie pushed herself higher up the bed.

"So, it was Tommy's doing then, not that sicko lesbian Lewis? I thought she'd just got it in for me 'cause I wouldn't let her have her sick, twisted way with me." Johnson didn't seem surprised by Elsie's insinuations.

"We have been aware of Prison Officer Lewis's, shall we say, activities for a while now, but unfortunately no one was prepared to make an official complaint against her."

"Can you blame anyone? They're all either a bunch of screaming lesbians or just downright bullies. Complaining to one of your PRISON OFFICERS about bloody anything is like taking your life in your own hands. They're bigger villains than us cons," blurted out Elsie.

"I can understand your way of thinking, Mrs Arnold, but not all of my officers are as corrupt as you might believe. But, that aside, I'm here to see if you'd like to press charges against inmate Irene Brownlow?"

"And what will happen to her if I don't? Or, more importantly, what will happen to me if I do?"

"Brownlow will receive an extra two months on her sentence for causing a, shall we say, disturbance, if you should refuse to press charges. You will remain here as a guest of her majesty. If you do decide to press charges, she'll be up on an attempted murder charge. You will be transferred to another prison regarding your safety.

"Prison Officer Lewis has been dismissed from the prison service and awaits sentencing as regards the attack on you."

Elsie pondered over what the governor had said then made her own request. "I know DCI Jack Wilde retires in a few days but before I make any decision can I see him or at least speak to him?" The governor rose from his chair and handed it to a nearby guard to return to the far end of the room.

"I shall see if I can get hold of DCI Wilde, immediately, then I'll send word of the outcome." Then Governor Johnson strode out of the prison's hospital wing with a guard close on his heels. Elsie slumped back onto her pillows and thought how close Tommy Jones had come to getting her erased.

***

Elsie had been returned to her cell in solitary the following day with news that DCI Jack Wilde had agreed to make the journey to come see her. He'd be here within the next few hours. Elsie had paced up and down her cell awaiting his arrival. Finally, after what seemed like days not hours, she was escorted to one of the interview rooms in the prison. DCI Wilde was already seated at the table with a styrofoam cup of what looked like black coffee in front of him. He watched as Elsie was led into the room and sat down in the chair opposite him.

"You are free to leave us now," he informed the guard.

"Are you sure, sir?" the young guard enquired.

"Positive," Jack assured him. The guard turned and left and once the door was slammed shut behind him, Jack spoke.

"Eight stitches, eh? Heard your attacker got twice as many."

Elsie smiled at the DCI. "Self-defence," she remarked. She waited for him to give a jibe about her reply but instead he took a sip of the black liquid from his cup.

"Tommy Jones was blown up in his car outside of one of his clubs along with his hired goon, Barney, on Boxing Day. The men you told us about regarding Douglas Moore have either turned up dead or simply disappeared. Douglas Moore himself was the victim of a knife attack on Monday. He sustained internal bleeding and died late yesterday afternoon. Prison Officer Lewis was found dead at her home this morning. The official verdict is going to be suicide, as several bottles of pills and a half-empty bottle of vodka were found by her side. I, myself, received a note at my office this morning, saying I was to let you know you're off the hook! From whom or what, I can't say." Elsie was dumbstruck by the amount of attacks that had taken place over a short space of time.

"IRA?" she asked.

"We think they are responsible, yes. Do we have proof? No!"

"And Irene Brownlow?"

"She's being released from the local hospital back into the hospital wing here. If you press charges, you'll be moved to a different prison."

"And if I don't?"

"You'll both remain here."

"Yeah, but what about me?"

"If you don't press charges you'll be seen as some sort of hero by the rest of the inmates. With the threat of Tommy Jones and Douglas Moore gone, you'll have the choice of either remaining in solitary or being moved into the general population. If you do press charges, you'll be moved to another prison and remain in solitary as it'll be too dangerous to let you mingle with the other inmates. They don't take to kindly to stitching up one of their own, as they see it, and no pun intended, by the way." DCI Wilde took another slurp from his cup.

"If you were me, what would you do?" Elsie asked.

Jack took another sip of his coffee then smiled at Elsie.

"I'd think Christmas had come at last. Not only are all my worse enemies dead but I get the opportunity to rub shoulders with my counterparts, instead of staring at the same four walls all day, every day. I'd drop all charges against Brownlow and even go as far as shaking her hand when I saw her again." Jack rose from his chair and crossed to the door. "Right, that's me done. As of now I'm a retired policeman with a plane to catch. Make the right decision, Elsie, for once in your life." Then he was through the door and gone. Elsie decided to take his advice. After all, she could end up top dog of this hell hole, if she played her cards right.

JACK

29th December 1982

Jack slid onto the passenger seat of the waiting unmarked police car and slammed the door shut.

"Everything all right, Guv?" asked the young PC, who'd volunteered to drive Jack from his home on the outskirts of Blackpool to Birmingham airport via this place. Jack looked across at the PC.

"No, Turner, it isn't! Now, let's just get off this driveway and go find a pub. I could do with a stiff drink." PC Mike Turner immediately turned on the engine, put the car in gear and pulled off the driveway. Jack Wilde was a decent bloke, so something must have upset him to put him in such a bad mood. After all, he'd seemed quite upbeat on their arrival at the house. Said it wouldn't take him long to pass on the information he had but he'd been inside the house for over an hour. Mike was dying to know what had gone on inside but wisely chose to avoid the question.

"I'm not too familiar with these parts, Guv, so I'll head for the airport and keep an eye out for a pub along the way, if that's okay?" Jack just nodded his approval and stared blankly out of the side window as houses and towns, turned to fields and farm buildings. All of them holding an interest to him. The clicking sound of the car's indicator going on brought Jack out of his stupor. PC Turner was indicating to turn right into the car park of a pub called the Hare and Hounds. He smoothly brought the car to a halt, right outside the front entrance, then turned off the engine.

"This do ya?" he enquired. Jack just opened the door and alighted from the car. Once again, he slammed the door shut. He never spoke a word as he entered the pub and made for the bar, with PC Mike Turner hot on his heels.

"Mind if I find the toilets, Guv? Only my bladder's bursting." Jack just waved his hand at him, so he set off to find a much-needed loo. When Mike returned to the main bar area he found Jack was hunched over a pint of bitter with what looked like a whisky chaser by its side. On the opposite side of the table was a bottle of coke and a clean, empty glass. Jack looked up as he approached the table.

"Hope the drink's okay?" was all he said. Mike sat down opposite Jack and gently poured the coke into the glass.

"I'd have preferred a lager, but this will do. Cheers," he said as he raised the glass to his lips. Jack didn't respond.

They sat in silence for a few more minutes, Jack staring blankly into his pint and Mike taking in his surroundings. Eventually, Jack spoke.

"That was Harry Arnold's house we called at. Are you familiar with the case, PC Turner?"

"Didn't the wife kill the son and you found her in Portugal?"

"Aye, that's the one. I went to tell them that Elsie, that's the mother, had been attacked in prison and that virtually all the people she'd used to get away had, one way or the other, met their maker over the last few days. I thought I'd let them know before I left the country."

"Weren't they pleased to hear the news, then, Guv?"

"Can't say as they were, and I don't blame them, after them telling me their piece of terrible news." Jack took a swig of his pint, quickly followed by a gulp of the whisky. Mike wanted to hear what the news was but waited patiently for Jack to continue.

"Elsie Arnold was – is – a ruthless woman. She left one New Year's Eve with her lover, Derek Collins, and left behind a dutiful husband and four children. Freddy, the eldest son, tracked her down and she stuck a knife in him for his trouble and framed Derek for the murder. Harry's sister, Bea, came to the family's rescue. It wasn't an easy decision for her to make, as years before she'd been thrown out of her family's home for taking up with a man her elder sister was in love with. Thing was, this man had neither feelings nor doings with the elder sister. So, Bea found herself out on her ear. Eventually, she was reunited with this man; Arthur was his name. They married and after many fruitless years Bea fell pregnant. It should have been the happiness moment of their lives, but Arthur was tragically struck down with a brain tumour and died within a few weeks. Bea was distraught and subsequently miscarried the baby. Life had dealt her another blow but, on hearing about her brother's dilemma, Bea decided to face the family and come home to help her baby brother." Jack paused for another slug on his pint. "Bea faced down her elder sister and mother and took charge of her nieces and nephew but then tragedy struck again. Arthur had a sister and niece in America. They'd visited them during their time together and Bea was godmother to their daughter, Megan. Just prior to Megan's thirteenth birthday, her mother shot dead her husband and then turned the gun on herself. The father had been sexually assaulting the young girl. Bea flew to America and brought Megan back here. She was welcomed by Harry and his children and has grown into a well-mannered, thoughtful, clever young lady. She recently started university, she wants to become a vet and I do believe she'll succeed." Jack took another gulp of his pint and this time he drained the whisky glass as well. Then he continued to tell his tale.

"The whole family were so relieved and pleased when Elsie was found and convicted of murdering Freddy. It was like a fresh start for them. Harry and his other son, Charlie, were expanding the family business. Anne, the eldest daughter, had recently had a little boy. Janie, the youngest daughter, was about to set off in a few weeks to travel the world with her boyfriend and Megan was settling in at uni. I thought that letting them know that all Elsie had got for Christmas was a three-inch scar down her face might just be a welcome parting gift from me! But how wrong was I?" Mike Turner watched as Jack lifted the empty whisky glass.

"Refill, Guv?" he offered, standing. Jack handed over the glass and watched as the young PC ordered him a refill at the bar. On his return, he noticed it was a double measure.

"Thought you looked like a single wouldn't do."

Jack nodded and took a mouthful of the amber liquid. It burnt as it slid down his throat. "They're a good honest family, are the Arnolds," he continued. "Have always made the best of everything that's been thrown at them, but Bea, well, Bea's in a class of her own. She's the strongest woman I've ever known. Life has certainly thrown her a curve ball or two, but she's never held a grudge. She's never wallowed in her own self-pity, just always put others first. And now life has thrown her the worst curve ball imaginable. She's got terminal cancer. Just a matter of a few months to live. Makes you wonder if there is a God, doesn't it? Thirty-odd years I've been a policeman. I've seen things and witnessed things that no God-fearing man should ever see. I've helped put away murderers, rapists, all kinds of lowlifes and do you know what they all have in common, Turner?" Mike shook his head. "They're all in good health. Banged up they might be but they're all drawing breath. Then you've got people like Bea who are about to face an agonising death who have done nothing but good. Doesn't make sense, does it?" Jack finished off the whisky in one go and pushed the glass away from him.

"You know what, PC Turner? If I hadn't already retired I'd have resigned on the spot after hearing Bea's news. I've lost all faith in God, in justice, in everything I believed in as a police officer." Jack rose from the table. "And they say crime doesn't pay! Sure as hell feels like it does to me right now. Let's get me to the airport and on this plane. The further away I am from this way of life the better."

PC Mike Turner followed the retreating retired DCI Jack Wilde with one thought in his head! "IS THIS JOB REALLY WORTH IT?"

CHARLIE & GEORGE

"Wished they'd slit her throat," remarked Charlie to his grandad. The mood that day inside the house was at an all-time low, so when George had suggested that they slip out for a breath of air Charlie had readily agreed, knowing his grandad had meant for a sneaky pint or two.

"Aye, lad, I'm with you on that score, but it was good of that copper to call in and let us know."

"I bet he wished he hadn't now," replied Charlie.

"Aye, lad, I'm with you on that one as well. Seemed to take it hard, he did, about our Bea."

"He did, Grandad. I could tell. He's been coming and going since Freddy died. Dad said he was a rare thing. A good cop, he called him. I didn't quite understand at the time. Thought he meant that all cops were bad, but he didn't, did he, Grandad?" George eyed up his young grandson. He was looking more and more like his dad every day, except for the blonde hair of course, which he'd inherited from his mother. He had the same jawline. The same intensity to his eyes. The tall, muscular build and, most importantly, the same thoughtfulness towards others. It never ceased to amaze George how his only son and youngest daughter had such a capacity to love, to forgive, to move on, despite all the horrors they'd undergone. He liked to think he was a good man. An honest man. But he wasn't so quick to forgive and forget. He hadn't spoken to his ex-wife or his eldest daughter, Mary, since he'd walked out on them the day Bea re-entered their lives. Now there was a pair who could hold a grudge and spit venom at the drop of a hat. Never had he known such hatred ooze from two people. And why? George asked himself. Ethel had never had it so good on meeting him. Her family had nothing. Lazy sods and all, if his memory served him right. She'd landed on her feet when she'd hooked him, everyone would say. Yet, Ethel was never satisfied. Always wanted more and never had a good word to say to anyone, least of all him. And Mary was no different. Born angry at the world, his old mum used to say. Boy, that was true. Then along came sweet-natured Bea and her brother, Harry. Where Mary would stomp about, grizzle, cry or do all three, Bea and Harry would smile, laugh and skip around the house. Anne, Harry's eldest daughter, could be a mardy so-and-so at times, but Charlie and Janie were eternal optimists. Freddy had been that way too. The glass was always half full with them. And now, after what seemed such a short space of time, he was going to lose his beautiful Bea all over again and for good this time.

"Did he, Grandad?" Charlie's voice brought him out of his reverie.

"Sorry, son, what did you say again?"

"I said he didn't mean that all coppers are bad?"

"No lad, no. There's a few bad'uns but there's also some that go that extra mile, like that Jack Wilde." Charlie guessed that his grandad had tuned out, thinking about Bea and who could blame him.

"Another, Grandad?" asked Charlie, raising his empty glass. George looked at his half-empty glass of beer and inwardly laughed at the irony of it.

"You go ahead, son. I'm still ploughing through this one."

Charlie turned his back on his grandad and stifled back the tears that were bubbling close to the surface. He knew the news of his Aunt Bea's terminal cancer had hit his grandad really hard. Charlie knew he still blamed himself for all those years that Bea had been kept away from the family. When Bea had come back to look after them he'd begun to see a different side to his grandad. Before that, his grandad had just spent his days either down on his allotment or getting under his dad's feet at the garage. On visits to his grandparents' house, Charlie had only seen his grandad ensconced in his old armchair, his gran constantly berating him. Since he'd walked out on his granny, Charlie had seen his grandad come to life. He'd joined a local bowls club, volunteered at the local animal shelter, played dominoes for the pub they were now enjoying a pint in and had a small army of old ladies vying for his affections. Charlie could now identify with the man that his father spoke of from his childhood. Charlie just hoped that this latest bombshell regarding Bea wasn't going to send his grandad back into himself again. Charlie paid for his pint and turned back to face his grandad.

"Our Janie will make sure Aunty Bea is well cared for, Grandad."

"Aye, that she will, lad, that she will. I just wish Bea had longer. We had longer with her. We've been playing chess on a Wednesday morning these past few years. I taught her how to play when she was seven years old. I used to play with my old dad and when he died Bea asked straight away if I'd teach her how to play. She told me that she'd taught Arthur how to play. Said she found it gave her a connection to me, to the past, to the good times. I'm not ashamed to say, I cried when she told me. Now, now I'm losing her and those lovely mornings of playing chess all over again. It's hard, lad, very hard." Charlie placed an arm around his grandad's shoulders.

"I used to play chess at school, Grandad. No one else in our house was interesting in playing so I stopped going as I just wasn't getting enough practice. Maybe I could give you a game?" George smiled at his grandson. He was still amazed by how much he didn't know about his grandchildren.

"I'd like that, lad, very much, but I doubt your dad will give you the morning off to play chess with me."

"Probably not, Grandad, but I could come round yours one evening a week and have a game – if you've got one spare, that is," joked Charlie. George smiled at his grandson. In one small gesture, he'd lightened his heart.

There was nothing he'd like more than to start spending some quality time with this delightful young man.

"I'll have to check my diary," he jested, "but I think I can squeeze you in on a Tuesday evening if you're free?"

"I'm free," Charlie replied, mimicking John Inman's character from TV series, *Are You Being Served?*

JANIE

Janie had been deliberately avoiding Josef since she'd overheard the conversation between her Aunt Bea and her dad. She'd put him off with saying she wanted to spend quality time with her family before heading off in the New Year for the start of what would be an eighteen-month tour around the globe. Now he was knocking on the front door. Janie steeled herself for what was to come and opened the door to him.

"Christ, Janie, thought I was going to freeze to death on the doorstep waiting for someone to answer it," he remarked as he stepped into the hallway.

"I was upstairs and no one else is home," replied Janie.

"That's gotta be a first, hasn't it? I mean, everyone out?" Janie closed the front door and headed along the hallway to the kitchen.

"Dad's taken Bea to see some old film at the Clifton.

Charlie's having a pint with grandad and Megan has gone out somewhere with Dave. Tea?" she asked as she began to fill the kettle.

"Please. Any of Bea's delicious fruit cake going?" he asked.

"There might be some left-over Christmas cake in that red tin over on the dresser." Josef busied himself with cutting off a large slice of the cake, while Janie poured them both a mug of tea."

"What do you fancy doing tonight?" asked Josef between mouthfuls of cake.

"Nothing, Josef. I've got something very important to tell you."

"Christ, you're not pregnant, are you?"

"No," replied Janie, "nothing as simple as that."

"What do you mean by that?" Josef asked.

"Something could be done about that, but nothing can be done about this." Josef finished off his mouthful of cake and swilled it down with a swig of his tea.

"What's with all the cryptic clues, Miss Marple?" he joked. Janie took a deep breath.

"Bea's cancer isn't getting better. She lied, Josef. She's only got a few months at the most to live." Janie watched Josef's face as he digested what she had said. It was almost as if she could see the wheels turning in his mind, figuring out what she'd just said. Finally, he spoke.

"I'll speak to the band in the morning. I'll tell them that we might have to pop home at a moment's notice due to your aunt dying. I'm sure they'll be cool with it, so don't worry, Janie, it'll be fine."

"FINE?" screamed Janie. "FINE? You think it'll be fine?" She was yelling now but couldn't help it.

"For Christ's sake, Janie, get a grip. I know you're upset about your Aunt Bea but there's no need to get hysterical." Josef got up off his chair as he spoke and made to wrap Janie in his arms, but she was on her feet, batting his arms away.

"Do you really think I'm going to swan off with you, traipsing around after some second-rate band that have duped you into photographing their journey – for free, I might add – while my Aunt Bea is alone in her cottage dying an agonising death from cancer." She knew she was getting hysterical now but his off-hand response to her devastating news had sent her fractured emotions over the edge.

"For FUCK'S SAKE, Janie, Bea isn't going to die alone. Your family won't allow it for a start and we made a commitment to the band. We said we'd take the photographs and chronicle the tour. We made a commitment, Janie. A COMMITMENT, REMEMBER. You can't just walk away from a commitment."

"You made the commitment, Josef, YOU, NOT ME! You turned our backpacking adventure around Europe into an unpaid job for some fucking band that no one's ever heard of. You did that, Josef, and I was expected to go along with your plans. It was supposed to be our adventure, not someone else's, but you didn't care about that, did you? You thought your desire to be some hotshot photographer to the rich and famous was far more important, didn't you?" Janie shouted at him.

"I was thinking of our future, Janie, thinking about making a name for myself so we could have a good life. Forgive me for trying to make something of my life. I want the finer things in life, Janie. The fast cars, designer clothes. I want to eat in the best restaurants and stay in the best hotels. I want that for us, Janie, for you and me."

"I don't want any of those things, Josef, and if you really took the time and thought about me from time to time you'd know that. All I want is to be happy. To be with people who I love and love me. I don't need fancy clothes and plush hotels. And, right now, I need to stay here and look after Bea. I need to make sure that she's got everything she needs. To hold her hand when the time comes and let her know how much I love her and how much I'm going to miss her. I need to do that, Josef. I need to do it just as much for me as I do for Bea. If you truly loved me you'd understand that." Janie collapsed back down onto the kitchen chair and rested her arms and head on the table. She prayed that Josef would see the sense in what she was saying. See the need for her to stay and take care of Bea. Janie's prayers went unanswered as Josef exploded in a fit of rage.

"If you really loved me, Janie, you wouldn't be leaving me and the band in the lurch. I'd pegged you for a lot of things, Janie, but being selfish wasn't one of them. I'm trying to do the right thing by you so now I need you to do the right thing by me. Spend the remainder of your time here with Bea but come the twenty-fifth of January you need to be packed and ready to leave. Do you hear me,

Janie? You need to be ready to leave and carry out your commitment to me and the band."

Janie lifted her head off the table and stared deep into Josef's eyes. Oh! How she used to love to stare into the depths and warmth of those deep, dark brown eyes. To see the love, or what she'd believed to be love, in them. Now they just look cold and hard. Had he ever loved her? She was no longer sure! She'd thought that he was her knight in shining armour, yet now he looked more like the evil baddie in a movie. How had she ever fallen in love with him? Because she had. She still was in love with him, despite all of this, but she didn't like him anymore. She didn't like that he thought 'the band' and his plans were more important than her dying aunt. Janie surprised herself with how calm her voice sounded as she spoke.

"I won't be packed and ready, as you say, to leave on the twenty-fifth to chase around after you and some godawful band. I'll be down living at the cottage in Talybont with Aunt Bea and seeing to her needs. My only commitment is to her, Josef. To her and my family to make sure her last days are happy ones. If you choose to go ahead with the commitment you made to the band, then that's your choice. I made no commitment to them. You made a commitment for me without even consulting me. I'm doing you the courtesy of telling you what I'm committed to doing. Something you never gave me. Now, please do me the courtesy of leaving." Without another word, Josef stormed out of the kitchen and made for the front door. He stood there with his hand around the door handle, waiting for Janie to stop him. When she didn't he finally broke the silence.

"If I leave now, Janie, I won't ever be coming back, do you hear me? I'll be gone for good. Is that what you want? What you really want?" Janie placed her head down on the table and waited for the inevitable to happen. And then it did! In one single action the door was wrenched open and Josef was outside, with the door slamming shut on him. He was gone, and Janie's tears fell like raindrops onto the kitchen table. Inside, her heart was breaking. Her Josef had gone. She'd hoped he'd understand. She'd hoped he'd be supportive. She'd hoped he'd loved her enough to stay. Janie was beginning to get the feeling that all those she loved would leave sooner or later. First it was her mum, then Freddy, now Josef and soon, too soon, it would be Bea's turn to leave.

Josef stomped his way through the snow out of the driveway, heading towards his parents' home.

"Damn you, Janie," he shouted out into the cold winter's night. Damn you for letting me down. Damn you for being so weak. Because that's exactly was she was. Weak where her family was concerned. She should be putting him first, after all in the future he'd be her family. Well, not anymore. He didn't need a selfish wife holding him back, keeping him from reaching his full potential, from achieving his dreams. He knew a dozen girls who'd kill to be with him and join him on this once-in-a-lifetime tour. Who needed Janie Arnold anyway? He sure as HELL didn't. Josef changed the direction his was heading in. Amber Murray would probably be working behind the bar of The Barley now. He'd go there and ask her if she fancied a jaunt around the world with him.

MEGAN

10th January 1983

Megan shut the boot of her little yellow Mini and made her way back into the house. She would be heading back to university in Aberystwyth within the hour but a cup of tea with her Aunt Bea was calling. As she entered the kitchen, Bea was pouring boiling water from the kettle into a china teapot. On the kitchen table were two cups and saucers, a milk jug, a sugar bowl and a plate of assorted biscuits. Megan sat down at the table with a heavy heart.

"It should be me going to the cottage to look after you." Bea turned with the teapot held firmly in her hands. She spoke as she crossed the kitchen and placed the teapot in the middle of the table.

"We've gone over this a thousand times, Megan. You've got university, Harry and Charlie have the garage. Janie will take good care of me and you're only an hour or so's drive away. I'll, we'll, look forward to your fortnightly visits."

"But what if you—" began Megan.

"I'm a stubborn old thing, Megan, you know that. I'll not let him upstairs take me until I've seen each and every one of your ugly mugs."

"But—"

"No buts about it, Megan. I promise, I won't go anywhere, sweetheart, without saying goodbye. I promise." Bea reached across the table and tenderly rubbed Megan's hand, before taking a seat opposite her and then pouring the tea

"You were my saviour, Aunt Bea. When all those terrible things were happening to me. You were the one thing that kept me going." It was Megan's turn to gently caress her aunt's hand. "The only time I ever felt love, felt special, felt safe, was when you'd come and visit. You'd take me on shopping trips for beautiful dresses and you'd brush my hair until it shone. Then you'd let me snuggle down beside you in your bed for the night and you'd read me those wonderful stories of beautiful princesses and happy ever afters. I'd cry for days, weeks, after you'd returned here, to England. The charade of our happy home would be over. Mum would be hitting the bottle by the time you'd closed the cab door. Within a few days, she'd be back in her alcohol-fuelled haze and dad would be entering my bedroom again."

"Ssshhh, child, that's all in the past. There's no need to torture yourself with it now. It wasn't your fault what happened."

"I know that, Aunt Bea. I just need to get it out. To tell you about that night. Please let me, Aunt Bea, before it's too late…" Megan held Bea's hand tight and looked into her aunt's eyes. She nodded her assent and Megan continued her account.

"Mum was totally spaced out when I got home from school that day. The house was a mess. The breakfast dishes were still on the table and she'd been sick all over the family room couch. I knew dad was going to hit the roof when he got in, so I started to clean it up, in the hope I'd get it done before he got home. I'd managed to clean off the couch and was just drying up the breakfast dishes when he walked through the door. He told me to go to my room. I knew it was best to do as he said so I put the tea towel down and went straight to my room. The shouting started before I even made it to the top of the stairs. Dad was hollering, calling mum a drunken whore but this time, for the first time, mum was hollering back. I was about to head back downstairs when mum appeared in the hallway. I quickly ran into my bedroom. I slammed the door shut then curled up into a ball in the far corner. Mum was coming up the stairs and dad was hot on her heels. She'd made it into their bedroom before he caught her then the beating began. At first, I could tell she was fighting back but then she went quiet and all I could hear was dad kicking her. Then he stopped. I could hear him calling out her name. He called out to her several times then he went back downstairs. I got up off the floor and crept across my room and slid open my door. I tiptoed across the landing to their bedroom. The door was wide open. I'd never seen so much blood before. It was all over the room. And on the floor lay mum's lifeless body covered in blood. I thought she was dead. I really did. I stood frozen to the spot. Dad dragging me by my hair back into my bedroom and, throwing me on the bed, brought me out of the trance I was in and straight into a living nightmare. His eyes were full of pure evil. He looked at me lying prone on my bed and let out this horrendous chortle. I thought this is it! I'm going to die! He's got nothing to lose! Mum's dead and he's going to rape me and kill me too! I prayed for it to be quick. For it to be over with. He didn't just rape me that evening. He made me do terrible things to him. He beat me. He bit me. But I wouldn't cry out. I thought only of you, Aunt Bea. Of all the kindness you'd shown me, and I prayed for Uncle Arthur to come get me. Dad had punched me several times in the face to get me to perform sexual acts on him. Both of my eyes were swollen, but out of the corner of my left eye as he was raping me for what seemed the umpteenth time, I saw a shadow enter the room. I thought my prayers had been answered. Uncle Arthur had finally come for me. Then there was this ear-shattering bang. My ears were ringing, and I felt this liquid drip down onto my bare chest. Dad slumped over to the side and then there was mum's beaten-up face smiling down on me. "It's over sweet Megan," she said, then raised the gun and shot her own brains out. Right there in front of me. The last thing I remember before waking up in hospital was calling out your name." Megan hadn't taken her eyes off her aunt as she spoke.

She watched as the real horror of that fateful night began to sink in and bring tears to her aunt's eyes. Megan wiped one of those tears away with her index finger.

"Oh, Megan!" Bea began. "I knew it was bad, but I never imaged it was so, so…"

"Violent? Horrendous?" Megan offered.

"All of those things and much, much more," replied Bea.

"When the welfare lady told me you were coming to get me, I cried. She thought I didn't want to go with you. I told her that the minute you walked through the door and held me in your arms, this nightmare would be over. And I was right, Aunt Bea. You, uncle Harry, grandad George, Charlie and Janie gave me my happy ever after but now you're…" Bea placed a finger to Megan's lips to prevent her from saying more.

"You'll have lots of happy times in the future, Megan, but everyone's life is tinged by sadness at times. It's the nature of things. You, Arthur, Harry, Charlie, Janie, dad and so many, many more special, wonderful people have given me happy times. My happy ever after is coming to an end but not yours, sweetheart. Yours is only just beginning. You said you called out for Arthur to come get you? Didn't you?" Megan nodded in agreement. "You believed he would come get you? That he was out there, somewhere, perhaps watching over you, didn't you?" Again, Megan nodded in agreement. "When my time comes, I'll be with my Arthur again and together we'll watch over you, Megan. I'll always be with you, sweetheart. Not in the flesh but in spirit. In your heart, in your mind and in your memories.

Just like my Arthur is with me right now. You've got your whole life ahead of you, Megan. I've had mine. It's had its dark times, its tough times, but it's also had so many good times, happy times. I've experienced heartache, pain, joy, laughter, tears but most of all I've experienced love. And each emotion, each experience has made me, me. Has brought me to where I am now. I'm not afraid of dying, Megan. I've had a good life. A full life. And you can make this easier for me by carrying on. By making the most of your life. You've got the help and support of a good family now and I reckon Dave plans on being a big part of your life too." Megan smiled.

"He does, Aunt Bea, he does. Apart from you, he's the only other person I've chosen to tell about that day. And you know what, Aunt Bea? He cried like a baby, then held me so tight, I thought he was going to suffocate me. I even told him that the chances of me carrying a child full-term were a million to one. He just said, 'we'll cross that bridge when we get to it.'

"I knew I liked him. I thought Josef was cut from the same cloth as Dave, but I got that wrong."

"We all did, Aunt Bea. Dave doesn't want anything more to do with him. Says he thought better of him. Josef just told him to mind his own business and then informed him he's already found a replacement for Janie on the tour."

"Charlie said the same. Only he used more colourful language when describing this Amber Murray.'"

"He has a way with words does our Charlie," giggled Megan.

"He's either all prim and proper or swearing like an old fishwife, he is," giggled Bea. Bea took a sip of her tea and immediately spat it back into the cup.

"Tea's gone cold," explained Bea.

"Or, as Charlie would say, 'fuck me, this tea is bloody cold.'" With that they both fell about laughing and all thoughts of death and horrendous deeds slipped from their minds.

JANIE

1st February 1983

Life at the cottage with Bea had settled into a routine quickly. Weekends were taken up with either Janie's dad and grandad or Charlie or Megan visiting. On Mondays, the village busybody, Mair Morgan, would pop in at 10am prompt and relay all the local gossip and goings on to Bea. Wednesdays were when Bronwyn Evans would call in with books and magazines for both Bea and Janie. Friday mornings, Bea's next-door neighbour Mavis Banford would come sit with Bea while Janie went and got the week's shopping from either Barmouth or Porthmadog. That left Tuesday and Thursday afternoons, which were filled up by Gwen Hughes, the district nurse and long-time friend of Bea. Gwen had taken to keeping those afternoons between two and four free to bathe and see to any medical needs of her dearest friend. Gwen was already running the bath for Bea as she ushered Janie out of the cottage, encouraging her, as always, to make the most of this time for herself.

It was a dry afternoon and wrapped up against the chill of the sea breeze Janie had headed down through the cottage's garden and out through the little wooden gate and onto the beach. The tide was almost completely out and there wasn't another soul to be seen in either direction. Janie turned left and headed down the beach towards all the caravan parks. They were all shut up for the winter. She loved walking through them when they were so quiet and peaceful. Occasionally, she'd see a gardener or a maintenance man working on a caravan or the gardens but that was about it. She'd follow the lane, leading out of the parks, up and over the railway bridge and then out onto the main road that would eventually lead her back to her aunt's cottage. It was a good couple of miles' round trip, but Janie loved the solitude. It gave her time to think. To clear her mind.

As Janie walked along the sandy beach her thoughts turned to what Charlie had said during the weekend. He'd been so angry at himself for letting it slip that Josef had indeed flown off with Amber Murray in tow to photograph that, 'fucking shite band', as he'd called them. It had hurt her to hear it but nowhere near as much as his callous disregard for Bea's fate had. That anger had still not subsided. How could she have been so blind to what he was really like? How could she have not seen that selfish side to him? After all, there had been clues along the way. They'd always seemed to do what he'd suggested. He'd break dates with her at the drop of a hat if one of his friends invited him out. He'd not stopped to ask how she felt about totally changing all their plans for their great adventure around Europe. When they'd discussed doing the whole wide world she'd beamed with delight. They'd be about to leave Australia now if they'd gone in the October like they'd planned to do. They would have spent Christmas Day having a barbecue on the beach but instead she'd spent Christmas Day hiding the pain of what she'd learnt about Bea's cancer from the rest of her family. The beginning of tears stared to tickle her nose and form in the corner of her eyes, but she refused to shed another tear over Josef. Janie took a deep breath of the crisp cold sea air, filling her lungs and stemming the flow of any tears. She took a tissue from her coat pocket, dabbed at her eyes and blew her nose, then looked out at the deep blue sea and yelled at the top of her lungs, "FUCK YOU, JOSEF WOJTASKI. I don't need a selfish little git like you. And fuck you too, Amber-fucking-Murray." Then she burst out laughing as she thought Amber probably was being fucked right now by Josef. With a new resolve to forget all about Josef, the band, the tour and Amber-fucking-Murray, Janie ran towards the surf's edge, waving her hands in the air like a mad woman. But she didn't care. She was Jane Elizabeth Arnold and she wasn't going to waste precious energy on a shite like Josef when she had her beautiful, beloved Bea to take care of.

Gwen was just filling up a tea tray with ham sandwiches and home-made scones when Janie entered through the back door of the cottage straight into the kitchen.

"Hang your coat up, sweetheart, then join us by the fire for a bite to eat," announced Gwen as she took the tea tray through into the small living room. "Be a love and bring the teapot with you; it's already filled." Janie hung her coat on the back of the kitchen door, washed her hands in the kitchen sink then carried the teapot through, complete with its woolly jacket. Bea was sitting in the large armchair next to the fire. Her hair was newly washed and shone in the glow of the fire. She'd applied a touch of lipstick to her lips and she smelt of baby talcum powder. All clean and fresh.

"Enjoy your walk?" she asked.

"I did, thank you," she replied while trying to find a place on the crowded coffee table for the teapot. Gwen helped by moving the side plates out of the way.

"Anyone about?" enquired Gwen. Janie placed the teapot on the table then sat down beside Gwen on the small two-seater couch.

"Not a soul on the beach. I met Mr Lloyd walking his dog on the railway bridge and Mrs Banford waved from her kitchen window as I walked by but that was it."

"I used to love walking on the beach at this time of year," began Bea. "Collecting shells for decorating the borders alongside the footpath. I'd pick up pieces of driftwood and stones too, if I could see faces in them."

"Oh, that reminds me," said Janie, getting to her feet. "I found a stone for you, Aunt Bea; it's in my coat pocket. I'll go get it." In no time at all Janie was handing the stone over to her aunt. Bea could instantly make out the face. It was an angry little face. Cuts in the stone appeared as angry eyebrows. A small blemish on the surface below as a nose then a deeper, longer cut beneath that portrayed a down-in-the mouth look. It did indeed look like an angry little face. Even sceptic Gwen could see the resemblance to that of an angry person.

"I'd been cursing Josef when I looked down onto the sand and there looking straight up at me was this stone. It made me laugh out loud."

"We'll name him Joyless Joe then," remarked Bea. "We'll keep him on the mantelpiece to remind us how we look when we scowl or get angry and hopefully it'll make us all laugh out loud." Bea handed the stone back to Janie for her to place it on the mantle. Janie propped it up against the wall for stability then sat back down to admire it.

"Well, Joyless Joe," began Gwen, "you're going to be even more miserable now watching us a lot tuck into this lovely tea." They all started to laugh as Gwen began handing out the sandwiches.

Joyless Joe had looked on as they stuffed their faces with ham sandwiches followed by scones topped with butter, jam and thick fresh cream. Bea had managed to eat a fair bit and that had brought joy to both Gwen and Janie. All too soon it had been time for Gwen to go. And, while Bea snoozed in the armchair by the fire, Janie had cleared away the tea things. It's the first of February, thought Janie as she wiped down the work surfaces in the kitchen. Spring is around the corner. A new year has barely begun, bringing with it yet another year of sadness and heartache to endure. She'd be twenty at the end of the year. No longer a teenager, yet still a child in so many ways. Only nineteen, with so much heartache already under her belt and a belly full of sadness waiting on the horizon. She had no idea what the future held in store for her. All her plans had turned to dust. Where she went from here, she had no idea. But she wasn't going to turn into a Joyless Joe. She was going to face life and whatever it threw at her with a smile on her face and love in her heart. If not for herself, for Freddy and Bea.

BEA

28th February 1983

Bea opened her eyes as Janie placed a tea tray on the table beside her bed.

"You said tea at three," remarked Janie. Bea smiled at her niece then hauled herself up into a sitting position in the bed. Janie was immediately at her side, plumping up the pillows behind her.

"Did you bring two cups?" she enquired.

"Yes," replied Janie as she placed an extra pillow behind her aunt's head. "Did you sleep well?" she continued.

"Very, thank you. Now would you be a dear and pour that tea, my mouth is all dry and furry." Janie stirred the tea in the pot then filled both the teacups, adding milk and two sugars to Bea's cup. She handed over the cup and saucer to her aunt then crossed over to the window.

"I've never understood why you chose to have the bedroom at the front of the cottage overlooking the driveway and the road, when the back bedrooms have those beautiful sea views," exclaimed Janie, as she stared out at the fading daylight casting shadows over the mountains in the distance.

"Arthur and I decided straight away that we'd let our guests wake up to those views of the coastline. We get to see them every day; our guests don't. Besides, Arthur also said we had better things to do in our bedroom than admire the view." Bea smiled at what the memory had evoked. The cheeky grin on Arthur's face as he'd spoken the words then how he'd grabbed hold of her and kissed her. Oh, how she missed those kisses, those embraces, their love-making.

"Are you all right, Aunt Bea?" she heard Janie say. Bea shook the memories from her head and focused on Janie.

"Just remembering something, sweetheart," she offered by way of explanation.

"From the grin on your face I can imagine what!" Janie replied with mock horror in her voice. Bea sipped at her tea at first then, finding it had cooled down enough, she drained the cup then offered it to Janie, requesting a refill.

Janie was a good girl. She'd taken the offered cup and saucer and had refilled it straight away. She never moaned about all the chores, the running around, the taking care of her personal needs. No. Janie just seemed to take it all in her stride. With Harry and Charlie busy with the garage, Megan engrossed in either her studies or Dave and Josef sloping off aboard with that BLOODY BAND,

Bea worried about Janie. How she'd cope after her death. Janie had forsaken her future to come here and care for her; she needed to give her something back. Something for her future. Today, she would set the wheels in motion. She beckoned for Janie to come sit beside her on the bed. Once she was comfortably settled, Bea reached across and held her niece's hand in hers.

"There's a big old key on a red ribbon in the bottom left hand drawer of my wardrobe. It's right at the back, hidden under a pile of scarves. It's the key to the wooden chest at the bottom of my bed. Inside, all wrapped in bundles with date labels, are mine and Arthur's private love letters. Our first contact was a note. Arthur slipped it into my coat pocket, asking me if I'd meet him on the Saturday night outside the church gates at 6pm. I wrote on a scrap of paper that I would and as I handed over the key to the supply shed I pressed it into his hand. After that we wrote each other notes often. It was a way to communicate in working hours without raising suspicion. We both knew how possessive and jealous Mary was over him, right from the start. In fact, that's how she discovered our relationship. She'd been rummaging through my bedroom and found the notes. Mother never scolded Mary for going through my private things, just hurled abuse at me and hit me several times with an umbrella as I walked through the back door."

"That's dreadful, Aunt Bea. Mary is going through your stuff and lying about her having a relationship with Arthur and yet you are the one punished."

"Mary was mother's blue-eyed girl. She could do no

wrong. Mary could lie, cheat, steal and bully but mother would chastise anyone but Mary. It was just how it was. Mother lost all her friends over Mary. As for Mary herself, she had no friends. She was just a nasty, scheming bully. Everyone gave her a wide berth."

"But grandad! Why didn't he stick up for you?"

"Oh, he did when he was home, but then he was away for the biggest part of the war. By the time dad returned, I'd been cast out of the family home, sent away. I wanted to write and let dad know I was okay. To tell him I was safe and at last I'd got my Arthur. But those two would have found the letters and I couldn't risk my happiness, my Arthur's happiness again. Harry was afraid for all those years that they'd find out he was in contact with me and our lives would be turned upside down again. So, he never spoke to Dad either about it."

"Grandad has changed so much since he left gran."

"Not changed, Janie. He's just the man he used to be before the war. The man who I grew up with. Happy, kind and thoughtful. I just hope this Rose Whittaker doesn't turn out to be a wrong'un."

"He seems quite taken with her, doesn't he? Dad says she's quite shy and follows grandad around like a lost sheep. Charlie says she's a hell of a good cook and you know how fussy he is with his food!" They both laughed at how Charlie would push his food around his plate, inspecting every last thing on it before daring to put it in his mouth.

"Well, let's keep our fingers crossed for grandad, eh? Now, back to these letters."

"Okay," replied Janie, then she snuggled up closer to Bea.

"Arthur and I wrote to each other from the moment we meet. Even whilse we were apart, we wrote to each other. Obviously, they were never sent to one another but when we found each other we both presented one another a bundle of unread letters. We wrote and sent letters to each other throughout our marriage as well. Then, after Arthur died, I continued to write letters addressed to him. It helped me cope with my grief, my loss. It was like, by writing down my thoughts, my fears, my days to him, he was still here with me. A way to communicate with him, somehow. I still write to him to this day. I've told him all about you, Megan, Harry, Charlie. About your mum, about poor Freddy's untimely death. I asked him to take Freddy under his wing for me. It was Arthur I told first, in one of my letters, about the cancer. Now I've told him that I'll be joining him soon. That I'm not afraid because I know he'll be there waiting on the other side for me." Bea looked across at Janie and saw the tears streaming down her face. She took her lace hankie from under her pillow and gently wiped away the tears from her niece's face. "Don't cry, Janie, please. I've had a good life. Coming to stay and take of you all filled the enormous void in my life left by Arthur dying. But soon I'll be back in his arms for all eternity. That's why you mustn't feel sad. I'm going home Janie. Home to my Arthur. Tell me you understand." Janie snuffled back her tears.

"I do, Aunt Bea, but I'm sad because I won't have you anymore. I'm sad for all the time you and Arthur were apart. For him being taken away from you so suddenly. For the loss of your child and all those years you should have had as happy, loving parents." Bea could feel the tingle of her own tears beginning, so she took a deep breath.

"I want you to sit and read those letters once I'm gone, Janie. When it's all over and you're alone, I want you to sit down and read those letters. I think your future lies in those old love letters. I think you have the ability to turn them into a wonderful story of two people's love for one another."

"But, Aunt Bea, aren't they private?"

"Not once I'm gone, Janie. I want you to tell the world of how love can conquer all. How it can make you strong. Make you feel like you're walking on air. That it can get you through all manner of tough times and things. You've always had a way with words. A natural talent for storytelling. Tell our story, Janie. Maybe it'll help you to forgive Josef too."

"Oh, Aunt Bea, how could the love you and Arthur shared help me to forgive a selfish pig like Josef? He's a—"

"A product of his upbringing, Janie." Bea stepped in. "When you used to go to Josef's house, what was his mum doing?" Janie gave her aunt a puzzled look. "Just answer the question, Janie." Janie shrugged her shoulders before answering.

"She was always doing one chore or another. Either cooking, cleaning or sewing. Always something about the house."

"And his dad?"

"He was either at work, watching TV or having a pint down the pub. Why?"

"Did his parents ever go out together, regularly?"

"Not that I can remember, no. WHY?"

"And what about his sister and his elder brother?"

"Sofia was always in trouble for something or other. Usually for wearing make-up and mixing with the wrong girls. Michal was always fighting and falling out with his wife and running back home to mummy, as Josef would say. But I still don't understand what any of this has got to do with forgiving Josef!"

"Am I correct in thinking that his dad is Polish and his mum Maltese?"

"Yes. They were both evacuated over here during the war. What has this got to do with—"

"Everything, Janie, everything. Josef's parents come from different backgrounds to ours. In their countries, women are second-rate citizens. Women are not equal. Josef's dad goes out and earns the money. His mum stays at home and looks after the family. His dad comes and goes as he pleases. His mum stays at home. That is her place. Sofia has grown up here and wants to be like the other girls. English girls. Wearing the latest fashions, make-up, being independent, but that isn't how her parents believe she should be. Hence why she is always in trouble. Michal has an English wife. She was brought up as his equal. I know his wife, Susan's mother, Carol. She told me how much they fight and fall out because he doesn't like the fact that Susan has a good job and earns good money. He wants her to give it up. To stay at home, to have his children and look after them all. Carol said that Susan wants kids, but she also wants to return to work afterwards. Michal refuses to allow this to happen. He says a woman's place is in the home."

"But what does this have to do with Josef? He's always been happy for me to work."

"What were you working so hard for, Janie?"

"So, we could travel round the world. You know that."

"Josef didn't mind you working while he benefited from it but—"

"Now, wait a minute, Aunt Bea. Josef was happy for me to pursue a career of my choice." Bea cut in again.

"Really, Janie? Weren't you going to write a travel book on those travels and Josef take the photographs?"

"Yes, but then the band asked him to be their official photographer so he—"

"Changed your plans. But how come you were only going to be the chief cook and bottle washer, Janie? How come you weren't going be their official writer? Why weren't you going to write the story to go with the photographs Josef was taking?"

"Because they'd already got someone doing that…" Bea watched as finally Janie was putting it all together piece by piece.

"He didn't want me to write, did he?"

"I don't think he did, sweetheart. Josef wants a woman just like his mum, deep down, as does his brother. He loved you for being you, don't get me wrong, but at the same time he wants you to be what he wants. You're supposed to go along with whatever he decides. He's the man. He makes the decisions about your future together, not you. It's what he's been brought up to believe, Janie. You unknowingly decided to defy his plans. That was wrong in his eyes. You didn't know you were defying him. You were just doing what you'd been brought up to do. To care about your family and help them out in times of need. You weren't aware that you needed to ask Josef's permission. You didn't know that he thought he owned you. You just did what was second nature to you. You decided to help me. You thought Josef would understand. Different upbringings, Janie, different cultures. Neither of you took these things into consideration. You saw Josef as you see your dad, as you see Charlie. Josef saw you as he sees his mum, how he believes Sofia and Susan should be. They're not joking when they say love is blind, you know. When you fall in love with someone you see only what you choose to see and nothing else matters. But, at some point, you have to open your eyes and see the whole story. You're going to start doing that right now, Janie, as we speak.

I should have seen what was going on way back when Josef changed your plans, but I was too consumed with my diagnosis to see beyond my own fears. Josef doesn't have an Aunt Bea to point these things out. He only has his dad and mum pointing out you were in the wrong. If you love Josef the way I believe you do, you'll find it in your heart to forgive him. To find a way of making it work. Just don't give up on him, on you both so easily." Bea lay back further into her pillows. All the talking, all the conjuring up of old memories had drained her. She was so tired now. Her eyes just wouldn't keep open.

"Aunt Bea," whispered Janie. "Do you really think that's why Josef acted so out of character? I remember how upset he'd been when you'd come clean about the c…" Bea couldn't find the strength to open her eyes as she spoke.

"Josef came to me, not long after you'd been told. He said he'd asked his mum, a devout Catholic, why God had been so cruel to me. She'd told him that God must have a greater plan for me. He'd replied that God hadn't ever been kind to me and if that was how God treated good, innocent, caring people, then she could take her God and stick him where the sun doesn't shine. I told Josef that I believed that God had dealt me all these things because he believed I was strong enough to deal with them. That I held no malice towards God. He'd taken my hand in his then and gently kissed it. He said he wished he had an ounce of the courage and grace I had. That's why I know Josef is deep down a good soul. He's just a misguided one, that's all."

"I didn't know about that; he never said. Did he ever come to you about anything else?" asked Janie. Bea gently shock her head. She was so tired now. Janie went to speak but Bea squeezed her hand.

"No, he didn't. I'd like to have a nap now if you don't mind." Bea felt Janie stir on the bed beside her then a gentle kiss was placed on her forehead before Janie alighted from the bed. And, as she fell asleep, her thoughts were once again filled with her darling Arthur.

GWEN, MAVIS & JANIE

Wednesday, 30th March 1983

Kneeling beside the sleeping Janie, Gwen brushed a stray curl of hair that had fallen across her eyes. Janie stirred. It didn't take a fully qualified nurse like herself to diagnosis that this poor child was both physically and mentally exhausted. Gwen hauled herself back up onto her feet and turned to enter the kitchen.

"Are you off now?" asked a sleepy Janie. Gwen turned to face Janie. She was rubbing the sleep from her eyes and uncurling her legs, stretching them out before her.

"Only for a short while, sweetie."

"I don't understand," began Janie as a yawn gripped her and forced her to stop talking and stretch out her upper body.

"I'm only popping home to fetch a few personal items

and to collect Bea's medication from the chemist. They rang earlier to say it had arrived. I'll be back shortly Janie and I'll be staying here for the foreseeable future." Even within her cloudy, sleepy head, Janie knew what that meant. It had been discussed when they'd first arrived at the cottage.

"You mean…"

"Yes," replied Gwen perching herself on the arm of the couch. "Bea's entering the final stage of her illness. I need to be here around the clock to manage her meds and pain relief." She leant forward and placed a motherly hand on Janie's knee. "I'll ring Harry and the others to come as soon as they can." Gwen rose to leave. The act of saying it out loud cut like a knife through both their hearts. Gwen had been friends with Bea since she'd taken over as district nurse for this area. Her first assignment had been Arthur. Their friendship had started with the untimely death of Arthur and now it was to end with Bea's own untimely death. Two wonderful people cut down in the prime of their lives. Life had a nasty habit of being cruel.

"H-h-how long?" stammered Janie.

"A few days, no more, a week tops," she whispered.

"I always thought she'd make it to the summer," began Janie. "I imagined she'd make it down onto the sand. That she'd be in a deckchair, the sun warming her face and a gentle sea breeze ruffling her hair. She'd have one of those big beautiful smiles on her face while she looked out to sea. I thought there would be more time." Janie began to cry and as Gwen rushed to hold the poor girl in her arms she felt the sting of her own tears. They held onto each other and let all the pain and the strain of the last few months wash over them.

Mavis Banford popped her head round the living room door to find Janie and Gwen huddled together on the armchair. It was obvious they were crying. Fearing the worst, she tiptoed across the room and up the stairs to Bea's bedroom. The door was wide open. Mavis strained to see if Bea's chest was moving up and down beneath the bed covers. In what seemed like an eternity, but in reality was only mere moments, she spied the light rise and fall of her best friend's chest. She crept into Bea's bedroom and without a sound she closed the curtains, shutting out the darkening sky. Re-crossing the room, she flicked on the standard lamp in the corner. It cast a pink, hazy glow around the room. Mavis took one last peek at the fall and rise of the covers, then as quiet as a church mouse descended the stairs. As she entered the lounge she found Gwen, who was now perched on the couch, and the two of them busy drying their eyes and blowing their noses.

"Just been to close Bea's curtains. Noticed they weren't drawn as I came across the driveway." Neither Gwen nor Janie mentioned their mini breakdown or that they really knew why Mavis had gone upstairs. It was obvious to them both that she'd feared the worst and had hastened to see for herself.

"Right," began Mavis as she strode across the room and off into the kitchen. "I've brought round a pot of home-made chicken and vegetable soup and some fresh crusty bread to go with it. One of you can wash their hands and butter the bread, the other can lay the table. It won't take me five minutes to warm this soup back up," Mavis spoke as she busied herself warming up both the soup and the bowls.

"I'll butter," offered Gwen. "So, you set the table, Janie. A bowl of hearty soup will do us all the world of good."

"But I'm not really hungry," protested Janie.

"Nonsense, child," remarked Mavis as she stirred the pot of soup. "You'll have a bowl of soup and a thick slice of bread with lashings of butter on it, then while we clear up in here you can go get yourself a nice soak in a hot bath."

"But, really, I'm—"

"Fine," Gwen finished off for her. "But you're clearly not. Now, do what you're told. You'll be of no use to Bea or anyone else for that matter unless you start eating and taking care of yourself. Now get and lay that table." There was authority in Gwen's voice, but it held a hint of tenderness in it. Janie resigned herself to the fact that she was going to have to at least try and eat a little of what was on offer.

Janie had not only surprised herself by polishing off two large bowls of the delicious soup and three rounds of bread and butter but Gwen and Mavis also.

"I don't know where you put it all," teased Mavis as she began to clear the table.

"We could have polished off just as much in our day," remarked Gwen.

"Eh, I suppose we could," admitted Mavis. "Now go get that bath and we'll have us a nice cup of cocoa ready for when you're done. We'll get that fire up and roaring in the lounge too. I reckon it's going to be a cold one tonight."

Janie rose from the table and headed upstairs. Both Gwen and Mavis knew she'd check in on Bea before running her bath. Gwen left the table and grabbed her coat off one of the hooks on the back door.

"I'll have to leave the pots and fire to you, Mave," explained Gwen as she donned her coat. "I need to catch the chemist and pop home for a few things." That meant Gwen would be staying here full-time now. The knowledge of what that implied filled her with dread.

"You'll be here when I get back, won't you?" asked Gwen. Mavis cleared the table as she spoke.

"Eh! Take your time, Gwen, and go safe: there's fog out there. I'll be here no matter what the time, watching over them both."

"I knew you would be, Mavis. You're a good friend to them and to me. I reckon we're going to need good friends over the next few days to get us through this. It's just lucky for us that we've got those on hand, eh?" Mavis turned to face Gwen as she buttoned up her coat.

"It is, Gwen, it is." Gwen smiled at Mavis then turned and headed out the door, leaving a gust of freezing air in her wake.

On returning to the lounge, Janie was welcomed by a roaring log fire. The curtains had been drawn and the lamps emitted a warm glow. On the coffee table lay a newly opened box of chocolates.

"Get yourself comfy, child, I'm filling up the cocoa mugs. Help yourself to chocolates. I thought we all deserved a treat." Janie decided to curl up on the right side of the couch facing the fire. She slipped off her slippers, lifted her feet up onto the couch and tucked them neatly under her dressing gown. She'd just settled herself nicely when Mavis, carrying a tray with two mugs on, entered the room. Placing the tray on the table, she offered one of the mugs to Janie. It was full to the brim with steaming hot cocoa. Mavis took the other mug, then nestled into the armchair beside the fire.

"She's okay?" Mavis asked.

"Umm," replied Janie as she blew across the top of her mug to cool the cocoa down and carefully took a small sip. It was still far too hot to drink so she asked Mavis a question as she waited for it to cool.

"Bea told me you moved in next door a few months after her, but she's never mentioned how you became such good friends." Mavis placed her untouched cocoa back down on the tray.

"At first it was just a friendly hello when we were out in the garden or passed one another in the street. I'd saved up some money, so I could replace the horrible shabby curtains in the house, but I didn't have a clue on either what or how much to buy. I knew Bea ran a sewing service from home so one morning I knocked on her door and asked if she'd come with me to Porthmadog shopping. She said yes straight away." Mavis picked up her cocoa mug and took a sip to check its temperature, then swallowed a bit more. She laced her fingers around the mug and held it in her lap.

"After that we spent a lot of time with one another. Bea taught me how to sew and I taught her how to bake bread. Brin, my husband, was a policeman. We'd moved here from the city, thinking it would be safer here, away from all the IRA terrorists with their guns and nail bombs. Brin had left that fateful morning same as always. It was his day for popping out to the more remote farms and small holdings to check everything was okay. There'd been a lot of sheep being stolen over the past few months, so they were making regular checks. Brin spotted two men manhandling a ewe into the back of a van. The ewe's lamb was crying out in distress and the ewe was putting up a hell of a fight. Brin put the call into the station, saying where he was and what was going on, and asked for immediate assistance. He was told to stay put and keep an eye on them. Before the backup arrived the two men had managed to load both the ewe and lamb into the van and were driving the van across the field towards the gate just up from where Brin was parked up in his panda car. He radioed that they were on the move and they told him to block their path; they were on their way. So Brin drove his car alongside the gate to prevent them from getting away. But the van kept coming and it was picking up speed. Brin realised they were intent on ramming the gate and his car out of the way. He didn't want to make things easier for them by moving the car so instead he climbed over to the passenger side to get out. The van came hurtling at the gate, ramming itself into the gate and Brin's panda car. They'd managed to lodge the van on the broken gate so it wouldn't move either forwards or backwards. At this point the two men jumped out of the van. One of them was holding a gun. He pointed it at Brin and just opened fire. When the backup arrived minutes later they found Brin dead on the side of the road. He'd been shot straight through the head. His police car was gone. The two men were tracked down and cornered in an old farm building. They shot two other officers before they were finally captured. The other officers survived."

"Oh, Mavis," exclaimed Janie. "I wished I'd never asked now." Mavis gave her a weak smile then finished off her cocoa. She began to continue the story as she placed the empty mug back on the tray.

"Bea was helping me to hang the new curtains we'd made together in the lounge when they came to tell me. She never left my side until mine and Brin's families arrived. Even then she'd pop round with pots of stew or a bag of shopping. I'd have gone back to the city with my family if it hadn't been for Bea. They didn't want me staying out here alone, but Bea said if I wanted to stay here, then she and Arthur would watch over me and they did. We've been through a lot, Bea, Gwen and me. They've been more like sisters to me than friends. Bea, as the eldest, always thought she had to care take of us. And she did. Now it's our turn to take good care of her, I guess."

"I'll second that, sister," piped up Gwen from the doorway that led into the kitchen. "But I'm going to need some of your famous hot cocoa to keep me going," she playfully added. Both Mavis and Janie were grateful for the distraction from all the morbid talk.

"I wouldn't mind a refill either," exclaimed Janie as Mavis took the tray with its two empty mugs out into the kitchen.

"I'll just go check in on Bea while you make it, Mave, okay?" called Gwen as she headed for the stairs." Janie slid her feet back into her slippers and crossed over to the fire and placed another log on it. She'd known that Mavis was a widow just like Bea but as he'd died before Arthur had and Bea had lost Arthur in her early thirties, that meant she'd been widowed in her mid-twenties. Mavis is a very attractive woman, who doesn't look like she's a few months shy of fifty, thought Janie, so why had she never remarried?

"No one could ever replace my Brin, dear," came Mavis's voice from behind her.

"I didn't mean to—"

"Think out loud?" offered Mavis. "You're not the first to think it or even say it. I've been asked that question more times than I care to remember, but the simple truth is, I've never come across a man who's a patch on my Brin. And, as my dad always says, 'why settle for scrag end when you've tasted best beef?'" Janie laughed at the phrase. She'd heard Bea use it often enough.

"I thought Gwen was one of us, but it seems she thinks your dad is a nice piece of prime beef," chuckled Mavis. Janie was glad their conversation had turned to something more fun.

"I think dad thinks the same on the quiet. Perhaps we'll have to do a spot of matchmaking."

"I think Bea would like that. She told me once, when Harry was down on the beach playing cricket with you kids that he was just the man Gwen didn't know she was looking for and vice versa. I didn't know your dad very well at all then, but I understood what Bea meant. I think they both know now but are too scared to make the first move."

"Dad's quite shy deep down," began Janie. "People call him the Gentle Giant. I can tell he likes Gwen a lot because apart from family members he hardly ever talks to women. But he natters away with Gwen, ten to the dozen."

"Talking about me, ladies?" asked Gwen. She'd crept down the stairs and had overheard a lot of their conversation.

"Ask me no questions and I'll you no lies," chortled Mavis. Gwen gave Mavis a fake hurt look then making her way over to the sofa she grabbed a chocolate from the opened box on the coffee table and stuffed it in her mouth, trying not to choke as laughter broke out between them.

Upstairs, Bea stirred. Their laughter wafted up the stairs to greet her. She thought she'd never hear them laugh again, so it came as a welcome surprise.

BEA

Easter Sunday 1983

"I think spring has finally sprung," announced Gwen as she opened Bea's bedroom curtains and light streamed in through the window. Bea struggled to open her eyes. Every fibre of her body seemed to be screaming out in pain. Gwen must have crossed over to her bed as she felt the pain of her lifting her wrist slightly to check her pulse. Bea forced her eyes open. The light hit her retinas with a searing force, causing them to close again. Bea swallowed down the nausea building at the back of her throat and once again summoned all her energy to open her eyes. Gwen's beautiful smiled greeted her this time. Gwen released her wrist and instead gathered Bea's frail hand into both her own. Bea tried in vain to speak. Just a noise like a baby gurgling seemed to emit from her mouth.

"It's time, is that it?" asked Gwen. Using all the strength she could muster, Bea gave Gwen's hand a gentle squeeze.

"I'll up the morphine dosage, Bea, just so I can dress you appropriately and the boys can move you without too much pain and discomfort. Then I'll lower the dose as much as I can, so you are as aware as possible without being racked too much with the pain, is that okay?" Bea just managed to move her hand slightly this time. Gwen placed a kiss on Bea's forehead then set about her task. As the morphine was absorbed into her body, Bea drifted away into oblivion.

Bea felt like she was floating on a boat out at sea. Her body moving up and down in time with the swell of the tide. Only, with each movement, her body ached more and more. The boat must have run aground, thought Bea, as a violent jolt sent needles of hot searing spikes through her entire body. Now she could hear a familiar voice calling to her. As it grew nearer she became aware of what was being said to her. It was Harry's voice, calling.

"Bea, darling, you're here as you wished. Try opening your eyes now." Bea struggled to open her eyes. Her whole body was gripped in a non-stop wave of crippling pain. She knew it was the cancer. She knew it was eating away at her very core. That her whole body was so very close to shutting down completely. She didn't want to fight it anymore. She couldn't fight it anymore but then she smelt the sea air. She felt a soft breeze caress her cheeks and she knew if she found the strength to lick her lips that they'd taste of salt. Bea willed her eyes to open. The pain was almost unbearable but the sight before her when she did was the best reward on earth.

She was out on the top terrace of the cottage, looking out towards the pebbles and sand and the sea beyond the edge of the cottage's garden. The spring sun was twinkling on the water casting a beautiful glow. She tentatively turned her head to the right. The pain seared down her spine but the sight of seeing all those she held dear congregated on the terrace made it all worthwhile. She let her gaze fall over each of their faces in turn. Her dad's, Harry's, Charlie's, Megan's and Gwen's. At Mavis' and Janie's. Dear sweet Janie. She would miss them all so very much. Then she turned her head back to look out across the garden, the pebbles, the sandy beach and out over to the furthest end of the sea, where sunbeams danced on the crest of waves. Bea strained her eyes against those sunbeams, focusing on the shadow within that she could see. It came nearer and nearer until at last she could see it was Arthur. He was coming to meet her. He walked right up to where the sea lapped against the sand and waited for her there.

Bea turned once again to look upon her love ones but this time there was no pain. She whispered goodbye into the breeze and turned back to her beloved Arthur, waiting at the water's edge. He reached out his hand to her and Bea closed her eyes for the last time.

Gwen had watched as Bea had opened her eyes. How she seemed to smile at something far out to sea. Gwen searched the horizon but there didn't seem to anything there but the twinkling of the sun's rays on the water. She'd turned back to see Bea was now watching them. She seemed to be absorbing their very essence and like some kind of magic elixir it was erasing the pain from her face. Suddenly she no longer looked ravaged by the cancer but glowing with health. Then Bea had turned back to face the sea and closed her eyes. In that moment, Gwen knew she'd lost her friend. She wandered to her side and gently reached in, under the blankets and felt for a pulse. There wasn't one. She turned to the others with tears already clouding her eyes. Gwen could tell they all knew, as each of them were shedding tears of their own.

JANIE & HARRY

Friday, 22nd April 1983

The sun was beginning to fade on what had been a long emotional day as Harry sat down beside his daughter Janie. He'd eventually found her, down at the end of the garden huddled up on the small cane sofa in the sun house. She looked emotionally drained, as he suspected he did after all the events of the day.

Bea had had it all planned out to very last detail. Memorial service in the village hall at ten o'clock for family and friends. Then her ashes, placed in a plain wooden box with Arthur's, were loaded onto a fishing boat in Barmouth and, along with her close friends and family, taken out to sea. Once they were a few miles out and running horizontal to where the beach stretched out, in front of the cottage, the ashes were cast into the water.

They'd each then thrown a single yellow rose into the sea and offered up a silent prayer before returning to dry land and the cottage.

Gavin Smthye-Jones, Bea's lawyer, had been waiting back at the cottage for them to read Bea's last will and testament. It had come as a great shock to them all to found out how much wealth she'd left behind. There'd been generous cash amounts, along with an item of her jewellery left to each of her close friends. George had been left a sizeable sum of money with orders to marry Rose before she saw sense and to book a cruise to the Caribbean for their honeymoon. Charlie was now the new proud owner of Bea's beloved MG sports car and also a good wedge of cash. Anne had received a substantial amount of money and young Freddy junior had inherited a fund that he could access once he reached twenty-one. Megan had inherited the shop along with its two-bedroomed accommodation in New Quay. It came with instructions that the tenants were free to lease it from her for as long as they required. Megan also got a hefty sum of money to do as she pleased and another amount to pay for all her expenses while she was still in university. Janie had been left Sea View Cottage and the studio that was in its grounds and again a huge chunk of money. Harry had been left Arthur's treasured Morgan. He'd been carefully tending to it for the past fourteen years, ever since Bea had come back into their lives. He too had been left a considerable sum of money. But there'd also been donations to local charities and causes and, most surprising of all, there'd even been gifts of both jewellery and money to their sister and mother, despite all the pain and heartache they'd caused Bea and Arthur. It never seemed to amaze him how much of a wonderful, caring, forgiving human being Bea had been.

Harry placed a protective arm around his youngest daughter's shoulders and drew her close to him. Automatically, Janie nestled into her father's embrace.

"I didn't come to look after her to be rewarded," explained Janie. Harry gave her a gentle squeeze.

"No one thinks that sweetheart. It was only right you should have the cottage; after all, it's been your home on and off since Bea came into your life. You gave up a lot to come and take of her and Bea knew you did it out of love and for no other reason."

"But I don't understand."

Harry wrapped his other arm around Janie and she nuzzled in further to his chest.

"Remember when you came out of the kitchen holding up a picture you'd drawn of the cottage when you were perhaps nine or ten?" Janie nodded her head. "You'd drawn a plan of the cottage turned upside down. The bedrooms on the ground floor and a big open-plan kitchen, dining room-cum-lounge upstairs. You said it would be far nicer if you looked at the beach, at the sea while you ate your meals or sat on the sofa, rather than only seeing them as you opened and closed your bedroom curtains."

"I did, didn't I? And I still do. The views are wonderful from the terraces but from the rear bedroom windows they are spectacular. The sunsets are beautiful from those windows. I've often sat perched on the thick windowsill watching the sun go down." Janie sighed at the memory.

"And do you remember what Bea did after you'd shown her your plans?"

Janie could remember clearly now. "She went into the studio and came back out with a rolled-up sheet of paper. She laid it on the table over mine and unfurled it. It was a much more sophisticated drawing of the one I'd done. The heading read, 'ARTHUR'S PLANS FOR SEA VIEW COTTAGE' Bea said that Arthur had been planning to renovate the cottage but then he'd been struck down with the brain tumour."

"Do you remember what she said next?" Janie searched for the answer, but it evaded her.

"She said, she liked the cottage how it was but one day she'd let you fulfil both yours and Arthur's dream. Today she's made good on that promise." Janie thought about what her father had just said. She vaguely remembered her aunt talking about letting her change the cottage one day. Then it dawned on her why Bea had bequeathed her the cottage and all that money.

"She wants me to finally make those dreams come true, doesn't she, Dad?" Harry gave Janie a big, knowing smile.

"Of course she does, sweetheart. She loves Megan, Anne and Charlie as the nephew and nieces they are but you, you she loved like the daughter she never had. She'd often remark how you reminded her of Arthur. The way that you'd stiffly dip a toe into the sea as though afraid of it and then the next minute you're running full pelt into it, waving your arms about and laughing as you immerse yourself into its arms. She said Arthur would do the exact same thing. How when she first ever came to stay, and you hummed away as you laid the table. Bea, since a small child had also hummed as she set the table. Then of course there was the vision for the cottage. The same vision as Arthur had had. There always was a deeper connection between the two of you."

Janie had felt that connection too. Bea had been like a mother to her. She'd taught her to bake, to sew, to plant vegetables and flowers. She'd been the mother Elsie never had been. Now she was gone, along with her Freddy. Was that how Janie's life was always going to be? Losing those she held most dear? The thought scared her, and she wriggled out of her father's embrace, so she could look him straight in the eye when he responded to her question.

"Dad, you promise to tell me straight away if you're ill or worried about your health, won't you?"

"I'm not ill, Janie," Harry replied.

"No! I mean if you do feel ill you'll tell me straight away, promise me," begged Janie.

"Of course I will, Janie, I'm not as stubborn as Bea, or as brave for that matter. Now stop worrying over things beyond all our control and help your old dad back up to the house, I'm bloody freezing to death out here." Janie was about to chastise her father for making fun of her when she realised he was only trying to make light of the situation.

"I'm counting on you living past hundred," teased Janie back. "So, let's get you inside before you collapse with pneumonia."

"A hot cup of tea with a drop of whiskey in will see me right," Harry replied.

"I'm sure it will," agreed Janie as they made their way out of the summer house and up the garden path to the cottage.

GEORGE

June 1983

George looked around the room. It was the community room of the sheltered dwelling he'd been living in since walking out on Ethel. There were thirty-two bungalows on the close. Twenty of them were two-bedroomed and the rest all had one bedrooms. Up until tomorrow he was a one-bed occupant but after today he'd be moving across the green into Rose's two-bedroomed bungalow. He looked across to his left at his new blushing bride, Rose Whittaker, that was. Now she was Mrs Rose Arnold. She looked absolutely beautiful in her pale pink lace dress and matching jacket. George smiled to himself. He'd have never dreamt in his wildest dreams that at the ripe old age of eighty-two he'd be getting married to a lively seventy-seven-year-old. Oh, how much his life had changed since the day he walked out on Ethel.

Images of Bea came rushing into his head. Bea as a new born all wrinkly and pink. Taking her first steps unaided. Singing along to the radio while dancing around the room. Bea still waving as his train went out of sight of the station taking him away to war. Bea all grown up sitting in Harry's lounge. The endless talks, the catching up, the walks along the beach. Then Bea sitting lifeless in the lounger on the cottage terrace.

"George, honey," came Rose's gentle voice. He looked at his new wife. He didn't need to explain why he'd been so far away, lost in his own world. She just instantly knew.

"I wish she was here too, George; doesn't seem right, does it? You and me in our twilight years getting married and one so young already gone." Rose entwined her arm through his. "I bet she's looking down on us though, checking we're having a good time."

George smiled. That's exactly what she'd be doing, he thought. "I bet she'd be wondering when you were going to ask me to dance, as well." George smiled and nodded his head at Rose. She was a canny woman, this one, and he loved for it.

"I've no doubt she would, Rose, no doubt at all! So, let's hit the floor and show these young'uns how to dance properly, eh?"

"You bet we will!" giggled Rose.

George gently guided Rose around the community room floor and their guests gathered round the edges and cheered them on. George looked at the gathered faces as he waltzed around the room. For a brief moment, he thought he caught a glimpse of Bea's face smiling back at him through the crowd.

JOSEF

Bangkok, June 1983

Josef stumbled back into the flea-bitten bedsit he was renting and slumped up against the wall. The door slammed shut on the dinghy corridor outside. On the opposite side of the small, dirty room, framed against peeling wallpaper, hung a mottled old mirror. Josef staggered across the room to take a closer look at his reflection. Gone were the boyish good looks, the dark, sultry eyes and smooth olive skin. His skin looked like he was suffering from a bad case of acne and it had an almost yellow tinge to it. His eyes were just sunken, lifeless black holes. He looked like a vagrant. Liked he'd been sleeping out on the streets for weeks, months on end. What had happened to him?

'The band' had happened to him, that's what! For the first few weeks it had been fun. The band would perform, he'd take photographs then afterwards they'd party. At first it was just harmless drinking games. Then it was drinking and a few puffs of a joint. Then somehow it had spiralled into LSD, magic mushrooms, uppers, downers, coke and heroin. In the beginning, the band or one of the hangers-on had supplied the drugs for free. Then he'd started dipping into the money he'd worked so hard for to travel abroad with Janie. Sweet, sweet Janie. But now that money was almost gone so he'd phoned home to ask for more.

Josef hadn't been in touch since the day he'd left with the band. His mother had cursed at him down the phone for being such a selfish boy, then had handed him over to his father. His dad had promised to wire him some money first thing in the morning with the condition that he was to use it to return home. Josef had told his dad he would, but he had no intention of spending that money on anything other than drugs to feed his habit. His father had then informed him of Janie's Aunt Bea having died back in April. The call had ended with thoughts of sweet, sweet Janie filling his addled brain as he'd staggered back up the hotels stairs to his room.

Now, here he was, staring at his reflection wondering why the hell he'd ever let himself sink so low. He was nothing more than a drug addict. A DIRTY, GOOD-FOR-NOTHING DRUG ADDICT. Janie wouldn't have allowed this to happen! Janie would have taken him away, saved him. But Janie had been the one to abandon him! Hadn't she? She'd wanted to save dear old Aunt Bea! Well, that hadn't worked out too well, had it?

"FOR CHRIST'S SAKE'S, JOSEF," he screamed at his

reflection. "WHAT THE HELL ARE YOU THINKING? LOOK AT YOURSELF FOR FUCK'S SAKE! YOU'RE A FUCKING MESS! A FUCKING TOTAL WASTE OF FUCKING SPACE!" Josef dropped down to his knees and banged his fists on the floor. He was a total fuck-up. He'd gone in search of fame and fortune when he'd already been the luckiest guy alive having Janie by his side. Tears of self-pity rolled down his face. He didn't wipe them away. He let them fall. He needed all this self-righteousness to wash out of him. He needed to take back control of his life. He needed to get back to Janie. He needed to get clean. He needed to act now. He needed to stop the ache, the pain. He looked across at the small piece of folded foil on the coffee table. At the spoon, the lighter, the ashtray. Just one more hit wouldn't hurt, would it?

Josef crawled across to the table and with trembling hands began to unfold the foil to reveal the precious brown powder. Just this last hit, he thought. Just to help me think straight. Just to silence the pain, the ache. He dragged himself up onto the strained and ripped seat of the only chair in the room. A gentle breeze blew in through the open window, bringing with it the noises of the Bangkok street life below. It snatched the foil from Josef feeble grip and sent the heroin spiralling in its wake around the room. Josef relaxed back in the chair and for the first time in ages a smile danced across his face, lighting up his eyes. There'd be more no hits for him tonight. Tonight, he'd have to go cold turkey.

MEGAN & JANIE

Sea View Cottage, June 1983

"Dave's coming Saturday morning and stopping for the night, if that's okay?" began Megan. "We'll head off late Sunday morning to New Quay, to meet the Harris's. It'll be so nice to finally get to look around Aunt Bea's shop and maisonette." They were both lazing on loungers outside the sun house at the bottom of the garden. It had always been Janie's favourite spot on sunny days, the cool interior of the sun house a welcome retreat for the redhead.

"What a daft question, Megan!" replied Janie. "This cottage maybe mine but it's still a place for all the family."

"I'm just letting you know, that's all!"

"Yeah! For the hundredth time," mocked Janie, as she got up off the lounger and headed into the shade of the sun house. "Fancy a glass of squash? It should still be cold."

"I'm just excited, that's all," explained Megan, then added, "anything to eat with that drink?" She could hear doors and lids being opened and closed and then the squash being poured into beakers.

"I've found a packet of salted nuts and a bag of Quavers in the cupboard, and I've got a banana, an apple, two satsumas, a Mars bar and a Curly Wurly in the cool box," called back Janie.

"Oooh! A satsuma and a Mars bar, please," replied Megan. She heard Janie reopen the lid on the cool box and then close it. Moments later, Janie appeared at her side, blocking out the sun, as she leant over with a beaker of squash in one hand and a Mars and satsuma in the other. Megan hauled herself up into a sitting position and took the items from her cousin.

They sat in silence as they enjoyed their impromptu picnic and admired the view. Janie had chosen to sit on one of the cane armchairs just inside the opened double doors of the sun house, enjoying a respite from the heat of the midday sun. Once Megan had finished her little feast she lay back on her lounger, face down so she could tan her back, while still being able to both talk and see Janie.

"I'm excited about the shop but I've also got a surprise for Dave as well," began Megan. "But you have to promise not to say a word to him when he arrives."

"You're not pregnant, are you?" asked Janie.

"No, of course not," giggled Megan.

"Don't know what you find so funny," Janie snapped back. "That would really throw a spanner in the works." Megan wondered when the girl she had thought of as her sister had suddenly got so serious.

"It just made me laugh that you thought that was my surprise," remarked Megan. "You'd normally come up with something more bizarre than that! You saying, 'are you pregnant?' is the sort of response I'd have expected from Aunt Bea or Uncle Harry, not you." Megan looked on as Janie processed what she'd just said. A look of sadness now appeared on her face.

"You're right! I would have normally come up with something silly, but I guess the last six months have taken its toll on my sense of humour."

Megan tried to appease Janie.

"It's understandable, sweetie, but with time you'll be back to your old self. A little wiser, a little more care-worn, as Bea would say. But you'll be you again, Janie, I'm sure of it."

Janie smiled down at Megan, "I hope so, Megan, I really do."

Megan reached out a hand to Janie and she stretched out and took it, giving it a comedy handshake.

"Now, if you're not pregnant, what's the big surprise?" she asked, letting go of Megan's now-aching outstretched hand. Megan manoeuvred herself round so that she was sitting up on the edge of the lounger facing Janie.

"Dave asked me to pop into the estate agents in Aberystwyth to drop the cheque off for the deposit on a small one-bedroomed flat we're going to rent together next term, now that I'm moving out of the university halls. Anyway, when I got there it was packed with other students either leaving or collecting deposits, so I had to wait a while to be seen. So, I started looking at the houses etc. being advertised for sale and for rent. I'm not really paying that much attention just scanning across the photographs that's all, when I come across this little rundown cottage. I'm so taken by the photo that I start to read the details. Turns out, it's a little smallholding with few farm buildings and a couple of acres of land attached to it. 'Idyllic, isn't it?' comes this voice over my shoulder. I turn to see its one of the estate agents. He goes on to tell me its situated about five miles out of New Quay and, along with a small farmyard, veggie patch and five acres of pasture, it's also got three acres of woodland. By New Quay! Can you believe it, Janie? Close to the shop Bea left me."

"Now that's spooky," butted in Janie. Megan had told her of the idea that she and Dave had of one day turning the shop and its accommodation into a veterinary practice.

"You can say that again," remarked Megan.

"So, did you tell the estate agent?"

"Well, not everything, just in case, you know, I – we – decided to buy it. Didn't want it looking too perfect. I remembered uncle Harry telling us to always play our cards close to our chest when thinking of make a big purchase."

"Sound advice coming from a man who making a living selling cars," chortled Janie.

"Exactly," began Megan. "So, I just said that I had a family member looking to move over that way and would it be possible for me to view it, so I could see if was as suitable as I thought. Anyway, to cut a long story short, I set up a viewing for the next day and talked Barry, a friend of both mine and Dave's from uni, into coming with me."

"Won't he have told Dave?" enquired Janie.

"Nah! Barry guessed straight away what I was up to and decided to play along. It was everything I'd hoped for and more, Janie. It's up a lovely private lane and the views are something else. The cottage itself is in dire need of renovation. There's a hole in the roof, no bathroom, no central heating, but it's wonderful. Even Barry could see its potential and, believe me, Barry has little or no imagination."

"You didn't go ahead and buy it, did you?" gasped Janie. Megan gave Janie a cheeky grin.

"No, I didn't go ahead and buy it. I could have though! In cash as well, and still have had enough left over from my inheritance to do all the work on it."

"So, what's the big surprise then?" asked Janie.

"Well, I've made arrangements for the estate agent to meet me and Dave there on the Monday morning before we go to afternoon tea at the shop. Only I haven't told Dave."

"Why not? Why all the secrecy?" asked Janie. Megan took a sip of her now-warm squash.

"Because Dave has got a chip on his shoulder already about me having all this money and the shop to boot. He worries that I won't need him, that he's got nothing to offer me now!" Now it was Janie's turn to laugh. "It's not funny, Janie! Dave—"

"Dave told me that Josef was a chauvinist fool who needed to grow up and get with the programme. That women today have minds, money and careers of their own and that men are no longer the be all and end all. Yet here he is acting like a male chauvinist himself." Megan laughed too but then the reality of what Janie said came back to her.

"So, you see my problem, Janie? Dave will think he can't afford to buy it right now so end of."

"OH! MEGAN!" screamed Janie at her. "Don't give in before you've even begun. Dave might not be able to afford it now. He's working hard like you to become a vet. He's a few years further on in his studies so he'll be qualified before you. By the time you've qualified he'll be an established vet earning good money. He'll be the one supporting you. Then, say in the future you decide to have kids. He'll be the one out earning the money whilst you're at home looking after the little ones. You just have to explain to him that you're investing in your future together now. He'll be the one who'll be investing in it after that."

"Do you really think that'll work? I mean I have the trust fund from Aunt Bea that supports me while I'm in uni." Janie came and sat beside Megan on the lounger.

"Truth is, I don't know, Megan, and neither do you! But if this place is as perfect as you say it is, it's gotta be worth a try. You just have to make Dave see that it's for both of you. That if it wasn't for him and the dreams you share, you wouldn't be looking at the place. That it's a home you can build together. He loves you, Megan, and he may have a few chauvinistic traits but he's not as single-minded as Josef. And he hasn't got a selfish bone in his body, so don't write it off just yet. Go take him to see it. For Christ's sake, if Boring Barry can see potential then I'm sure as hell

Dave can." Megan wrapped Janie in her arms and pecked her cheek.

"I hope so, Janie. I hope so, 'cause I've fallen in love with the place."

"Then so will Dave," added Janie.

***

Janie was sitting at the desk in Arthur and Bea's old studio working on the book that she'd promised Bea she'd write after reading all their love letters, when Megan came hurtling in through the door.

"There you are!" she managed to get out between gasping for breath. Janie shuffled round in her chair to see what all the urgency was about.

"Of course I'm here! Where else would I be?" Janie looked on as Megan caught her breath back. Her cheeks were bright red and she had a grin from ear to ear.

"Dave loved it," she panted. "He loved it so much he let me go right ahead and buy it."

"Say you offered a lower price, tell me you just didn't sign on the dotted line?" begged Janie. Megan's breathing was becoming less laboured now.

"What! And face the wrath of uncle Harry? No way! In fact, Dave even pretended we had to think things over. Told him we had to do some sums, get some professional advice. We went and had afternoon tea with Mr and Mrs Harris at the shop. Even had the guided tour, before we went back to the hotel and rang them. We put in a cheeky low offer then waited for a response. An hour later they rang us back to say it wasn't quite enough. At this point, we informed them we were cash buyers and could proceed straight away at the offered amount. Half an hour later our offer had been accepted. Yesterday we got the ball rolling and employed a lawyer to oversee the purchase, surveys, all the legal stuff. This morning we spent looking around all the land and its boundaries and coming up with ideas. Oh, I'm so, so happy, Janie," Megan finished, flinging herself onto Janie's knee. Janie wrapped her arms around Megan's waist to stop her sliding off her knee.

"So, all that worrying was for nothing?" enquired Janie.

"No! The investing in our future and the kiddie thing swung it," came Dave's reply from the doorway. The pair of them looked across at him. He moved into the studio.

"I was just about to say it was perfect BUT… when Megan started giving me this grand speech about our plans for the future about having kids and how we'd take care of them and each other and well… all my foolish macho pride took a hike. It made sense. Megan wasn't buying it for herself; she was buying it for us, our future, our kids. Good job she told you all about it, Janie, else we'd still be arguing about it now." Janie blushed, and Megan gave her a big squeeze before jumping off her lap and into Dave's waiting arms.

"We owe you a big thank you, Janie," they both said in unison.

"Those cheesy grins on your faces are all the reward I need," Janie replied. "Now get out of here, I've got a story to write."

"I'll cook us something special for tea," called Megan over her shoulder as they exited the studio. "That's if it's okay for us to stay?" she teasingly added.

Janie just shook her head and turned back to face the desk and the typewriter. She was happy for Megan, she really was. She was happy for grandad George and Rose. She was even happy for her dad and his romance with Gwen, but it still left a bittersweet sting in her heart. Would she ever be happy? Would she ever find the kind of love she was now so busy writing about? She'd thought she'd had it with Josef. Even the thought of him still sent butterflies into flight around her stomach. Would they ever stop? Would she ever stop loving him? Would she ever love again?

"Snap out of it," she said out loud to herself. Janie ran her fingers through her hair and had a good stretch of her shoulders, her arms, hands and fingers. She felt the tension in them ease away. She didn't have time to feel sorry for herself; she had a book to write.

HARRY

September 1983

Harry swung the Range Rover onto Bea's driveway and parked up beside Janie's Vauxhall Chevette in front of the double garage. He mentally corrected himself for thinking of it still as Bea's driveway, when in reality it was Janie's now. He reached across and opened the glove compartment and retrieved the car's paperwork from it. Harry placed the documents on the passenger seat and closed the glove compartment. He took the keys out of the ignition and was just reaching for the door handle to open the door when it shot open. Harry looked up to see Gwen holding onto the open driver's door with a face like thunder.

"You might have rung to let me know you was coming," she almost shouted at him. Harry leant across and took the car's documents off the passenger seat then swung his leg out of the open door and eased himself up and out onto the driveway. Gwen had taken a few steps back to allow him to alight from the car. Harry closed the car door and turned to face Gwen.

"I've come to deliver Janie the Range Rover and take her little Chevette back home. It's more of a business visit than a social one."

"OH! So, you won't be calling in to see Janie then?" snapped Gwen. Harry took a deep breath before answering, mainly to keep his growing aggravation with Gwen's irrational behaviour at bay.

"Of course, I'll be seeing Janie, Gwen. There's papers to be signed for one thing and she is my daughter and I don't get to see her very often, as you well know!" explained Harry. He could see his answer had only infuriated her more.

"And what about me, Harry? I thought we were a couple. Yet here you are! You've travelled all this way and you wasn't even going to stop by and say hello! How do you think that makes me feel?" Harry let out a sigh.

"How many times in these past few months have I been to see you, Gwen, and not my own daughter? Eh?"

"That's different," shrugged off Gwen. "You're not supposed to be having a relationship with her!" Harry just couldn't help laughing out loud at the absurdity of her reply.

"How dare you laugh at me," screamed Gwen at him. Now it was time for Harry to raise his voice.

"I'm laughing at how absurd your last remark was," began Harry. "Janie is my daughter, for God's sake! We have a father–daughter relationship. It's perfectly natural Gwen, for me to want to spend time with her."

"But why do you have to leave me out?" exclaimed Gwen.

"I'm not leaving you out. I'm just spending time with Janie today, that's all. I'm just making sure my little girl has got a safe motor for when the bad weather comes, that's all. But really, Gwen, I shouldn't have to explain myself to you. I don't have to ring Janie every time I come down to see you. It's nothing to do with her and me visiting Janie today has really nothing to do with you either. Now, if you'll excuse me, I'll carry on in to see Janie as I've wasted enough of my time here with you over this already." Harry turned away from Gwen and started towards the gate at the side of the building. Beyond it were the steps that led down to the back of the cottage and its kitchen door. He'd managed two paces when Gwen grabbed his arm and tried to turn him back round to face her. Harry spun round to confront her. He wasn't a violent man. Christ! He was usually an easy-going bloke, but Gwen had more than tried his patience. It had been fun when they'd first hooked up. They'd laughed, talked, danced and even sung along to the radio together but there'd always been this sort of neediness about her. She always seemed to want to know his whereabouts. If he hadn't rung when he'd said he would, she'd be on the phone straight away asking why. Always asking when he was coming down to see her but never saying she'd come up to see him. Then she seemed to be envious of any time he spent with his family and she'd go all moody if he spent time with his friends. He liked Gwen but not that side of her. Elsie had had two sides to her and look where that had got him. It was no good. He was going to have to call it a day with Gwen. There was no way he was ever going to go back down that road again.

"Don't you dare walk away from me." Gwen was now in full hysterical flow. Her cheeks were bright red and her eyes were almost popping out of their sockets with anger at him. "It damn well is my business what you get up to, Harry Arnold, and don't you ever forget it. We're a couple and I have a right to know EVERYTHING YOU SAY AND DO! DO YOU UNDERSTAND ME?"

"Well, we're not anymore," replied Harry.

"OH! YES, WE ARE," yelled Gwen. "WE'RE NOT THROUGH UNTIL I SAY SO, DO YOU HEAR ME?" DO YOU HEAR ME?" she repeated.

The front door of the cottage swung open and Janie appeared in the doorway with Mavis at her side. They both strode out onto the drive.

"What the hell is going on?" asked Janie.

"None of your damn business," spat Gwen at her. "So, piss off back inside and keep your nose out of my affairs." Harry watched the fire rise up in his daughter. Janie was a redhead in every sense of the word. From her fiery red curls, right down to her fiery quick temper.

"Get the fuck off my property," shouted Janie at Gwen, "Before I call the police on ya!"

"Oh, shut up, you stupid little girl," screamed Gwen back at her.

"Now now, Gwen, I think you should come with me,"

began Mavis, taking Gwen by the arm and trying to lead her off towards her house next door. Gwen just lashed out at Mavis, catching her full-on across the face sending Mavis toppling to the ground. Janie rushed over to check on Mavis and Harry, dropping the folder of paperwork onto the driveway, caught hold of Gwen's arms before she caused any more damage.

"Let me go," screamed Gwen at Harry.

"Not until you calm down and apologise to Mavis and Janie then I'll let go so that you can get the hell out of here." Gwen just twisted and turned and kicked out at Harry, but he held onto her. Janie helped Mavis to her feet and then led her back into the cottage. As she closed the front she called out to Harry.

"Make sure that nutcase leaves in the next five minutes, Dad, else I'm calling the police, okay?"

"I will, love. You just take care of Mavis."

Once the front door was shut, Harry released his grip on Gwen and as she was still thrashing and kicking about the momentum sent her hurling to the ground. She immediately got to her feet and ran at Harry, pummelling his chest with her fists and shouting.

"How dare you let that little cow speak to me like that?" Harry once again grabbed her arms but this time he just pushed Gwen away from him before releasing her.

"Just go, Gwen, and take a long, hard look at yourself in the mirror and think about what's happened here today, will ya? I don't know what the hell has got into you but it sure as hell ain't pretty. You've just attacked your oldest friend, insulted my daughter and ended our relationship and all because of what, Gwen? Go ask yourself that!" Harry took one last look at Gwen, picked up the folder from the ground and headed for the front door of the cottage.

"You should have told me you were coming," shouted Gwen to Harry's retreating back. Harry just opened the door and without looking back walked through it and slammed it shut behind him. He waited in the hallway, listening for Gwen's footsteps on the driveway. Finally, he heard them turn and walk away. He slipped into the front bedroom and peered through the net curtain down the drive. Gwen was just turning out of sight. A few minutes later her car sped past the top of the driveway. Harry let out a sigh of relief then made his way down the stairs to the kitchen.

Janie was just handing a cup of tea to Mavis, who was seated at the kitchen table. Her left cheek was showing the first signs of a bruise and there was a graze running down her right arm where she'd fallen to the ground. No doubt she'd have a similar graze on her right leg, thought Harry.

"I'm sorry, ladies," began Harry. "I didn't mean for you to get caught up in our argument."

"No need to apologise, Harry," offered Mavis. "When Janie and I heard the commotion up on the driveway I knew that Gwen had lost the plot, so, to speak."

"What do you mean?" asked Janie puzzled by Mavis's remark.

"Gwen moved here after a failed marriage. Her ex-husband was a womaniser. Gwen had trusted him wholeheartedly and had swallowed all the lies he'd fed her. Then one day a young girl turned up at the house. She was heavily pregnant and Gwen's husband was the father. He had the audacity to tell the girl she could move in and Gwen, being a nurse, could look after her. Gwen packed her bags and left. She's had a trust issue ever since. It used to drive me and Bea mad in the beginning but we kinda got used to it and, as we were females, she eventually started to trust us and the problem seemed to have gone away. Then along comes Harry and it seems he's brought the green-eyed, untrusting monster back to life."

"But she knows dad's history. She knows he's been lied to, cheated on and worse. So, why think or believe he's capable of doing those things to someone else?" asked Janie.

"Jealously and mistrust aren't logical, that's why, Janie," began Harry. "They're a disease, an illness, just like alcohol is to some. They don't see it as a problem. They don't see things as we do. I just wish she'd told me. Maybe we could have avoided all of this. Maybe we could have worked it out. But now? I don't know!"

"It's not for you to work out, Harry, that's Gwen's job. She's a sensible old thing underneath all that silliness. She'll realise sooner or later what a complete arse she's been then she'll come crawling back with her tail between her legs asking for forgiveness. And when she does, I for one will give it," ended Mavis.

"Me too," added Janie. Harry said nothing. He wasn't so sure he could! Gwen's behaviour had been a stark reminder of his life with Elsie. He liked Gwen, he liked her a lot, but another irrational, selfish woman in his life was something he definitely didn't need.

ANNE

December 1983

Anne took a good look at her father as she cleared away the dinner plates. He looked older, somehow, from the last time she'd seen him back in August, when he'd visited with Gwen. He'd looked really happy that day but now he looked so lost, so low. Janie had filled her in on what had happened with Gwen and how she'd since been round and apologised to her. Strange how people never seem to be what you expected of them. Take her Eric, for instance. He'd been her rock for the past six years. He'd taught her how to forgive and to ask for forgiveness. To rid herself of the stubbornness and spite that her aunt Mary and gran had nurtured in her. Eric had blossomed in those years too. Age suited him well. It had enhanced his looks and the hard, manual labour of running a grocery shop had done wonders to his body. He'd been her meal ticket to a new life away from the grip of her aunt and gran. Away from the family that she had so cruelly treated but now he was the love of her life, the man she admired above all others, save for her father, and that was why she was saddened by his appearance.

"Are you okay, Dad?" Anne asked as she removed the empty plate from in front of him.

"I'm fine, love, especially after that lovely meal. Still got room for a spot of pudding if there's any going though!" Harry quipped as he rubbed his swollen belly.

"There's some home-made rice pudding cooking in the oven. It'll be another ten, fifteen minutes before it's ready though," replied Anne as she stacked the dirty plates in the sink.

"Plenty of time for you to tell me what it is you want to ask me and what you want to tell," responded Harry, leaning back in his chair. Anne wiped her hands on her apron then resumed her place back at the kitchen table. Eric reached across and held her hand.

"We're expecting another baby come June," blurted out Anne. Immediately a smile spread across Harry's face.

"How wonderful, another grandchild, oh, Anne what a lovely surprise." Harry reached across the table and placed a kiss on Anne's cheek, then he shook Eric's hand.

"So, I'm guessing the next thing you want to tell me is you're moving into a bigger place?" Anne looked over to Eric and gave him the nod to speak.

"Well, Harry, the next thing we wanted to ask was

if that talk about me joining the team at the garage was serious?"

"Too, right it was serious, Eric. Charlie has big ideas for the garage beyond that new flash car showroom. He wants to move into motorbike sales as well. We own a decent-sized plot to the side of the workshop and been offered more land behind that for a fair price off the old bloke who owns it. With you on board it would be a definite goer. You've got a good business head on your shoulders, Eric, and we need someone with those skills to forge ahead. Just say the word and we'll welcome you aboard the family business." Harry beamed at Eric.

"We were hoping you'd say that, Dad, weren't we, Eric? Cause we've got something else to tell you," continued Anne. "Eric and I have sold the shop and flat and bought a three-bedroomed house a couple of streets away from your place. It used to belong to old Mrs Ferriday, the infant school teacher, remember her, Dad?" Harry nodded at Anne.

"Well, she died over a year ago, but the estate has only just been settled and the house put up for sale. We'd asked about it and logged an interest in it not long after she died and last month they got back to us. Gave us first refusal. We got someone to look after Freddy Jnr and the shop and literally just drove down, viewed it, then came straight back." Eric took over from Anne then.

"The house is a mess inside and out. The old lady never did anything to it all the thirty-odd years she lived there and it standing empty for over a year hasn't done it any favours but the minute we walked through the door we fell in love with it."

"It's got a huge garden out back, Dad, and all the bedrooms are a generous size," interrupted Anne.

"Anyway," continued Eric. "We made a slightly lower offer than they were asking and after keeping us waiting for a few days they agreed to it. We put the shop and flat up for sale as soon as we got the news and within hours of word getting out the young couple who help us out in the shop came up with the funds to buy it."

"Isn't it wonderful, Dad?" exclaimed Anne. "I'm finally coming home." Harry was grinning like a Cheshire cat. He'd always hoped that one day Anne and her little family would move closer to home; now it seemed it was all happening.

"And you'll be wanting to move back in with me and Charlie while you wait for it to be done? Is that what you're leading up to?" asked Harry. Anne nodded her head, as did Eric.

"I can do all the chores for you, cook, wash, clean and Eric will be able to start straight after the handover at the garage." Harry started to laugh.

"Of course, you're all welcome to stay for as long as it takes and there's no need to be running around after me and Charlie either."

"But we – I want to help, to do my bit," argued Anne.

"We'll all work together as a family, Anne. Now, where's that rice pudding you promised me?" Anne rose from the table and heading towards the oven she stopped by her father and gave him a hug.

"You're the best dad in the world," she said, then set about serving up the dessert.

GEORGE & HARRY

January 1984

"Be glad when all this icy weather has gone," remarked Harry as he stepped out of the warmth of The Honeysuckle public house. George pulled the collar of his coat up tight around his neck and buried his chin into his chest.

"Good for killing off the germs and us old folk," he jested.

"Take more than a cold to kill you off, Dad," joked back Harry. "You're made of sterner stuff."

"Thought your mum was, Harry, but they reckon it was a cold that took her."

"Only thing in her life she couldn't beat the stuffing out of, eh?" quipped Harry.

"She was a cold woman, so it makes it appropriate that it was a damn good cold that got her in the end."

"Eddie Norris reckons her death caused our Mary's husband to grow a pair of balls! I reckon Eddie must be right to have got our Mary to sell up and move," finished off Harry.

"Aye!" was all the response that George gave.

"You know, Dad, you've never mentioned how you felt about mum's death or Mary moving away," queried Harry. George lifted his head and took a sharp intake of the cold icy night air.

"Guilty is how I felt about Ethel's death at first," George began. "Guilty for feeling nothing when Mary came to tell me. Now? Now I feel nothing. That woman caused nothing but heartache and misery to everyone she ever encountered. The world's a better place for not having her in it as far as I'm concerned, son. Harsh, I know, but there it is. As for Mary, a bit of sea air and some straight-talking northerners might just be the making of her."

"Eddie Norris said, 'there'll be one more cunt in Scunthorpe, once she gets there,'" replied Harry. A smile broke out on George's face.

"He's not far wrong there, lad, he's not far wrong."

"I must admit it made me smile too, Dad."

"After everything this last year threw at us, son, we could with something to smile about."

"I think this year is going to be a good'un, Dad, I really do." George looked across at his son as they walked along side by side.

"I'm glad you've still managed to stay optimistic, Harry, I really am. After everything that life has thrown at ya over these past few years, you're still managing to see the best in things." He patted his son on the back.

"What's not to be happy about, Dad? Anne has come home and is expecting a baby. Megan and Dave have got engaged and done wonders with that old rundown cottage. Janie has been offered a book deal and Charlie is building us our own little empire at the garage. And you, Dad, you've got a diamond in Rose."

"When you put it that way, son, I can't argue with ya. And, talking of Rose, there's my turn off to home. She'll have my slippers warming by the fire and a pan of milk simmering on the stove for our bedtime cocoa. So, I'll bid you goodnight, son and I'll pray that you get a happy ending when I go to bed." George patted Harry once again on the back and turned in the opposite direction to his son, for home.

"There's no need to pray for me, Dad," shouted Harry after him. "I've got everything I need for my happy ending. It's called the FREEDOM TO DO AS I PLEASE."

George waved his hand in the air to Harry as he continued on his way. Maybe that was all that Harry needed for now, he thought, but I'm still going to pray for him. If only for God to go easy on him!

JANIE

March 1984

Janie scoured the line of people behind the barrier in the arrivals hall of Faro airport in Portugal. Her eyes swept across the faces searching for a familiar face. Then there it was! Jack Wilde! Only he looked less harassed and gone was his pale pallor, replaced by a sun-kissed golden glow. His hair was almost entirely white. A little longer, a lot less manicured. Gone was the worn overcoat and business-like suit. He was dressed in casual jeans and a polo shirt with a jumper slung over his shoulder. He'd spotted Janie too now and was waving her frantically over to him.

"Didn't recognise me at first, did you?" His voice still held those distinctive detective tones.

"No, no, I didn't," admitted Janie, as Jack relieved her of her suitcase. "You look so, so…"

"Chilled? Relaxed? Unpolicemanly?" he offered.

"All three," replied Janie and they both laughed as Jack led the way out of the airport. Jack talked away as they walked.

"My car's just over here," he pointed to a car point just up ahead of them. "It's roughly a forty-minute drive back to Albufeira. I've booked you into the hotel your mum was working at when I found her. It's a lovely place and you've a suite overlooking the main square. You can see my humble abode from your balcony," he continued.

"A suite?" cut in Janie.

"Aaarh! When I booked the room, Juan – that's the hotel manager; he's also my weekly chess opponent – realised who I was booking it for and insisted on giving you a suite free of charge."

"But why would he do that?" asked Janie.

"When the news of where I'd found Elsie hit the news, people flocked to the hotel. They wanted to see and stay where the 'monster' had worked. They've been busy ever since. It kind of put them on the map, so to speak. Now people come here because of its excellent service and nothing more."

"They won't expect anything of me?" Janie asked. Jack just laughed as he loaded the suitcase into the boot of his car.

"No, Janie, they won't. It's just their way of apologising for having employed your mum in the first place. That's all! The Portuguese people are a very proud race and a very friendly one. I'd not have booked you in there if I thought for one minute you'd be used in anyway. You do trust me, don't you, Janie?" he begged. Janie smiled across the roof of the car at the ex DCI. Of all the men in the world he was probably one of only a small handful she trusted.

"Hope the food there is good as I'm starving," replied Janie.

"There's a small fishing village that serves the most amazing seafood dishes, just a short detour away from Albufeira. It's called Olhos de Agua. How about we stop of there for a bite to eat before we head to the hotel. You can fill me in on the news while we eat looking out to sea. What do you say?"

"Fabulous," replied Janie as she climbed into the passenger seat of the car and within minutes they were out on the open roads of Portugal.

The food had been divine, and Jack had listened whilseJanie had told him all about how emotional the sprinkling of Bea's ashes out at sea had been. How she'd inherited the cottage and how shocked they'd all been by the wealth Bea had had. She told him about the romance Harry had had with Gwen and its subsequent break up. Of how much the garage had grown and Anne's return home with another baby on the way. Of George's marriage to Rose and of Megan's engagement. She spoke of Charlie's never-ending parade of girlfriends and lastly, she spoke about the book she'd written at Bea's request. Then she produced a copy from her bag and handed it over to Jack Wilde.

"It's not really your kind of book but I wanted you to have one. It's not out on the shelves until the third of April, the first anniversary of Bea's death. The publishers gave me a few copies to hand out to anyone special I chose. I've signed it so if it's the 'big success' that they're predicting, it might be worth a few quid in a few years." Janie tailed off. Jack took the book from Janie and opened it to the page with the dedication on. It read:

Thank you, Aunt Bea.
For giving me the love I was so in need of.
For the strength to follow my dreams
And the words on which to do it.
Give Arthur a hug from me
Love Janie x

"What a beautiful thing to write for a truly beautiful woman. When I came that last time to Harry's and was told of the sad news it made me question the way of the world. It saddened me so to know that someone who had done nothing but love and care about others could be dealt such a cruel hand while vile murderers sat in cosy cells in the best of health. That was the first time I'd cried in years. Any doubts I'd had of walking away from the police force, my country, my life, to come here and start afresh were washed away in that instant. I knew I had to cease that day. I had to find some peace in my life. After all, you don't know what's around the corner. The only good thing that ever came out of young Freddy's untimely death was Bea coming back into your lives. It also meant I got to know one of the most remarkable, resilient families I have ever come across. Freddy's death didn't tear you apart it made you all stronger, somehow. And, from the look of this book, Bea's death is doing the same. I take my hat off to you all, I really do." Jack raised his glass of beer and offered up a toast to Bea, to Freddy, to all the Arnolds for them to have a happy future. Janie clinked her glass of wine with his.

"And we're eternally grateful that you never gave up on finding Elsie, Jack. Knowing she's paying the price for what she's done has helped us all move forwards." They clinked glasses once more.

"You know I paint, don't you Janie?"

"Umm, so I've been told."

"I'm no van Gogh or Picasso but I've done a watercolour of Bea on the veranda at the cottage. I did a quick sketch from the beach after the memorial service. You'd all left to catch the boat by then. I had planned on popping by before I returned to Portugal but there just didn't seem to be any right words to say."

"It meant a lot to us you come all that way."

"Harry rang me a week later to say thanks. We chatted for a while about nothing really. So, I decided to paint a picture. I'll show you tomorrow after you've had a good night's sleep."

"I'd like that," replied Janie through a stifled yawn.

"I'll go pay the bill, then we'll be on our way," Jack spoke as he rose from the table. "I'll meet you over by the car, okay?" Janie gave him a sleepy nod of her head. It had been a long day and that hotel bed was going to be a very welcome sight.

***

True to his word, Jack gave her a guided tour of his gallery, studio and apartment. Then he produced the most beautiful watercolour painting of Bea and the cottage. It showed the cottage nestled in its tiered garden, with its little path winding down to a gate that opened out onto the golden sand. On the bottom tier was the sun house, its doors wide open and the loungers on its decking. Janie let her eyes follow the path back up through its manicured terraces to the veranda at the back of the cottage. Sitting in a large wicker chair, with a book on her lap, a straw hat on her head, was Bea. It wasn't a detailed painting of her but just enough so that those who had known her could easily recognise her from the way the hat tilted to the one side, her legs stretched out before her, and the way her dark locks caressed her shoulders. Jack had captured the essence of Bea, of the cottage and its garden. Tears pricked at Janie's eyes as she gazed in wonder upon it.

"It's for you if you want it?" Jack began. "I thought you could hang it in the cottage." Janie was overcome not only his by talent as an artist but at his generosity.

"The cottage is undergoing a major renovation now," she began to explain. "It was both Arthur's and my vision to turn the whole place upside down. Bea made me promise to do it. Once it's finished, I want you to come and stay, and bring this amazing painting with you. Then you can hang it on the wall. Bea would like that." Jack agreed.

For the next few days, Jack was Janie's guide. He took her to museums, vineyards, drives along the coastline, marketplaces and a fiesta. All too soon her stay was over, and they were back at the airport, Janie with her suitcase in hand.

"Thanks, Jack, for everything, not just this visit but everything."

"It's been a pleasure and a welcome distraction. It's also made me fall in love with this place all over again," he gestured, holding out his arms towards the sky.

"You won't forget to come? Will you?"

"I'll be there as soon as you're ready for me," he smiled.

"Jack?" Janie tentatively asked. "How come a man like you never got married?" Jack beamed.

"Lucky, I guess!" he replied as he headed off to his car. "Just lucky."

CHARLIE

March 1984

Charlie held up his home-made placard with "MISS J ARNOLD" boldly written on it. He'd jokingly borrowed a chauffeur's uniform from one of their regular customers at the garage. He knew Janie would appreciate the joke. His arms were starting to ache from holding up the sign for so long. He was beginning to wonder if he'd got the wrong arrival time when Janie emerged from round a corner.

Her long, red, curly locks fell with a glossy sheen onto her shoulders. Her eyes shone like emeralds and her face had a lovely healthy glow behind all those freckles that the sun had obviously coaxed to the surface. Janie looked the healthiest and happiest he'd seen her look in a long while.

Charlie watched as a big cheesy grin broke across her

face as she'd spotted both the placard and Charlie in his uniform and cap. She hurried across to him, dropping her suitcase on the floor and wrapping him up in a bear hug then planting a sloppy wet kiss on his cheek.

"You really shouldn't kiss the staff, ma'am!" teased Charlie. "Whatever will the natives think?" he finished.

"Oh! Charlie, you're such a card," exclaimed Janie, giving him a playful punch on his left bicep.

"Now, really, ma'am. I must insist also that you don't resort to violence towards your staff. We're in a union now, you know?" Janie's face took on a serious look.

"Very well, Charles. Point taken. Now collect my suitcase and lead on to the car, I'm absolutely exhausted." Janie spoke in posh accent and marched off towards the exit. Charlie, smiling to himself, picked up the case and strode off after his sister. It was good to have her back home!

Once safely inside the car and they had cleared the traffic around the airport, Charlie broke the silence.

"You look well, sis, did you have a good time?"

"Hmmm," replied Janie. "Jack Wilde was the perfect guide. He drove me to some lovely places. Told me where the best places were to eat and shop of course. Oooh! He's also done this fabulous watercolour of Bea sitting on the veranda of the cottage. He wanted me to bring it back, but I insisted that he brought it himself. He's agreed to come over towards the end of September."

"So, dad getting Jack to look out for you on your first trip aboard wasn't such a bad idea after all?"

"No, it wasn't. I know I acted like a spoilt brat when

dad said that if I was going to take myself off alone to Portugal at least I should let Jack Wilde look out for me. I thought he was treating me like a child, but I know now he wasn't. Knowing that I had a friendly face to meet me turned out to be very reassuring. I got to see and do things I'd not have done otherwise. I had lots of time to myself and Jack took me out to some wonderful places I'd never have dared go on my own."

"Not fallen for an older man, have we?" asked Charlie.

"NO! Don't be daft. It was kind of like having dad there with me, in an odd sort of way. Sort of like an uncle. Do you get what I mean?" Charlie nodded. "It made me feel safe while I was out there, yet still at the same time not smothered. Am I making any sense?"

"Yes, I get what you mean. You're an attractive young lady, sis, and dad wanted to make sure you were safe. Jack being an ex-copper and us having known him for so long seemed the perfect solution. There's some nasty people out there, sis, and dad just wanted to protect you."

Janie smiled at Charlie.

"So, what's new in your world, Charlie?" she enquired. Charlie felt a lump rise in his throat. He had a huge secret, bursting to be shared, Janie was his best option but just where should he begin?

"Janie?" he began. "How do you see me? I mean really see me?" He stole a glance across at Janie before returning his attention back to the road.

"Do you mean how would I describe you to a stranger, for instance?"

"Yeah, yeah, that's right."

"Well, let me see. You're a very caring, loving person. Not afraid to show your emotions, unlike most guys. You take pride in your appearance. You're brilliant to take clothes shopping. You're a good dancer and you have a wicked sense of humour. Ooh, oh and freakishly neat and tidy for a man."

"So, you wouldn't describe me as macho or manly?"

"I know you would stand up for me, for Megan, for anyone really, but I don't think of you as a man's man. You're not a wimp, Charlie, but you're not like Freddy was or the twins or even like Josef. It's like you don't feel the need to act all manly or macho. I'm not explaining this very well, am I, Charlie?" begged Janie.

"You've described me beautifully, Janie. That's how I see myself too! Doesn't that description remind you of anything else though, Janie?" He watched as Janie searched her memory for someone of similar qualities.

"No, Charlie, it doesn't. I'm afraid I don't understand what you mean!" replied Janie. Charlie let out a sign. Up ahead there was a lay-by, so Charlie pulled into it and parked up the car. He turned to face Janie, who by now looked bemused.

"Janie, would you still love me or want to know me if I told you a secret about me?"

"Of course, I would, Charlie, but you're beginning to scare me a little now." Charlie took Janie's hand in his and gazed deep into her eyes.

"I'm gay, Janie," he blurted out. He watched as a smile crossed Janie's face.

"Now you're messing with me, Charlie. I've lost count

of all the girls you've taken out over the years."

Charlie frowned.

"Oh, I like girls, Janie. I like talking to them, being around them, but all the physical side leaves me feeling cold and dirty."

"That doesn't mean you're gay," responded Janie. "It just means you haven't found the right girl yet, that's all, Charlie."

Charlie rubbed Janie's hand in both of his.

"No, Janie, I haven't met the right girl, but I have met the right boy!"

"I don't understand, Charlie."

So, Charlie began to explain.

"There's been this guy who's been coming to the garage for a year or more now. His dad owns a hire car business. He does weddings, anniversaries, that sort of thing. Greg drives for him. That's who I loaned this uniform off. He brings the motors to the garage to be serviced and we kinda got talking. Seemed we had a lot in common. Then a few months back he came in looking for a new car for himself. Obviously, he came to me and I took him out on a test drive. At one point his hand brushed my thigh as he changed gear and it was like I'd been hit by a bolt of electricity. My leg went all tingly and my heart began to pound away in my chest. Greg pulled over to the side of the road and just turned and looked at me. It was like a eureka moment, sis! The next thing we kissed like it was the most natural thing in the world to do. I – we've been seeing each other ever since. I'm in love, Janie. I'm in love with Greg and he loves me and I'm happy and afraid all at the same time. Happy because when I'm with Greg I feel free. Like I'm finally being me, Charlie. Then I think of you, of dad, grandad, Anne, Megan and everyone else and I'm afraid you won't love me anymore. That you won't want to know me anymore, that you'll all turn your backs on me, that you'll all disown me, and it scares the hell out of me, Janie, it really does." Charlie realised he'd started crying somewhere along the line. He looked though the tears at Janie. Her hand was still cradled in his. She wasn't looking at him in disgust or with horror; she was smiling at him.

"Oh! Charlie, don't be so daft. I don't care if you like girls or boys or both for that matter. I just care about you and your happiness. I've lost one brother and nothing on this earth is going to make me give up the other one, do you hear me, Charlie? Do you?" Charlie wiped away the tears then hugged Janie like his life depended on it.

"Somehow, I knew you'd understand," he began. "But what about dad? grandad? The rest of the family?"

"They'll understand, Charlie, I'm sure they will. Dad services that really camp bloke that lives with his disabled mother. He won't have a bad word said against him. Thinking about it, I reckon grandad already knows, or at least has his suspicions."

"What makes you say that?"

"Rose told me that grandad suggested you helped out with all their wedding arrangements. He told Rose you had an uncanny woman's eye for those sorts of things."

"I wondered why she asked me to help, not you or Anne or Megan. She told me it was because you all lived so far away. She obviously didn't want me to know what grandad had said." Charlie laughed at the thought of his grandad making those remarks to his wife-to-be! Then a memory of his grandad telling him to be himself no matter what others thought came to mind. He'd thought it an odd remark at the time but now it made perfect sense.

"Why don't we get all the family together this weekend coming? I'll make sure Megan comes. I'll cook us all a nice meal then afterwards I'll help you break the news to everyone, if you want. Let's get it out in the open, eh? You know how important it is in this family to be upfront about things. No secrets, Charlie. Nothing good has ever come from this family harbouring secrets. You know that, so what do you say?"

"Okay, Janie, okay! If you'll just hold my hand, I'll can do the rest." They hugged once more, then Charlie started up the engine and eased back out onto the road. He felt like a huge weight had been lifted from his shoulders. Good old Janie. She always seemed to know how to make everything right!

ELSIE & HARRY

May 1984

Elsie squinted at the ceiling in her cell. Her left eye was closing up fast with the swelling around it and she could taste the metallic tang of blood from her bust lip on her tongue. She didn't need to look in her small mirror to know that she looked a fright.

"Damn you to hell and back, Jane Elizabeth FUCKING Arnold," she screamed at the top of her voice. She glanced around at her little cell. With its grey peeling paint on the walls, heavy-duty metal door and small barred window set up high, it was no palace, but it was hers, but for how much longer? The TV news had run a story on the fastest-selling book in twenty years. It was a harmless enough story except it had then gone on to outline the life of the author! The author being Janie! So, there for all the wing

307

to see, was Elsie, the mother who had killed her eldest son, brother to this wonderful writer. It had all kicked off then, with most of the kicks being landed on Elsie. Elsie tittered to herself at that thought. Ironic, really! Most of the women on this wing were murderers! Oh! You could murder your husband, his mistress or your lesbian lover. Christ! you could even murder your own mother and father or some random stranger out on the street and no one in here would bat an eyelid. But murder a child, especially your own, and you were a monster. One step up from Hindley, the other inmates had chanted as the screws fought to shield her and leed her back to the safety of her cell. Now the whole wing was in lockdown.

For almost a year now she'd been the queen bee on the block. Oh! They knew she was in for murder, but they hadn't known it was her own son she'd run a knife through. Elsie had made sure of that. She'd enjoyed her run of the wing, the freedom, but now that was all over because of Janie. Now she'd be back in solitary, shipped out to some godforsaken hellhole of a prison. All because of that fucking ginger bitch!

"Warden," Elsie screamed at the top of her voice. "WARRRRRDENNNN." She continued to yell until the hatch in her cell door dropped open and a screw' face appeared in the gap.

"SHUT THE FUCK UP," spat the prison officer at her.

"I WILL WHEN I'M ISSUED A VO," spat Elsie back her.

"And just who do you think is gonna want to visit you?" taunted the officer.

"My ex-husband, if he knows what's fucking good for him. Now make sure I get one ASAP."

"Oh, I'll get you one, Elsie, just to see the look on your face when he doesn't turn up!" laughed the screw as she slammed shut the hatch on the door and rammed the bolt across.

"Oh! he'll come," whispered Elsie to the closed door. "He'll come."

***

Harry sat upright in the hard-plastic chair in the visitors' room of the prison, his hands firmly clenched together on his lap. He knew the minute he saw the prison emblem on the envelope what was inside. He'd half been expecting it since the day Janie's book had hit the bookshelves. Now here he was waiting to come face to face with Elsie.

Harry watched as the inmates filed into the room. They seemed to drag their feet and looked like they had the weight of the world on their shoulders. And then Elsie appeared. Her head was held high, with her shoulders back and a look of pure defiance on her face. She strode across the room and elegantly sat down at the table opposite Harry.

"You look rather handsome, Harry. Do you ever miss me, I wonder?" Elsie smiled sweetly at him, as if butter wouldn't melt in her mouth.

"About as much as you'd miss being locked up," replied Harry.

"I see you've developed a sense of humour," Elsie shot back.

"I've developed a lot of things, Elsie, while you've been rotting away in here." Harry noticed a slight squirm from Elsie. She wasn't used to Harry answering her back.

"I hope you've developed a healthy bank account, Harry, because if you want me to keep our little secret about Janie quiet, it's going to take a whole wedge of cash to do it!" Harry just smiled at Elsie. He'd gathered this was why she'd suddenly sent for him.

"I guess you know about Janie's book deal?" he offered.

"Oh! I know. I took a beating because that little ginger bitch got her fucking face plastered all over the fucking TV, dragging up the past." The mask had dropped now. There, in all her glory was the real Elsie.

"You're the one who committed murder, Elsie, not Janie. You can't blame her if the other inmates turned on you."

"OH! YES, I FUCKING CAN," she yelled at Harry. He watched as a prison officer made to come across and restrain Elsie. Harry waved and nodded to say everything was fine. The officer stepped back to her post. Elsie relaxed back into her chair.

"They're going to move me come the end of the month. Ship me off to some maximum security prison and then lock me up with a bunch of child killers. They say it's for my own safety. I ask ya? How can being locked up with some freaks who've done despicable things to little kiddies be the best thing for me? I ain't NO FREAK."

"You killed our son, Elsie. Our little Freddy. He idolised you. How could you just take his life and move on with your own as if it was nothing?" Elsie leaned across the table and looked into Harry's eyes.

"If you'd kept an eye on him, none of this would have happened, but no, you let him go around poking his nose into other people's business. MY BUSINESS. He shouldn't have come looking for me. If he'd stayed away we'd all be living out our lives in peace, but the little BASTARD couldn't let it drop, could he? Had to keep coming after me, spoiling my plans. He left me no choice, Harry. He really didn't." Harry was shocked by how cavalier she was with it all. Blaming away her vile selfish actions on others. Placing Freddy's death on him and Freddy himself. Anger welled up inside him, but he fought to keep it contained. He wasn't about to lose his self-control in front of her, not now, not here, not today!

"Freddy wanted to tell you to keep away from us, that was all! He hadn't come to drag you back home or spoil your plans, as you say. All he wanted was for you to stay away from us. He didn't deserve to die for that, Elsie."

"Yeah, well, I haven't asked you here to discuss Freddy; you're here to make arrangements for me to get regular money and parcels and in return I'll not go blabbing that you're not Janie's father." She'd slumped back in the chair now and casually began lighting up a cigarette. Now it was Harry's turn to lean across the table.

"I AM JANIE'S FATHER, always have been, always will be, end of. Go ahead and blab as much as want, Elsie, but be it on your head what happens to you. I mean, if those other prisoners didn't take to kindly to you doing your own son in, how do you think they'll feel about you bragging you left your daughter with another man? I'm imagining that won't go down well at all, will it? Now let's look back at what the judge said, shall we? He said you was to serve a minimum of fifteen years before parole could be considered. That parole board won't take to kindly to you destroying your daughter's life, will it? Because that's what it will do, Elsie, believe me. I'm going to get up and go now. God only knows why, but I've left you a parcel and a postal order for a hundred pounds at the main office. It'll be passed on to you once visiting is over. If you know what's good for you, you'll go back to your cell and forget all about us and then maybe, just maybe you'll live to walk out of prison one day." With that Harry pushed his chair out and stood up.

"You ain't seen or heard the last of me, Harry Arnold." Harry turned to look one last time at Elsie.

"Oh, I hope I have, Elsie, for your sake, I really do. Let's both hope our next meeting is one in which you're wearing a pine overcoat." Harry turned and walked towards the exit. The sooner he got out of this place the better.

***

At the third time of asking, the parcel from Harry was delivered to Elsie. Inside were a carton of cigarettes, two pouches of tobacco, several books of matches and fag papers. A hand rolling cigarette machine, soap, shampoo, deodorant and a small bottle of her favourite perfume. It also contained a sponge bag, sponge, flannel, hairbrush, a bag of mints, some chewing gum and a packet of assorted toffees. All Elsie's favourites. There was also a brown prison-issue envelope with a small accounts book inside with her name and number on it. The amount inside read 'one hundred pounds only'. Elsie laid all the items out on the bed. They wouldn't last her for the rest of her sentence, but they would make a start on making her life inside more comfortable. It's 1984, thought Elsie; come July 1997, she'd be eligible for parole, like Harry had said. She'd be sixty-two. If she kept out of trouble and looked after herself, she could still make a life for herself, couldn't she? And once she was out, there'd be no reason not to let the cat out of the bag would there? Maybe she'd be able to get a book deal, just like darling little Janie.

JOSEF

July 1984

Josef bumped along in the passenger seat of the old utility truck. It was about a five-hour drive into Perth from where he'd been living this past ten months in Marvel Loch, Western Australia. Steve Reilly, his saviour, was at the wheel.

Steve had found Josef beaten half to death in some alley in Bangkok. He'd carried him back to the small shanty he was renting and had not only nursed his cuts and bruises but saved his life. He'd been the one to help Josef kick his drug addiction and clean his life up. For two whole months, he'd never left Josef's side. Steve had cleared out his room at the squalid apartment block he'd been lodging in. He'd provided Josef with food and clothing and had paid for everything. When Josef had asked him why, he'd gone on to explain that, just like him, his kid sister Irene had gone off in search of adventure. When she stopped calling home, Steve had gone in search of her. He'd found her, there, in Bangkok. Unfortunately for Steve and his family they'd been too late. She'd been gang raped and then beaten to death. The police had arrested her several times for prostitution prior to her demise. That had been over four years ago, and still no one had been charged with her murder. Steve had returned to Bangkok every year since to rescue vulnerable people like his sister.

When it was time for Steve to return to the family sheep farm he'd asked Josef if he'd like to join them or he'd pay for his return ticket home. Josef had instantly chosen to go with him. At least that way he could make a small dent in all that he owed Steve.

Josef had been expecting to work for the Reilly's, but he hadn't expected to be welcomed into their home as part of the family. Phil and Jean Reilly had treated him like one of their own from the minute they'd met them at Perth airport. For the past ten months, he'd not only learnt how to be a sheep farmer but how to ride a horse and fly a small plane and had also been encouraged to take up photography again. The last part had been the easiest. The scenery was breath-taking and there was so much to photograph. He'd made a lot of money selling his photographs to the small store in town and the wider community. He'd made more than enough for a return ticket home and that's where he was heading right now.

"We're making good time," commented Steve. "Should make Perth in plenty of time to pick up Mum's books, check into a hotel, shower and get us some grub, washed down with plenty of grog. What'dya say, Joe?"

"Sounds good. One last night in Oz with my best buddy."

"We'll go check out the flights back to the UK first thing tomorrow, that's unless you change your mind and decide to stay here with us!"

"I'll be back, Steve. I just need to put things right with Janie, that's all. I need to tell her I was wrong to go off like I did. I need to tell her that I still love her and will do anything to win her back. I have to give it a go, Steve, I really do."

"No worries, mate. I understand. After all, I keep going back to Bangkok to try and put things right."

Josef patted his companion on the back.

"You've done a fantastic job with me, Steve. You saved my life. In fact, you gave me back my life, only better somehow. Maybe you can forgive yourself now and concentrate on your own life. Plenty of sheila's would jump at a chance with you, mate." Steve looked across at Josef and smiled.

"I tell you what? You come back with that girl of yours on your arm and I'll go find me one of my own! What'dya say? Deal?" Steve held out his hand for Josef to shake.

"Deal!" replied Josef, shaking the extended hand.

In no time at all, Steve was parking up the ute outside a large bookstore on one of Perth's busy high streets. Both men clambered out of the vehicle and into the store. Steve headed straight for the counter to collect his mum's order. Fifty books of different genres packed into two boxes for her to read. Josef wandered a little further into the huge store. As he turned to go around a large bookcase into another aisle he came face to face with a life-sized cardboard cut-out of Janie! There she stood in all her glory! Red curls, emerald eyes, freckles and a smile that you just knew reached her eyes. Josef stopped dead in his tracks and stared at Janie. Why? How?

"She's absolutely gorgeous, isn't she?" a female sales assistant remarked. "She's the bestselling author of the book *Letters Straight from the Heart*; here, would you like a copy?" Not taking his eyes off Janie, Josef took the offered book.

"She's taken the UK and Europe by storm and has made a huge impression in the United States. We've only had the books a couple of days and we're close to selling out already."

"It's Janie Arnold, isn't it?" Josef managed to get out.

"Yes, sir, it is. You say it as if you know her?" she commented. Josef glanced at the photo of Bea on the books dust jacket.

"I do. I did," stuttered Josef.

"Did you know the lady the book's about?" she asked. Josef nodded.

"Yes, yes, her aunt Bea. Janie always called her either Busy Bea or Beautiful Bea. She looked like a dark-haired version of Diana Dors. She was good to me. I let her down…" Josef tailed off.

"In what way, sir?" enquired the sales assistant.

"Joe, there you are, crikey mate, I'd thought I'd lost you there. Holy mother of God, Joe, that's your sheila?" exclaimed Steve as he realised what had captivated his buddy. "No wonder you wanna go get her back! She's bloody gorgeous!"

"Sir, can I ask that you keep your voice down?"

"Yeah, yeah, just got a little excited that's all, no harm done, eh?" Steve ushered Josef back towards the counter. "Come on mate. Let's grab mum's books and pay for that one, you're gripping it like your life depends on it and go get ya a stiff drink, eh?" Josef just let Steve lead him to the counter. He watched as he settled his mother's bill and paid for the book he was still holding on to.

"I'm gonna need a hand here, mate," Steve said as he offered a box up for Josef to take. In a dreamlike state, Josef placed the book on top of the box then took the weight of the box from Steve. Like a robot, he followed him out into the street and across to the ute. They loaded up the two boxes and he retrieved the book off the top, they made their way across the street to a bar. Steve sat Josef down at a table and ordered a brandy and two large cold beers. He made Josef knock the brandy back in one go. Josef began to flick through the pages of Janie's book. He let it stay open on the page outlining a brief profile of the author. He eagerly read through it.

"The lady in the shop said it's a bestseller. A massive hit around the globe. It says here that she lives in the cottage she inherited from her aunt by the sea. It says she's single…" Josef finished.

"There you go, Joe, she's still single, could be waiting for ya, buddy."

"I doubt it."

"Now, come on, mate, you don't know how she feels, Joe! She just might be hoping, wishing you'd get in touch, turn up."

"I'd look like a gold-digger Steve. That's how I'd look. I've got nothing to offer Janie now! I've got a few dollars in the bank and that's it, Steve! I've no job, no home, no nothing to offer her!"

"Aye! Now look here, mate, you've got a job and a home here, with us, for always, okay? You're a talented photographer and a damn good farmer, though it pains me to say so. You've got a lot to offer to her. Okay? She might be rich and famous with a house by the sea but she ain't got you, buddy, and you've got a lot to offer her, I can tell ya!" Josef just shook his head.

"It's not enough for me, Steve. I want to be on equal terms with Janie. I want to be as successful as she is when I ask her to be mine. I can't do it any other way, mate, I just can't."

"So, what'dya wanna do now?" asked Steve.

"Go back to Marvel Loch with you and make something of my life." Josef downed the last of his beer. "Can we leave now, Steve, please?" Steve drained his own beer glass and got up from the table.

"If you're sure that's what you want, buddy, if you're sure that's what you want!" Josef got to his feet. He picked up the book and turned to leave the bar.

"It is, Steve. Right now, that's all I wanna do, but one

day I'm going to go back and get my girl, if it's the last thing I do!"

***

Across town, Derek Collins was exiting Perth airport with his new wife, Emma. She was a born-and-bred Aussie and knew everything there was to know about Derek. Emma had been just the saviour he'd needed. He'd agreed to move to Australia when the book Janie had written started to send news reporters to their door. The sudden intrusion had awakened the dormant feelings for Elsie he still held inside! The thought of her had begun to arouse him again. There were moments when he wanted to squeeze the very last breath from her body, and others when he wanted to hold her and never let her go. She plagued his dreams and seemed to wander into his wakening thoughts. He'd spoken openly to Emma about it. How his emotions had been stirred and how Elsie still seemed to have a hold over him. "I've enough love and strength for the both of us," she'd replied and suggested the move here. Derek just hoped that she was right, that journeying halfway round the world was enough to keep Elsie at bay, he really did!

JANIE

August 1984

Janie stood on the beachside of her garden gate and admired her home. The cottage and its tiered gardens looked beautiful in the late evening sun. The renovation of the cottage had given it a whole new lease of life. With the help of an architect, Janie had turned the building upside down. Where once there were bedrooms there was now an open-plan living area with all the latest mod cons installed in the slick new kitchen. The bedrooms were now downstairs, and each had the luxury of its own bathroom. The outer walls had been extended and new large windows and patio doors let the light flood in, while making the most of the incredible views along the coast line. Arthur's old studio had been connected to the main house via a corridor but was now a well-appointed one-bedroomed self-contained annexe. Janie had even given it its own terrace area. Sea View cottage now really did live up to its name.

Janie pushed open the gate and weaved her way up through the manicured gardens, climbed the outer stairs at the side of the property and took a seat out on the large balcony to watch the sunset. As the sun dipped down below the horizon, Janie thought about her life so far.

She wouldn't be twenty-one until the end of the year and look at her... a successful author and home owner with a very healthy bank account. Wasn't that everyone's dream? But it hadn't been her dream, had it?

She'd dreamt of days spent exploring unfamiliar places, nights under star-filled skies, different cultures, different customs, different people. Of writing a travel journal of all the amazing places she'd seen and of the colourful characters she'd met along the way. She'd dreamt of walking hand in hand with Josef on faraway shores. Of climbing mountains, crossing deserts on a camel and sailing on the wide-open seas. She'd dreamt of new tastes and of new sounds that would flood her senses. Of exotic birds, of getting up close and personal with wild animals and diving along the Great Barrier Reef. It had all been so very close. So very close that she could almost touch it but then, as always, her hopes, her plans had been spirited away by someone else's hand!

Elsie had caused most of her dreams, her hopes to fail. She'd taken away a huge chunk of all the family's freedom with her thoughtless, selfish, vicious actions. At school, she'd been 'the girl whose mummy had left her'.

After Freddy had lost his life at Elsie's hands, she'd become 'the murderer's daughter'. Since the day Elsie had walked out on them all, everything they ever did was preceded by the name Elsie. She wasn't even known as just 'Jane Arnold Author'; instead she was referred to constantly as 'the authors' daughter of the murderer, Elsie Arnold, Jane Arnold". But somehow everyone else in her family seemed to have escaped its trappings and been free to live their own lives.

Anne had flown the nest long ago. She'd married, moved away, run a business, even started a family of her own. She'd returned to her roots now but still lived her life as she chose to. Charlie had thrown caution to the wind and announced he was gay. The family had just opened their arms and welcomed his boyfriend, Greg, into the fold. Megan had bought a smallholding and ended her studies at university to be a vet, instead choosing to pursue artistic pursuits. She'd started making clothing, doing up old furnishings and painting and even taken up pottery. No one had even raised an eyebrow. Janie envied them, she really did. Where she lived, what she'd written, had all been down to Bea. Beautiful, bold, busy Bea. Oh! she would be eternally grateful for it all but that didn't make it her choice, her dreams, did it?

And now, here she was, sitting alone on a beautiful summer's evening with a decision she'd made weighing heavy on her mind. It hadn't been a rash decision. She'd spent many sleepless nights going over it, again and again. It had all started with a chance meeting with Sofia, Josef's younger sister…

Janie had been walking back from her grandfather's bungalow, after popping in to drop him off a copy of her book, when she'd heard someone calling her name. Janie had carried on walking at first, thinking it was some journalist, out for a story. The book release having been a green flag to the press to open up the whole Elsie saga, again! As the voice called out her name more urgently now, Janie thought she recognised the voice and decided to turn around and see who it was. The young girl was Sofia but not the Sofia Janie remembered! Gone were the height-of-fashion clothes, the perfectly teased hair and face full of make-up. Her hair was simply tied back in a ponytail. She wore jeans and a t-shirt, and her face bore no signs of any cosmetics. Janie had thought how much more beautiful she looked but once face-to-face with Sofia she could see the tell-tale signs of sadness that clouded her eyes. They'd sat together on a nearby bench. First Sofia had talked about Janie's book, how her elder brother was disgracing the family by getting divorced. How she was studying to be a nurse at Keele University. Then finally she'd told Janie of Josef's disappearance! How he'd rung in the middle of the night asking for her parents to send him money and a ticket to get back home. He'd told them where to send it. The very next day they'd wired money to a post office in Bangkok and details of his prepaid flight back to England. As a family, they'd travelled down to London to meet him off the plane, but Josef had never made the flight. He'd never collected the ticket or the money. Her parents had contacted the authorities in Bangkok, every police station, every hospital in all of Thailand but there was no trace of him anywhere. It was if he'd just simply vanished into thin air!

Janie had walked away in a daze. Josef lost? No, it couldn't be. He had to be out there somewhere! She'd feel it, sense it somehow if he was dead! She knew she would. She believed he was alive – lost, yes, but still alive – she had to believe it for her own sanity!

She'd fretted over Josef night and day until the compulsion to act had become too much to bear. She'd walked into the nearest travel agents and paid for flights and accommodation there and then to Bangkok Airport. The tickets were lying on the desk in her new study, along with her passport, visas and Thai bahts, right now. She'd cleared her diary with her publisher for the next month and was due to fly out in two days' time. Tomorrow she would pack her suitcase and head for London's Heathrow Airport with a quick stop-off at her father's house to inform him of her plans and leave details of where she could be reached. For the first time in her life, Janie was about to embark on an adventure of her own making without the help or the influence of her family. She felt scared but exhilarated at the same time.

Janie woke refreshed the next morning, after the first good night's sleep she'd had in a long time. She quickly showered then began to pack her suitcase. She'd bought some cool linen trouser suits and long flowing dresses for her trip, along with a guide book to Bangkok and Thailand and a small phrase book. She'd try to master a few words on the flight over. For the first time in her short life, she truly felt free. She turned up the radio as she neatly stowed her clothes and toiletries into her case, singing along to an old Motown tune they were playing. Janie thought she could hear the phone ringing in her office, so she lowered the volume on the radio. The phone's shrill tones rang out from the room next door. For a second Janie thought of ignoring it but then her conscience got the better of her and she ran to answer it. Lifting the receiver to her ear, Janie began to speak.

"Hello," she answered.

"Janie, Janie is that you?" came Dave Evans, Megan's fiancé, down the phone. He seemed panicked, distressed even, to Janie.

"It's me, Janie, Dave, what's wrong?"

"It's Megan, Janie. Oh! Janie, I'm so scared. When I came down the stairs this morning she was lying on the kitchen floor. She was just lying there in this puddle of blood, Janie. It was all over her nightie, she wasn't moving, Janie, she wasn't moving." Both fear and panic had got the better of Dave now and he just seemed to be rambling on.

"Dave, Dave," called Janie down the phone. "Where's Megan now, Dave? Where is she?"

"I called 999, Janie, straight away; they seemed to take forever to get here. I sat on the floor by her, Janie. I really believed she was dead, but she was warm, Janie and I could feel a pulse." He was starting to ramble again.

"Dave, what happened when the ambulance arrived?"

"They took her to hospital, Janie, they took me in the ambulance too. She was asking for you, Janie. She just kept drifting in and out of conscientiousness and asking for you, Janie. Say you'll come, Janie, say you'll come."

"I will, Dave, I will, but I need to know where Megan is, Dave. You need to think, you need to tell me."

"She's in theatre, Janie, they're operating on her now. Please come, Janie." Janie felt the fear and panic rising in her own voice now. She fought hard to keep it and the rising feeling of nausea at bay while she tried to coax out of Dave which hospital Megan was at.

"I'm going to leave as soon as you tell me where I need to go, Dave. Can you do that? Can you tell me where to go?"

"Aberystwyth Hospital, Janie. She's in Aberystwyth Hospital, Janie, come quick, Janie, come quick!" the line went dead.

"Dave! DAVE!" she screamed down the phone. But it was no use: he'd hung up.

Janie carefully placed the receiver back in its cradle and lifted her flight tickets to Bangkok off the desk. She brushed them against her cheek before kissing them goodbye.

"I'm sorry, Josef," she whispered into the air. "You, me! We'll just have to wait. Megan needs me." And with that she dropped the tickets into the waste paper bin and exited the room.

ACKNOWLEDGMENTS

I'd like to start by saying thank you to my sons, Simon & Jak, for putting up with a mother who insisted on writing them stories & poems while they were growing up. You both were and still are magical.

To Dee Bruce, who read along as I wrote this book & gave me feedback both good & bad. It helped immensely. To Nan Walker, Sharon Hyland & Suzie Allen for taking the time to read my manuscript. Your thoughts, words, encouragement were priceless. Even the comment about you not realising I was THAT clever! Thanks for your friendship & honesty.

Kevin, my truly wonderful husband thank you for believing in me and this book. For pushing me to get this finished and providing the means to bring my dream into reality. Let's hope your dreams come true too.

Thank you to Hannah, Sophie and Fern at Troubadour. For your guidance and replying to my numerous emails and questions.

And lastly a big THANK YOU to all those that have purchased CUTTING THE CORD and read it. I only hope you've enjoyed reading it as much as I have writing it. Work has begun on the next book.

Lub Amanda.